Thoughts of Christmas evaporated from Caroline's mind. She slammed on the brake and steered frantically to the right.

"Wrong," her brain screamed. She released the brake pedal and hauled the steering wheel to the left. The Buick bucked into a spin, its tires now completely off the road, before veering sideways across the pavement. Caroline pumped the brake in an effort to go with the slide. She depressed the pedal a second time, felt it flatten uselessly to the floor. Horrified, she clung to the steering wheel while the car fishtailed toward the far embankment.

The forested slope was a blur of brown and white rushing straight at her. Caroline threw up her hands in an instinctive gesture of self-protection. The Buick plowed into a wall of brush, lurched skyward where it hung motionless for the briefest of moments, then slammed violently back to earth. It rocked forward and sank into the snow, its front bumper crumpling against a jagged tree stump.

Caroline's forehead met the steering wheel with enough force to send shock waves down her spine. She felt rather than heard herself cry out in pain before she passed into unconsciousness.

———————— ★ ————————

A MERRY LITTLE MURDER

MARY WELK

W⬤RLDWIDE®

TORONTO • NEW YORK • LONDON
AMSTERDAM • PARIS • SYDNEY • HAMBURG
STOCKHOLM • ATHENS • TOKYO • MILAN
MADRID • WARSAW • BUDAPEST • AUCKLAND

Recycling programs
for this product may
not exist in your area.

A MERRY LITTLE MURDER

A Worldwide Mystery/December 2012

First published by Echelon Press

ISBN-13: 978-0-373-26829-0

Copyright © 2007 by Mary Welk

Previously published as *A Deadly Little Christmas*

Printed in U.S.A.

Acknowledgments

In loving memory of my father,
Dr. Lawrence Anthony Thoennes.

*Voice of the dead whom we loved, our Lawrence,
the best of the brave.*

—The Defense of Lucknow
Alfred Lord Tennyson

PROLOGUE

December 14

FOR AN ARTIFICIAL Christmas tree, this one wasn't half-bad. At least that's what Martha Schoen said, and she ought to know. Having browbeaten her critics into silence years before, Martha reigned as the town's undisputed authority on all things great and small, fake balsams included.

"I chaired St. Mark's beautification committee for thirty-two years," the silver-haired matron sputtered when Gail Garvy rebuffed her offer to supervise the trimming of the seven-foot tree. "No one's more qualified for the job than I."

Martha snatched the box of ornaments from Gail's hands with a snort of contempt. Holding the box aloft like a worn but trusty battle flag, she marched across the room with the resolve of a crusader off to fight the Saracens, her progress punctuated by a running commentary on the stupidity of modern youth. Only when she spied May Eberle did she pause for breath, and then merely to refocus her outrage on the tiny woman standing slumped against the west window. Frail in body and spirit, May offended the sensibilities of the tough-minded Mrs. Schoen. Weaklings had no place in Martha's world. She firmly believed in survival of the fittest, and May was far from fit in any sense of the word. The elderly spinster existed as a shadow dweller, a woman more dead than alive whose terror of the real world confined her to the dark corners of her private universe. May rarely spoke except to whimper over some perceived slight or whine about life in general. She spent most of her waking hours wrapped in a cocoon of silence, her body held rigidly still, her face an inscrutable mask concealing all thought.

At present, May's attention appeared riveted on a glazed section of windowpane where frost fairies had traced icy tendrils on the glass. Martha doubted that the artistry of winter could so capture the other woman's fancy. It seemed more likely that senility had just punched another hole in the Swiss-cheese brain of little Miss Eberle. Much as she disliked May, Martha knew her duty when she saw it.

"Snap out of it, Eberle. You're daydreaming again."

May Eberle winced. The choir had begun its final hymn. Six men in black suits lifted her casket to their shoulders and processed solemnly down the aisle. In their pews, the little congregation wept.

"Did you hear me, May? Stop all that nonsense and come lend a hand with these ornaments."

The choir faltered, their sweet harmony disintegrating into cacophonous gibberish that grated on May's ears. She forced herself to concentrate, but the fantasy continued to fade. First her casket disappeared, then the mourners vanished. When she could no longer smell the incense on the altar, May turned from the window in surrender. No use fighting it; the cemetery would have to wait.

"I'm coming, Martha." May glared at her nemesis. Today had been ruined, but tomorrow she'd have her revenge. Tomorrow she would plan Martha's funeral. How different it would be from her own!

"Be careful now," Martha commanded when May sidled up to her. "I spent all morning making this." She handed May a string of popcorn and cranberries and pointed to the tree. "Drape it on the branches, but don't break it!"

May caressed the garland with bony fingers, momentarily forgetting her hatred of Martha Schoen as a wave of memories flooded over her.

"My sister, April, and I used to string cranberries at Christmas," she whispered. Her brow puckered in a frown. "But Papa was so particular. If even one berry didn't meet his approval, he'd make us take the whole string apart and start over."

·"Humph." Martha dismissed Papa Eberle with a wave of one plump hand. "I'd never put up with such behavior from a man." She tucked a dented Santa deep in the tree where it wouldn't be noticed. Satisfied with the result, she turned and studied the woman standing next to her. With her tight gray bun and beady black eyes, May reminded Mrs. Schoen of a field mouse that had wandered mistakenly close to a sleeping cat. Martha flexed her fingers, mentally extending her claws.

"But of course," she purred, "I've always said, one should do things right the first time. Sloppiness is a wicked habit. It springs from sloth, and you know what the Bible says about that."

May Eberle's head shot up. She stared at Martha, but saw Papa scowling back at her, Papa whose mouth twisted in condemnation. May clamped her hands to her ears to shut out the sound of her father's wrath.

"Watch what you're doing," Martha screamed as shredded popcorn fluttered to the floor. "You'll crush the garland."

May buried her face in the berries, terrified at the

extent of Papa's rage. She prayed he wouldn't hit her. Papa had hit April, and looked what had happened then.

"Oh, give me that!" Martha lunged at May, but the frightened woman pulled away. The garland tore in two and cranberries cascaded down May's legs.

"Now look what you've done," cried Martha. She fell to her knees and scrabbled at the berries. Horrified, May retreated a step. Thick drops of blood rolled past her feet. She cringed when Papa plucked some from the carpet and hurled them at her.

"You stupid woman!" Martha pitched another handful of berries at May. "You destroy everything you touch."

"For God's sake, turn it off."

The sudden intrusion of another angry voice so startled Martha that she pitched forward and sprawled unbecomingly on the carpet. Overcome with fury and embarrassment, she twisted around to lash out at the newcomer.

"Who do you think... Oh!"

Martha blanched at the sight of Thomas Adrian's clenched hand quivering inches above her head. Adrian's face was contorted, his olive skin suffused with an unhealthy reddish glow that extended from collar to hairline. The cords on his neck bulged like wire ropes with each ragged breath.

"Nobody gives a damn about you and your berries," Adrian snarled. "You're not as important as you think." He whirled around, almost colliding with May, who shrank against the tree in terror. "I'm the one they're after. It's me they're out to get."

Martha scrambled to her feet and fled to safety behind a worn leather recliner.

"You're mad," she gasped. "Absolutely mad."

"Shut up, you old souse." Adrian's eyes glittered darkly. Flecks of spittle dampened his lips and chin, and high on his left cheek a muscle twitched.

"You tell her, Tommy boy."

Will Chapell strolled into the room, his fists tightly balled in the pockets of his grease-stained jeans. A wicked grin creased his craggy features as he took in the scene near the Christmas tree.

"Havin' a little argument, are we?" Chapell approached the group, his gaze sliding over the two women and coming to rest on Adrian. Having chosen his victim, he edged nearer to Thomas and slapped him on the back. "Now, now, Tommy boy. Mustn't let these old biddies get under your skin. If they're causin' trouble, just shoot 'em 'tween the eyes and be done with it."

"Stay away from me." Adrian spun out of Chapell's grasp. He despised the big blond oaf with his work-worn hands and hillbilly accent. He let it show in the look he threw at Will.

"Ooh, Tommy! Aren't we touchy today," Chapell sneered.

"That's enough."

Gail Garvy appeared in the doorway, arms akimbo and eyes blazing. Anger gave her the voice of a drill sergeant as she bore down on the group.

"Keep it up and there'll be no Christmas party today, tomorrow, or any other day this year." Gail's gaze strayed to the mess on the floor, then moved up to the frightened face of Martha Schoen. For a brief instant she almost pitied the woman. "We'll clean this up later, Mrs. Schoen. For now, let's all get back to work."

Ignoring an eruption of complaints from the suddenly loquacious quartet, she herded them toward the tree, then bullied them into decorating it. Chapell and

Adrian traded gibes despite Gail's threats while May Eberle cowered in the background eyeing both men anxiously. Only Martha Schoen seemed to relax as she concentrated on the placement of each ornament. After setting the last one in place, she claimed the privilege of fixing the angel on the top branch.

"Now it's done," she exclaimed after backing ponderously down the stepladder. A perfectionist to the end, she checked the placement of the angel from all sides of the tree before nodding in satisfaction. "Nice and straight, exactly as it should be."

"Ain't a bad-lookin' tree if y'all like institutional trees," Chapell drawled.

"Bea-u-ti-ful! The tree is sooo bea-u-ti-ful!"

Curled in a fetal position on a corner sofa, Richard Canty had awakened from his nap and clapped his hands in delight. Martha pursed her lips and frowned at the pale little man with the bald head and watery eyes. She'd forgotten he was there in the room, almost forgotten he'd existed.

"Do something about him, Garvy. He's…he's… sick!"

"Ain't she the perceptive one," crowed Chapell. He grinned at Martha, then leaned forward and said softly, "Angel's crooked, Mrs. Mayor."

Martha threw him a withering look. "Mind your own…"

"Institutional tree! Institutional tea! You can pay a hefty fee to sit in here with tree and tea! I'm a poet, and don't I know it." Richard Canty rocked back and forth on the sofa. His high-pitched voice crackled with an adolescent excitement that belied his advanced age.

"Bet you could shut him up with this." Chapell

plucked a peppermint cane from the tree and tossed it to Adrian. "Unless you'd rather eat it yourself."

Adrian stared blindly at the striped candy, then threw it down and ground it into the carpet with a twist of his foot. His eyes met Chapell's and he grinned triumphantly.

"You think I'm some kind of fool? You can't poison me that easily."

Chapell opened his mouth to retort, but Gail held up a restraining hand.

"Enough! We need to light the tree before everyone arrives for the party. How about doing the honors, Mr. Chapell?"

"Got a match, Garvy?" Chapell waggled his thumb in the direction of May and Martha. "I bet the little ladies would enjoy warmin' their britches by a bonfire."

Martha's lips drew back in a silent hiss of disapproval. May's expression, though, remained benign. Absorbed in planning Richard Canty's funeral, she hadn't heard Chapell's crude reply. Gail disregarded the remark also. She'd grown tired of Chapell's word games, just as she'd grown tired of Martha's bossiness, May's tears, and Adrian's paranoia. Canty didn't count; she considered the man already brain-dead. The only one worth bothering with was the bronze-skinned ex-soldier standing quietly at attention near the electric fireplace. Much to Gail's frustration, even the inscrutable James Belding was fast becoming a bore.

"Could we get on with it?" Martha demanded. "Light the tree, Garvy."

"Light the tree," May Eberle echoed dreamily.

"Light the tree and serve the tea," sang Richard Canty.

"It's traditional to gather around it first," Gail insisted. "Then we can…"

"Traditions are all well and good," interrupted Martha. "But you're wasting your time if you're looking for a volunteer to plug in the lights. The outlet is near the floor, and I, for one, refuse to dirty my skirt crawling around under those branches."

"Let Mr. Belding do it."

Of course, thought Gail. *What better way to draw the recluse into the group?* She turned toward the fireplace, a pleased smile lighting her face, and motioned to Belding.

"How about it?" she said, coaxing the man forward. "Will you light our tree?"

Lost in a world where Christmas no longer existed, James Belding chanced a look at the present and saw in the eyes of his jailer the pain of empathy.

This one knows, his first self said.

James raised his index finger, then slowly uncurled the second, third, and fourth fingers. "Four to go," he whispered.

Gail inclined her head and nodded.

She only thinks she knows, warned his second self.

James Belding groaned. Resigned to captivity, he obeyed the order given him and walked slowly toward the tree. Gail pointed to the electric cord dangling from the trunk, then signaled the others to come closer.

"Si-i-lent night…" she sang.

Belding reached for the cord with trembling fingers.

"Ho-o-ly night…" caroled Martha Schoen.

He sank to one knee and forced himself to concentrate.

"All is calm…" May Eberle added sotto voce.

Fool, hissed his second self. *They've got you now!*

"All is bright…" they sang in unison.

I know, cried his first self.

"Thy will be done," James shouted. He plunged the plug into the outlet.

The explosion was immediate and devastating. By the time Caroline Rhodes reached the doorway, Recreation Room 2, Psychiatric Ward One, St. Anne's Hospital, no longer existed.

Neither did its inhabitants.

ONE

December 19

CAROLINE RHODES STOOD on the nursing dorm steps and plotted murder. The methods she considered were primitive—boiling oil, the guillotine, a quiver of arrows through the heart—but effective nonetheless.

"And exactly what he deserves," she growled.

He'd been bursting with confidence at noon, cocksure of his ability to predict the future.

"Take my word for it, Rhineburg. You can put away those shovels until after Christmas. We're in for a spell of blue skies and sunshine clear through the holidays."

Then at two o'clock a breeze ruffled the treetops along Wilhelm Avenue. A gray haze crept catlike into the western sky, thickening over time until dark shadows slunk across the fields outside of town. Still, the voice on the radio jeered at the doubters.

"Okay, you worrywarts. Lay off the lines. I told you no snow and I meant it. Relax!"

By four o'clock the weakening sun had disappeared behind a barricade of clouds. Gusts rattled the windows of City Hall and weather vanes spun crazily on farmhouse roofs. Rhineburg held its breath and waited for the next report.

"There's no need for concern, folks." The forecaster's bravado had vanished. Nevertheless, he stuck to his guns. "It's too warm for snow, although we might see some rain tonight. We could use it, though," he added cheerily. "Let Mother Nature clean up our roads."

"So much for weathermen," Caroline grumbled.

Good old Mother Nature was cleaning up all right, but not with any gentle rainfall. Ambushed by shifting winds, Rhineburg had surrendered to a squall so intense that previous blizzards paled by comparison. By eight o'clock five inches of new snow whitened the dirty mounds abreast of the highway. Drifts rippled across the roads, each crest and valley glistening with ice formed by the plunging temperature. Given another hour, the storm could transform the landscape into a mini version of Antarctica.

Caroline grimaced at the thought. She could cope with a normal winter, but like the ghost voters of Chicago, the snow had come early and often this year. Three weeks into December and already the hospital's snow gauge measured a two-foot accumulation. Rhineburg's youngsters were delighted. Caroline's generation was not.

"No putting this off any longer."

Caroline tugged the hood of her parka lower over her forehead and trudged down the unplowed driveway. The wind buffeted her until she felt like a punch-drunk boxer. It squealed through the treetops and spit showers of ice crystals onto her face and down her neck. She jerked at her scarf, already stiff with frozen snow, and pulled it over her nose. The smell of wet wool increased her annoyance.

"Damnation!"

Caroline longed for the protection of her ancient Buick, but the twelve-year-old car lacked the punch for tackling the storm. A fair-weather friend, it tended to balk at the slightest hint of cold. Right now it sat cringing in the hospital parking lot, a worn blanket protecting its battery from the frigid air. Caroline knew she must either walk or stay home; she had no intention of doing the latter. She'd promised Martin she'd appear at Bruck Hall for the university's holiday bash. Come hell, high water, or twelve inches of snow, she'd keep her word.

"If Hannibal could cross the Alps during the worst part of winter, I can surely make it across Bruck Green in a little blizzard."

Of course, Hannibal had elephants to carry him. Caroline had to rely on her own two feet, not the best mode of transportation tonight. A dog sled would have come in handy, or at least a pair of snowshoes. Ice lurked beneath the drifts and Caroline's boots crunched on it as she struggled against the wind toward Circle Road. Irked that the walk wasn't shoveled, she kicked at the remnants of a snowman littering the pavement. She immediately regretted the impulse. Her right foot skidded forward, her left one flew back. Like a drunk on a Friday night binge, she staggered the length of the path, lurching to a halt at the corner where a blast of wind pummeled her with sleet.

"This is ridiculous," she snarled. "I could be home in my warm bed, a stiff drink in one hand, and a good book in the other. But no, here I am tramping through this god-awful snow to some god-awful party with a bunch of god-awful people I don't even know. And all because of my damned son."

Caroline experienced a twinge of remorse for referring to her firstborn in those terms. Neither the storm nor the invitation could be blamed on Martin. A Ph.D. candidate vying for a teaching post at Bruck University, Martin was fortunate to be on the guest list. She wondered, though, why she'd been included. Her invitation had arrived late yesterday, the apologetic note accompanying it couched in effusive language that immediately aroused her suspicions. Could her sudden popularity be related to the bombing at St. Anne's Hospital? Had some committee selected her as the evening's entertainment, her role that of survivor eager to tell all? If so, they'd made a big mistake. She refused to play the part of the gruesome guest.

Caroline pushed that problem from her mind and considered a more immediate one. Across the road lay Bruck Green, a broad wooded oval separating the hospital from the campus of Bruck University. At the south end of the campus stood Bruck Hall. The building should have been visible from the corner. Tonight, the storm effectively camouflaged it.

Great, she thought disgustedly. She'd originally planned to take one of the many paths that crisscrossed the Green. In better weather that would have meant a five-minute trip to the Hall. Attempting it now, though, would be suicidal. Blinded by the blizzard, she could easily slip on the ice and collide with one of the massive oaks straddling the Green's cobbled walks. And if she fell into a snowbank, she'd have one helluva time extricating herself from its suffocating softness.

Caroline turned her thoughts to the street girdling the Green. Despite its oval shape, the town fathers had, for some unfathomable reason, christened it Circle Road, or The Circle, for short. Mounds of snow covered the pavement, but if she zigzagged between the drifts, Caroline could follow the curved surface all the way to Bruck Hall. Not a bad ides as long as she didn't encounter a snowplow along the way.

The only other route lay to Caroline's left. South of the road a sidewalk meandered past look-alike bungalows reserved for faculty housing. The walk curled in and out of cul-de-sacs before finally reaching the campus, making it the longest of the three approaches to the Hall.

Caroline hunched her shoulders against the biting wind and considered her choices. The snow lay as deep on the walk as on the street, but the former offered one advantage. Victorian-style gas lamps sprouted from the pavement at ten-yard intervals. To a native Chicagoan like herself, even this modest lighting provided a sense of security not found on the darkened road. People weren't mugged under streetlights. Muggings were reserved for shadows—alley shadows, park shadows, gangway shadows—but certainly not for streetlights.

But this isn't Chicago, Caroline mused. *This is quiet little Rhineburg, home to wealthy farmers and poor professors. Sedate as sedate can be.*

"Also," she said aloud, "home to a mad bomber!"

She shivered, more from the memory of recent events than from the cold, and hurried across the street. Psychopaths who blew up hospital wards probably didn't stoop to mugging middle-aged women struggling through snowdrifts. Still, she'd feel better once safely ensconced in Bruck Hall. If only the pavement wasn't knee-deep in snow!

"Doesn't anyone here believe in shovels?" Caroline shook her head in bewilderment. In Chicago, people would have been outside long before now, shoveling sidewalks and staking claim to cleared parking spaces with beat up old lawn chairs saved for such occasions. Children would be sledding on the streets while neighbors waved to each other and wondered aloud where the heck the city plows were. Caroline missed her old

home. She missed Chicago and the people there. Rhineburg was so very—different.

Lost in memories, Caroline barely noticed the shift
in the weather. The wind had died, and with it the snow.
The absolute silence accompanying this change ulti-
mately captured her attention. She paused beneath a
streetlamp, puzzled, then pulled back the hood of her
parka and gazed up at the sky. A single star glimmered
in the darkness. In the east, the moon slowly crept from
behind a bank of clouds. The storm had indeed ended.
Caroline heaved a sigh of relief.

Walking became easier without the wind battling her
every step. She quickened her pace and soon reached
the final stretch of sidewalk leading to the campus.
The houses in this section glittered with Christmas
lights. Wreaths of holly and ivy hung from the doors,
and several porches boasted plastic Santas or snow-
men. A common theme united the block: each lawn
featured a painted plywood reindeer studded with miniature white lights, a larger red bulb blinking merrily on
its umber nose. The animals stood posed beside over-
sized alphabet letters outlined in strings of red, blue,
or green lights.

Caroline passed three houses before the significance
of the display registered in her mind. A smile soft-
ened her features as she slid to a halt before a slightly
tipsy reindeer leaning against a four-foot-tall letter *P*.
The deer's nose flashed on and off like an errant stop-
light above his crooked grin. His left lid drooped in
a sly wink while his right brow arched over a notice-
ably bloodshot eye. One slender foreleg crossed the
other causing his body to tilt toward the *P* in a most
unreindeer-like manner.

Caroline turned and looked back down the path.

The letters *H* and *A* were barely in view, but she could clearly see the *P* next door. She walked past another house where a bright blue *Y* decorated the lawn. The head of a sleepy reindeer lolled between the branches of the *Y,* a bottle of champagne cradled in its antlers.

Caroline's smile grew to a grin. It took a real joker to dream up a line of inebriated reindeer toasting the New Year. Seeing them there almost made up for the long cold trek to Bruck Hall.

But only almost. Chilled to the bone, she plunged on through the snow while taking a quick mental count. Twelve letters, twelve houses. She trudged past a *Y* and an *E,* slipped on the ice near an *A,* then regained her balance as she passed the letter *R.* She slowed to more decorous pace when she approached the Hall's spacious lawn.

Bruck Hall looked impressive at any time with its pink stone walls rising to twin towers fore and aft. Tonight the storm had worked a kind of magic on the old building. It shimmered in icy elegance like a spun-sugar castle, moonlight bouncing off its mullioned windows and highlighting the snowcapped gargoyles perched above them. Caroline's spirits rose at the sight of it. They lifted even higher when the great oak door beneath the portico swung open and she saw other snowmen-and-women scurry inside. She shook the blanket of white from her own shoulders, then hurried down the Hall's freshly shoveled sidewalk and up the staircase.

Caroline barely touched the ornate bronze handle before someone unexpectedly flung the door open from inside. Off balance, she pitched headlong into Bruck Hall's brightly lit lobby. Saving her from a face-to-face encounter with the floor was a pair of strong hands that grabbed her from behind and yanked her unceremoniously to her feet.

"Mother! I thought you'd never get here." From a foot above her head, Martin Rhodes frowned down on Caroline. "Where in the world have you been?"

"I took the scenic route, dear," Caroline said irritably. She rubbed the back of her neck, conscious of a twinge in her upper spine. "You could have killed me jerking open the door like that."

"I was only trying to help. You were late."

"In case you haven't noticed, our latest blizzard has fouled up the streets again."

Caroline shrugged off her parka and shook the dampness from her ash-brown hair.

"Hey, watch it!" Martin ducked as a shower of melted snow spattered his suit. Dancing out of the way, he collided with his wife, Nikki.

"Don't mind your son," chuckled Nikki, her dark eyes sparkling with mirth. "He's just eager for you to meet his friends." She handed Caroline's parka to Martin, who grumbled something about impossible women before marching off down the hall. "He's a nervous wreck," Nikki said as she watched her husband wedge his mother's jacket onto an already crowded coatrack. "All the bigwigs are here, including the president's advisory committee on hiring."

Caroline felt a surge of sympathy for her son.

"I meant to be on time," she said apologetically. "But I had to walk. My old rattletrap wasn't up to the weather." Caroline collapsed on a bench, slid off her boots, and wiggled her cold toes. "This has been quite a day so far," she said as she slipped on the shoes she'd stored in the parka's pocket.

Nikki gave her mother-in-law a wry grin. "Bad time in the ER?"

"No more than usual. It's these constant interruptions by the police that are so irritating. They ask the same questions over and over. I'm totally fed up with them."

"Why are they badgering you?" Martin returned with a numbered ticket for the parka. He handed it to Caroline. "They must realize you've told them all you know about the bombing."

"Of course they do!" Caroline drew a deep breath, willing herself to stay calm. "Forgive me if I'm grouchy, but every time I turn around, there's an officer from some agency asking to speak with me. Today it was the ATF. I've already told my story to the FBI, the Rhineburg police, and the state police. I've even talked to a JCAHO investigator."

"JCAHO? What's that?"

"That, my dear boy, is the Joint Commission on Accreditation of Healthcare Organizations. JCAHO accredits hospitals. They have a Sentinel Event Policy covering unexpected occurrences involving death or serious injury. JCAHO sends an investigator to determine what happened and if the hospital could have prevented it. God only knows what they'll come up with. Probably a recommendation to ban Christmas trees on the wards."

Nikki rolled her eyes. "So which agency is in charge of the case? It can't be the Rhineburg police."

"Your guess is as good as mine. Seems like everyone has a finger in the pie. But I'd bet on the FBI." Caroline rose. "We'd better go in to the party. Your friends will be wondering where you are."

"Especially Professor Atwater." Martin's rugged face registered a mix of pride and amusement. "My boss wants to talk to you about the bombing. Carl's the town historian. These murders are grist to his mill. He's hoping to get some inside information from you."

Caroline's left eyebrow shot up. Before she could reply, the man they were discussing hailed them from the end of the corridor.

"My, my, Mr. Rhodes. Don't tell me this lovely young woman is your mother!"

If Caroline hadn't known better, she'd have sworn she saw Santa himself standing there. A massive man who nevertheless carried himself well, Carl Atwater wore his thick white hair collar-length and curly. His matching beard and mustache accented eyes the color of forget-me-nots in a face so plump and windburned that Caroline could almost hear the sound of sleigh bells. The fact that he claimed no waist—his top being as round as his bottom—added to the professor's Santa-like appearance, as did his red checked shirt, black corduroys pants, and knee-high laced hiking boots.

Caroline extended her hand while pointedly ignoring the professor's ridiculous compliment. She knew she looked like a half-drowned cat, limping down the hallway on frozen feet with damp hair clinging to her forehead and cheeks. As for the young part, she'd passed her fortieth birthday years before and felt no need to hide it.

"You must be Carl Atwater, Martin's mentor at Bruck. I understand you're chairman of the history department."

"Due to a lack of contenders, I earned that honor many years ago. Since then, I've simply outlived my rivals."

Caroline smiled. "I bet your ability has something to do with it."

"I consider myself a fairly good teacher," Atwater

replied with a shrug. "But as far as the chairmanship goes, that's more a matter of tenure and politics."

Caroline found herself pleasantly surprised by the professor's candor. Maybe Atwater was the paragon of virtue her son claimed him to be.

"So," Atwater said as they walked down the hall. "I hear you've moved to Rhineburg permanently. Thinking of buying a house soon?"

Caroline glanced at her son. His face registered nothing but innocence.

"Actually, I haven't decided if I'll stay. I've taken the position of nursing dorm housemother on a temporary basis only."

"Hmm. Martin told me you enjoy working with young people. Of course, living with them does have its drawbacks."

Caroline considered her answer. Keeping track of forty students could be troublesome, especially at night. There wasn't a trick in the book they didn't try when it came to breaking curfew. But she'd pulled the same tricks in her youth and had no problem anticipating the current generation's antics. All in all, she had no complaints.

"It's certainly not a dull job," she replied. "But I'm not sure I want to make it a lifelong occupation."

"I suppose not. You're a nurse also, aren't you?"

Caroline nodded. "I'm in the float pool at St. Anne's. I usually work in the ER, but I'll help out elsewhere if needed."

"Marty said you were on the psychiatric ward the day of the explosion."

So the perfect professor had at least one flaw: curiosity.

"Yes, but let's not spoil the party with talk of bombs

and blood." Caroline turned to Nikki. "What I'd rather discuss is that line of inebriated reindeer I ran into on my way here."

"Aren't they hilarious?" Nikki laughed. "They were Dr. Pauly's idea. He convinced everyone on the block to join in the fun."

"You should have seen the crowds the first night they were lit," crowed Martin. "Hundreds of students lined the street."

"Now, children, behave yourselves," said Atwater. "You know our esteemed president disapproves of said decorations. They're out of keeping with the character and dignity of this fine institution."

"I'm glad to hear you agree with me, Professor."

Martin and Nikki froze in their tracks like two statues bearing similar expressions of horror. They stared at Caroline, who in turn stared at Professor Atwater. The professor, on the other hand, didn't seem the least bit disturbed as he turned to greet the newcomer.

"Ah. President Hurst. Welcome to our little circle. May I introduce my teaching assistant, Martin Rhodes, and his lovely wife, Nikki." Atwater motioned toward Caroline. "And this is Martin's mother, Mrs. Caroline Rhodes. We were just discussing Dr. Pauly's reindeer."

"So I heard. For once you seem to concur with me."

Opposite of Atwater in size and stature, Hurst puffed up his scrawny chest and glared at them through horn-rimmed glasses.

"You misunderstand," Atwater said smoothly. "I wasn't agreeing with you, only stating your point of view."

The two men exchanged artificial smiles. With the atmosphere getting chillier by the minute, Caroline decided to change the subject.

"Bruck University is quite beautiful, President Hurst. I've always enjoyed visiting the campus."

She thought Hurst might ignore her, but then his hooded eyes swiveled to meet hers. Dark pools of granite, they radiated none of the warmth of his words.

"We try to maintain a gracious educational setting here at Bruck. It's a difficult chore since we're obliged to rely heavily on our alumni for financial support." Hurst glanced at Martin. "You're one of our graduates, Mr. Rhodes?"

"Y-yes, sir," Martin stammered. "I'm doing my postgraduate work under Professor Atwater. I hope to teach history on the college level after I earn my Ph.D."

"Really." Hurst's head bobbed in the direction of the chairman before his gaze returned to Martin. "Good luck, young man. I'm sure you'll do Bruck proud someday."

He favored the women with a tight smile, then excused himself and walked toward the faculty lounge. Atwater watched with narrowed eyes.

"Observe a master at work, Martin. If you hope to rise in the academic world, remember one thing: flattery will get you everywhere."

Caroline took note of the contempt in the professor's voice. She glanced at Nikki and saw her tug surreptitiously on Martin's sleeve. He looked down and the girl shook her head ever so slightly.

It didn't take a genius to understand the gesture. Still, men could be dense at times. Caroline wasn't one to take chances.

"I don't know about the rest of you, but right now I could do with a good stiff drink. Is there a bar set up somewhere, Martin?"

"How rude of me." The professor bowed to his guest

and extended a chubby arm. "If you will do me the honor, madam."

Caroline latched onto his elbow like a fish to bait. "Lead on, MacDuff!"

BRUCK'S FACULTY LOUNGE overflowed with revelers when the foursome made their entrance. Atwater cut a path through the crowd, his goal an unoccupied settee near the buffet table.

"This should do nicely," he shouted above the din. "Close to the food and the fireplace."

Caroline looked about the room in surprise. She'd expected it to be utilitarian in nature, furnished in chrome and vinyl with steel shelving for bookcases and sensible stain-free carpeting on the floor. Instead, the motif reflected down-home cozy. Tartan plaid easy chairs stood scattered in groupings near an enormous stone fireplace at the far end of the lounge. Matching sofas flanked the door on the opposite side. The plank flooring gleamed a burnished gold except where an occasional throw rug concealed the shine. Dead center in the room stood a large oak table, its surface hidden by an ivory tablecloth on which rested a smorgasbord of delights already being sampled by Professor Atwater. He gestured for Caroline to join him, but her attention had strayed to the room's holiday decor.

"How beautiful!"

Caroline gazed appreciatively at the various arrangements scattered about the room. Someone had lent a professional touch to the job of decorating and it showed. Massive pots of crimson and pink poinsettias crowded the windowsills bracketing the far corner of the lounge. To the left of the windows, a four-foot wreath embellished with scarlet and silver streamers dominated the chimneypiece of the fireplace. A line of vanilla-scented candles graced the stone mantel above an artistically draped balsam garland. Smaller candles flickered on pewter stands next to bowls of holly scattered about the shelves of the floor-to-ceiling oak bookcases.

The pièce de résistance occupied the corner left of the fireplace. There, a grouping of three pines, the smallest perhaps five feet tall, the largest almost touching the ceiling, sparkled with miniature red lights and silver glass balls. Nestled in the center of the trees stood a magnificently carved candle in peppermint shades of pink, deep rose, and white. Pots of scarlet poinsettias surrounded its wrought-iron stand.

"Very nice," exclaimed Caroline.

"Credit Mrs. Pauly," Atwater replied between mouthfuls. "This room is off-limits for days while she's transforming it from drab to magnificent. Well worth it, though. Our faculty party is the highlight of the social season at Bruck."

"That's understandable," said Caroline. "Life in a small town probably offers few opportunities for this kind of gathering."

The professor shot an incredulous look at Martin who merely shrugged his shoulders.

"Actually, you'd be amazed at the number of 'opportunities' we poor Rhineburgers have for celebrating," Atwater retorted. "We may be short on opera and ballet, but we manage to amuse ourselves in various backward ways."

Caroline blushed. "I didn't mean it that way."

Nikki rushed to her mother-in-law's rescue. "How about some hot cider, Mom? Marty!" She poked her husband in the ribs. "Go get us something to drink."

Martin didn't need any urging. "How about you, Professor? Cider or beer?"

"Beer, of course. Unless that cider is well spiked." Atwater snatched another canapé from the table and followed his protégé to the bar.

"What a gaffe," Caroline muttered disgustedly. "I must have sounded totally condescending."

"Don't worry about it," Nikki reassured her with a broad grin. "Most urban refugees consider Rhineburg a bit provincial at first."

Caroline smiled ruefully. She knew Nikki had easily adapted to life in the boonies. But could she, city born and bred, ever do the same?

"Tell me," she said, changing the subject. "What's up with President Hurst and Professor Atwater? They act like they're charter members of the Mutual Unadmiration Society."

"So you noticed. Well…" Nikki glanced at the people nearest them before drawing Caroline over to a deserted corner. "You have to be careful what you say around here. At Bruck, the walls not only have ears, but hearing aids as well."

Caroline laughed. Still, she got the message. She lowered her voice to match Nikki's.

"Did something happen recently?"

"Oh, no. Those two have been at each other's throat for years. It began soon after Hurst arrived here."

"When was that?"

"1985."

Caroline's eyes widened. "That's what I'd call a longstanding feud. What started it?"

"Jealousy on Hurst's part. Professor Atwater is practically an institution in Rhineburg. He went to college compliments of the government after his Army days, then came here to teach. He says he started at Bruck and he'll finish at Bruck, no date of retirement specified."

Caroline watched the subject of their conversation wend his way through the clots of people blocking the bar.

"Martin's boss could afford to shed a few pounds. But on the whole, he looks pretty good for a man in his seventies."

"Don't ever allude to his age, Mom. The professor goes bananas over the term *senior citizen*. Those are two words he never applies to himself."

"Young at heart, huh? Okay, I'll forgo any mention of white hair in his presence. Tell me more about Hurst's jealousy."

"The professor is a born historian. He's written several books about rural America, and they've all sold well."

"I've read two of them," said Caroline. "He delves into a particular town's past. The stories he digs up are fascinating."

"Marty's doing research on Atwater's next project, a book about company-owned coal mining towns. The professor has earned a pile of money on his books, plus a reputation for educating folks who normally don't read historical non-fiction. The university adores using his name to attract new students. His credits look impressive on those glossy brochures they hand out at open house."

"So Bruck needs Professor Atwater more than he needs Bruck."

Nikki nodded. "That's why our dear president despises him so. Hurst hates to share the limelight. It bugs him that Professor Atwater draws more attention from the press than he does."

"Come on, Nikki. There has to be more to it than that. Professional jealousy I can understand. But President Hurst is an important man in his own right. Why, he runs the entire university!"

"And quite poorly, if you ask me," Nikki countered darkly. "Look around this room. The faculty is almost evenly divided between supporters of the president and those who'd like to see Professor Atwater elevated to that post."

Caroline's eyebrows rose a fraction. "Is the professor gunning for the job?"

"He says he isn't, but he's not happy with the curriculum changes Hurst is making. The president is decimating the liberal arts program. He's slashed classes across the board, especially in history."

"I can see how that would upset the professor," Caroline remarked dryly. "There's nothing so irritating as having someone infringe on your turf."

"The professor's not like that," Nikki retorted. "He just doesn't think the liberal arts program should suffer because the Emperor—that's what everyone calls Hurst—wants a football stadium."

"Hold on, Nikki. You've got me totally confused. Since when has Bruck had a football team?"

"We don't now. But we will if Hurst has his way. He says emphasizing sports more will attract kids to the school, as if that's what college is all about."

Caroline saw a glimmer of sense in the plan. Bruck relied on its graduates for a portion of its funding, and everyone knew that alumni cherished their sports teams. Look at the dough Notre Dame raked in from its Knute Rockne devotees. There wasn't a college in the country that didn't wish Ronald Reagan had made them famous with his "win one for the gipper" line.

"The Emperor's in thick with Mayor Schoen," Nikki continued. "He wants the town to refurbish the old high school stadium that abuts the campus so he can field a team there."

"Rhineburg doesn't have that kind of money, does it?"

"A lot of folks here live and die by their sports teams. If Hurst can convince them of the need for a decent stadium, they'd hold bake sales from here to eternity to pay for it. He's already pledged reduced tuition for any kid from Rhineburg who attends Bruck. He's hinted at other concessions as well. Mayor Schoen's all for it since the quarry would supply new stone for the stadium walls."

Caroline vaguely recalled hearing of a quarry somewhere nearby. She'd never seen it, but it probably employed a good number of the town's residents. A contract to repair the stadium would benefit both the workers and the town treasury.

"Hurst claims Bruck can pay part of the cost by cutting what he calls 'non-essential classes.' He's pink-slipping professors who haven't earned tenure, but only in certain departments. The business school is actually growing because everyone and their uncle want to major in business."

"So the professors in the school of business are backing Hurst."

Nikki nodded. "And those in the liberal arts department are supporting Professor Atwater. The problem is, their numbers are shrinking every semester."

"I suppose some teachers are sitting on the fence, waiting to see which way the wind blows."

"Yeah. They're no help at all," Nikki said glumly. "I think the Emperor is going to win this battle."

"If he does, Martin stands little chance of being hired at Bruck."

"I know." Nikki smiled weakly at her mother-in-law. "We love Rhineburg. But we may have to move on once Marty graduates. I doubt there'll be any job openings here."

Caroline heard the pain in Nikki's voice. She put an arm around the girl and hugged her.

"Things will work out for you two. Martin's a bright young man. He'll get a job somewhere, believe me."

"Sure he will," said Nikki. "I shouldn't have laid all this on you. Please don't worry about it."

"Hey! Aren't moms supposed to worry about their kids? Someday you'll do the same thing with your children."

That brought a grin to Nikki's face.

CAROLINE WAS EXHAUSTED. In the two hours since her arrival at Bruck Hall she'd been bombarded with questions about the bombing at St. Anne's. It seemed everyone assumed that because she'd been present on the ward that day, she had an inside track on the investigation. She'd sidestepped all inquiries with a stock reply: "I'm sorry, but the police have asked me not to discuss the case."

The excuse sounded hackneyed even to her own ears, but it seemed to satisfy most people. It also lent a certain air of mystery to Professor Atwater's guest. Faculty members exchanged knowing looks with their wives, and professors were overheard muttering the words *prime witness* to their colleagues.

Caroline found it amusing when Martin told her of the speculation elicited by her remark. She gave little thought to it, though, concentrating instead on stifling yet another jaw-wrenching yawn. Her day had been tiring and the walk to the Hall arduous. Thoughts of a warm bed and soft pillow occupied her mind. Noting the time on her watch, she decided she'd done her motherly duty. She said as much to Martin, but phrased it more acceptably.

"I believe I've met everyone here, Marty. It's been a great party, but if you don't mind, I'm going to call it a night."

Distracted by laughter at one end of the lounge, Martin made no protest.

"Hmm? Oh, sure, Mom. If you want a lift home..."

Caroline shook her head. "The fresh air will do me good. Have a wonderful time with your friends and say bye to Nikki for me."

She squeezed Martin's arm affectionately and made a beeline for the door. Padding down the carpeted hallway, she noted with some surprise the quality of the paintings lining the walls. One particular landscape made her pause. The artist had captured the ephemeral beauty of a Maine sunset viewed from the ocean. Wispy pinks and oranges splashed the sky above a craggy coastline and served as a backdrop for the lazy flight of two seagulls. A double-masted schooner rocked in the tide, its deck deserted, its white sails furled. Nearby, two chunky lobster boats floated on the dark sea. The peaceful intimacy of the ships at rest contrasted sharply with the remoteness of the bouldered shore stretching back to wooded cliffs. Their presence seemed not so much an intrusion on nature as a complement to it.

The watercolor reminded Caroline of a happier time. She had walked those stony bluffs and sailed on a schooner much like the one pictured. She hadn't been alone then, hadn't even considered what alone could mean. Now, gazing at the painting, the pain of loss engulfed her. Life was transient, fleeting. Only the rocks and the hills endured the whims of nature and survived.

The picture opened a floodgate of memories for Caroline, not all of them pleasant. *Don't do this,* she warned herself. *He's gone. It's over.* The past was dead, despite its effort to reclaim her soul. She'd made it through the evening with poise intact. She refused to fall apart now.

"Damn it!"

The shouted expletive startled Caroline from her reverie. She turned and stared at the door opposite her. From behind it came a voice raised in indignation.

"It had nothing to do with us. Some maniac planted it."

Caroline heard a low murmur but couldn't make out any words. Curiosity dispelled all former thoughts from her brain. She tiptoed across the hall and stationed herself near the doorway. A soldier's portrait hanging on the wall provided a convenient excuse for her presence there. She feigned an interest in the picture as she strained to hear the conversation.

"That's a pile of crap, and you know it, Gary. And don't tell me to be quiet. I don't care if the entire university hears me."

The second voice broke in, once again indistinguishable except as a rumble of sound. Caroline leaned closer to the door.

"Listen to me," the first man shouted.

His voice faded, became stronger again, then faded once more as he apparently paced the room. She caught only bits and pieces of his sentences.

"Too much at stake…protect your interests…go off half-cocked."

Caroline almost gave in to her baser instincts and

put her ear to the door, but the knob suddenly turned. Heart pounding, she turned and bolted down the hallway. She reached the lobby unobserved, but in her haste, she caught her heel in the carpet, pitched forward, and collided with the coatrack. Simultaneously, she heard a door being flung open behind her.

"I'm warning you, Gary. Be careful what you say and to whom you say it."

Caroline clung to the swaying rack, pretending to search for her coat while at the same time shooting furtive glances over her shoulder. Her subterfuge was rewarded when a heavyset man emerged from the room and strode rapidly toward the lounge. Caroline couldn't see his face, but she recognized him immediately. A broad streak of silver zigzagging through an otherwise red head of hair gave away the administrator of St. Anne's Hospital.

What could Charles Paine be doing here? she mused. *And why is he so angry? Or frightened.*

Intrigued by the argument she'd overheard, Caroline searched distractedly for her parka. The two men—she assumed Paine had been talking to another man; he'd called him Gary—must have been discussing the bombing. Paine's reference to a maniac made that much clear. But what did he mean by "too much at stake"? Was he worried about the hospital's reputation? Or could there be a more personal reason for the confrontation?

She finally found her coat buried beneath two others. She slipped into the parka, exchanged her shoes for boots, and stepped out into the night still contemplating the administrator's words.

"Chilly out here, isn't it."

Caroline almost made a repeat performance of her

entrance into Bruck Hall. This time Professor Atwater saved her from tumbling down the stairs.

"I'm sorry if I frightened you," he said gruffly. "Are you all right?"

"I'm perfectly fine." Caroline extracted herself from the professor's arms with an embarrassed smile. "And you didn't frighten me at all." She looked at him curiously. "Why aren't you inside with the others?"

Atwater shrugged. "I'm not good at these affairs. Too many people trying to impress each other with their academic achievements. All very boring."

"Come now, Professor. Isn't that a bit snobbish?"

Atwater shrugged a second time as they descended the stairs. "That may be your opinion now, but attend a few more of these shindigs and then let's see how snobbish you think I am."

"To be truthful, I overheard a few conversations tonight that could only be labeled esoteric. Comparing Shakespeare's sonnets to modern rap music…"

"That had to be Andrew Littlewort," chuckled the professor. "Dr. Littlewort loves to shock folks with daring pronouncements on literature. His theories are so off-the-wall that arguing with him only dignifies his silliness. The best thing to do is simply avoid the man."

"I take it, that's what you do."

"Like the plague," Atwater said with a grin.

They reached the end of the path and turned onto the sidewalk bordering Circle Road. Caroline gazed in astonishment at the clean pavement stretching all the way to the hospital.

"What happened to all the snow? This sidewalk was buried in drifts when I arrived at Bruck Hall."

"Considering the severity of the storm," said the professor with a hint of satisfaction in his voice, "I'd say the troops did well tonight."

"The troops? Who exactly are the troops?"

"The troops, milady, are Bruck's answer to crime in the street. Law and order the Rhineburg way."

Caroline studied Atwater through narrowed eyes. The man sounded serious, but he had to be joking.

"You're related to Professor Littlewort, aren't you? I should be avoiding you also."

"No, no." Atwater laughed. He took Caroline by the elbow, swung her around to the west, and pointed to a small stone building at the far end of Bruck Green. "You see before you the home of the Archangels where miracles are born on a daily basis."

Other than raising one eyebrow, Caroline managed to contain herself. Too many beers or too long in the boonies, she thought. Unfortunately, the man beside her was Martin's mentor. She'd have to be tactful.

"How delightful. Someday you'll have to tell me all about your…your angels. But, it's pretty cold out here…" She hunched her shoulders to emphasize the point. "And it's been a very long day. So…"

"Nonsense," boomed Atwater. "The night is still young. You don't work tomorrow—Marty told me— and we have lots to talk about." He propelled her toward a line of parked cars. "Let's head over to the Blue Cat Lounge and get to know each other better."

Caroline silently cursed Martin. Why hadn't he chosen to work with someone more normal? Someone like an axe-murderer with a penchant for chopping up recalcitrant students?

"Really, Professor…"

They came to an abrupt halt beside a fire-engine-red

Jeep Cherokee. Caroline's resolve melted away as she stared at the Jeep, then at Atwater, then back at the Jeep.

"I should have guessed," she said, a smile tugging at her lips. "You go whole hog with the Santa Claus bit, don't you?"

Atwater stroked his snowy beard. "I always say, if you've got it, flaunt it. Ho, ho, ho!"

Caroline had been on edge all evening. Standing there in the crisp night air, though, seeing the man so obviously pleased with the image he and his Jeep created, she couldn't help but dissolve into laughter. Once begun, she couldn't stop.

"You're perfect," she gasped between giggles. "White beard, pink cheeks, and even a shiny red nose."

"You might even say it glows," Atwater replied with a wicked grin. He waggled his eyebrows at Caroline, who burst out laughing despite herself. Her unrestrained humor proved infectious. Within seconds the two were leaning against each other, choking back tears, and holding their aching sides.

"Oh, my!" Caroline gulped. She swiped at her eyes with the back of one hand. "You're truly something else, Professor."

"You aren't too bad yourself, Mrs. Rhodes. But why don't we drop the formalities? I'll be Carl and you can be Caroline, okay?"

Caroline hesitated, then nodded with a shy smile. Aware that some self-imposed barrier was crashing down around her, she took a deep breath before straightening her disheveled clothing. The professor opened the door of the Cherokee and waited. His grin appeared inviting, yet undemanding, and Caroline sensed he wouldn't hold it against her if she turned him down. At that moment, though, she couldn't think of anything more enjoyable than a ride through the country-side with this jolly companion. Without another word, she climbed into the Jeep.

"Tell me about your angels."

They had circled Bruck Green, and everywhere Caroline looked, the pavement had been scraped bare. Considering the state of affairs earlier in the evening, the transformation was nothing short of magical.

"Angels? Oh, you mean the Bruck boys."

"I'm not sure who I mean," said Caroline. "You mentioned angels and miracles, and I wondered..."

"If I was putting you on? Of course not." Carl checked his side mirror before turning onto the highway leading north. He gestured at the property around them. "All this was wilderness when Joseph Bruck arrived in America. He came from Germany looking for good farmland and found it here in Rhineburg. After a long and profitable life, he died the wealthiest man in the county."

"Until I moved here, I thought all farmers lived from hand to mouth. You know what I mean; a constant struggle to survive."

"Some do live that way," Carl replied. "The young ones who can't afford enough acres to realize a decent profit, and the old ones who overinvested in land back in the '80s, then couldn't pay the taxes on it. But the early settlers got their land cheap. If they were good farmers and good managers, they prospered.

"Joseph Bruck really prospered. Forest covered much of this area back then. He and his brothers cleared the timber and sold it to buy more land. Once their farms were in place, they branched out into other endeavors. They succeeded at everything they did. Old Joe was a natural born leader. He guided the family enterprises and made money for all of them.

"He made his greatest killing when the first locomotive arrived in Rhineburg. The original tracks cut right through his land. Even today there are people who claim he cut a deal with the railroad to solidify the family fortune."

"A regular land baron, hmm?"

"Don't let the Bruck boys hear you say that. They're a trifle sensitive about their family history."

"So a later generation named the university for Rhineburg's founding father."

"Actually, Joe masterminded the birth of Bruck," said Atwater. "I told you he was an intelligent man. He knew that the growth of the country depended on an educated populace governing it. He envisioned a center of learning in Rhineburg, something patterned on the great universities of Europe. Before he died, he made provisions for part of his land to be set aside for such a school. His will stipulated that his money stay in the family only if they agreed to build it."

"That had to be expensive. How'd the Brucks manage it?"

"They made various deals with other powerful people in the county. They also drummed up support for the school among the common folk in the area, many of whom valued education as a way for their children to better themselves."

"Amazing."

"What's amazing is what families will do if the incentives are great enough. The Bruck family had no intention of losing their inheritance. And while the present Bruck U. can't compare with the University of Heidelberg, it's still a decent enough college."

"Where do the Bruck boys, as you call them, fit in?"

"Joseph was determined to safeguard his dream," the professor explained. "His instructions called for a Bruck to preside over the Board of Trustees as long as the institution existed. He also demanded that university security be managed in perpetuum by his descendents."

"Interesting concept," commented Caroline.

"You have to remember, Joseph Bruck thought like a typical German. Hard work and education were high on his list of priorities, but so were law and order. He passed those values on to his progeny. The Bruck brothers who currently head up security are quite adept at keeping the more rambunctious students in line. They have unique penalties for infractions of the rules."

"How unique?" Caroline asked suspiciously.

"Let's just say they believe in the value of physical labor."

Caroline couldn't keep the astonishment out of her voice, or off her face. "You mean to say, students shoveled all that snow?"

Carl grinned. "We have the cleanest campus in the world. We have regular groundskeepers, but don't be shocked if you notice students manning snowplows in the winter, or picking up litter on the Green in spring. That's the way it works at Bruck."

"I'm surprised the students don't object. You'd never get away with such a policy at a Chicago college."

"It's all spelled out in the student handbook. You either agree to it or you don't enroll at Bruck. Mainly, kids here try to stay out of trouble."

They rode the rest of the way in silence, the professor intent on avoiding an accident on the icy road and Caroline busy contemplating the customs of small towns. She began to think life in Rhineburg might not be so bad after all.

"We're here." Carl steered the Jeep into a clearing left of the road and pulled up in front of a long, low-slung wooden building. "Welcome to the Blue Cat Lounge."

Caroline stared openmouthed at the old roadhouse. It had the seedy appearance of a business hanging on by the skin of its teeth. Blue paint flaked off the outside walls in long curling strips, exposing plank siding that looked like it had been pieced together from scrap lumber. At the far end of the building, cracked and grimy windows flanked a wooden door sagging on its hinges. Above the door a crooked neon cat flashed blue in the night. There was no sign; evidently the cat said it all.

Caroline scanned the clearing for other cars. "Are you sure it's open?"

"Of course." Carl pointed to their left. "There's a parking lot behind those trees. It's probably filled to capacity since the Parker boys are playing tonight. Hope you like jazz," he added as he climbed out of the Jeep.

As predicted, they found the lounge crowded with music lovers. Tables for two sported twice the number of chairs while every bar stool appeared occupied. Despite the large number of people, relative quiet reigned in the Blue Cat. As Caroline's eyes adjusted to the dim lighting, she realized why.

At the west end of the room a raised plywood platform supported three musicians preparing for a set. A tall willowy youth in faded denims cradled a tenor sax to his chest, his eyes closed, his fingers roaming the stops as he silently rehearsed a piece. Another boy, this one even younger than the first, stood hunched over a keyboard at center sage. The third fellow was older and stockier than the others. He huddled behind a drum set, adjusting the snare. Together, the three men presented a picture of concentrated energy waiting to explode.

Carl led the way to a reserved table near the bar. They were barely seated when an expectant hush descended on the room. Caroline took in the scene on the stage. Coated bulbs dangling from overhead wires glowed soft blue and illuminated the area where the musicians sat. Beyond this zone the light dimmed, causing shadows to dance on the platform edges. It was an oddly reverent setting, austere in its simplicity, and the audience seemed to sense this. They waited patiently until, without a word of introduction, the pianist swept his fingers across the keyboard, executing a complicated series of chords in a crescendo of sound. He paused for a fraction of a second, then the sax filled the silence with a muted wail before the drummer dragged his brushes across the snare head.

The wild fury of the prologue gave way to a dreamlike passage that dipped and rose in soulful strains. As the melody changed, so did the mood in the room. A sense of haunting intimacy seemed to fill the lounge, inviting the audience to feel rather than hear the message of the music.

Caroline closed her eyes and let the sound sweep over and into her. Each new melody caressed her mind with sensuous fingers until she was oblivious even of Carl's presence. Old memories died, new ones were created in her imagination. Time and reason became irrelevant. Pleasure existed solely in succumbing to the mood of the music.

Without warning, it was over. Caroline opened her eyes to find the professor staring at her. She unexpectedly felt herself blush. Ducking her head in embarrassment, she turned in her chair and joined in the applause for the three musicians waving their thanks from the stage. Mercifully, her cheeks cooled before she faced Carl again.

"They played a good long set," said Carl. "You felt it, didn't you?"

"They're very good," Caroline hedged. She looked down, unwilling to meet Carl's eyes. For some unexplainable reason she felt a reluctance to share the emotions laid bare by the music. Carl continued to probe.

"I've heard the band before, but I don't think I've ever enjoyed them as much as I did tonight."

Caroline perceived a double meaning in the professor's words. She smiled to hide her uneasiness while hoping her eyes didn't give her away. Atwater seemed to sense her discomfort, though. He pushed a menu toward her before opening his own. They spent the next few minutes silently perusing their choices.

FOUR HOT CHOCOLATES and a lot of small talk later, the professor finally got down to business.

"Martin's told me quite a bit about you, Caroline. He says you're a student of human nature."

Caroline's eyebrows rose. "I'm interested in people, if that's what you mean. I don't pretend to understand them, though."

"According to your son, you're very perceptive."

"Martin credits me with talents beyond my abilities. Lately," she added moodily, "I've had difficulty comprehending my own motives. I no longer speculate on those of others."

Carl stroked his beard thoughtfully. "I guessed wrong. I presumed you were over it, but apparently you still haven't reached the stage of acceptance."

Caroline almost bolted from her chair. "I've no idea

what you're talking about, Professor Atwater." She heard the nervousness in her voice. She had to get out of there before she began babbling. "It's quite late, Professor. I'd like to go home."

"A second ago I was 'Carl.' Now you're back to 'Professor Atwater.' I must have struck a raw nerve to turn you against me so quickly." Atwater leaned forward and touched Caroline's hand. "I may be an old man, but I'm not a fool. I can see when someone's hurting."

Caroline pulled her hand away, her stomach churning. Fear tore at her. What did this man know? Martin had probably told him about Ed, but had he revealed her secret, too? She'd told no one at St. Anne's, not even when she'd applied for her job. Like the professor, she wasn't a fool. She knew they'd have never hired her if they'd suspected the truth.

She struggled to hide her agitation. "I'm fine, Professor. Just a little too tired for an introspective conversation."

"My timing usually isn't this poor." Carl sighed. "I thought after five days you'd be handling it better."

Agitation gave way to confusion. *What's he talking about?* Caroline wondered. *It's been months, not days, since Ed's death.*

"But you see," Carl continued, "Martin led me to believe you could help me figure out this little mystery. I'm convinced the bombing wasn't a random act of violence. With your knowledge of the hospital…" He paused when he saw the astonishment on Caroline's face. "Now I've upset you again."

Caroline pressed her fingertips to her forehead. She'd leaped to all the wrong conclusions. Instead of prying into her secrets, Carl had been prattling on about the damned bombing. It was painful recalling that hellish day, but less threatening than a recital of her personal history. She had to pull herself together, apologize somehow.

"Forgive me…Carl." She lifted her eyes to meet his. How could she explain her coldness? Her downright bitchy behavior? "I didn't mean to be rude. Things have been…difficult lately. I've been going through a lot of changes, trying to straighten out my life. I'm a bit on edge at times."

Carl nodded in empathy. "Life can be tough. I know about your husband's death. Martin took it hard. We had some long talks after the funeral."

Caroline wasn't surprised to hear Martin had confided in his mentor, but she wondered how much he'd confided.

"It appears you've adjusted to living in Rhineburg. I presume that means the depression has eased up. You're getting back on track."

Caroline frowned. Apparently Carl did know the entire story.

"It could happen to anyone," the professor said quietly. When she didn't answer, he went on. "If it would help to talk about it, I'm a pretty good listener. And I know how to keep a confidence."

Caroline hesitated. She hardly knew this man. Still, Martin trusted him. It couldn't hurt to tell him a small portion of the story.

"I didn't cope well with widowhood," she finally said. "Ed and I grew up in the same neighborhood. We dated in high school and married soon after graduation. We were very young, but so much in love." She paused as memories of those early days engulfed her. "I thought we'd live happily ever after, like lovers do in the movies. It sounds silly, I know, but everything seemed to work out for us. Ed took some college classes, then applied to the fire department. By the time they accepted him, he had his degree. After he settled into his job, I returned to school. I received my nursing degree when Martin was seven."

She told Carl about the house they'd bought in Chicago and how her daughters, Krista and Kerry, had been born there. She told him stories of camping trips to Kentucky and birthday parties at the Foster Avenue beach, of friends and family and jobs she'd held in nursing. When at last she paused for breath, she discovered, much to her surprise, that they were the last patrons left in the lounge.

"Oh, dear. They're closing up around us."

Two members of the waitstaff were whisking empty glasses and full ashtrays off the tables around them. Caroline acknowledged the hint by half rising from her chair, but the professor shook his head. He signaled a waiter for refills.

"Don't worry," he said with a sheepish grin. "When you've put money into a place, you can stay for as long as you like."

"You own the Blue Cat?"

"Part owner. Jazz is my hobby. Fortunately, my bank account is sufficient to support both me and this." Carl gestured to the room at large. "But my life story can wait. Why don't you tell me about Ed's accident?"

Caroline had been avoiding the subject. She much preferred recalling the good days to the bad.

"Ed jogged almost every day," she said slowly. "He preferred to run in the evening when the streets were quieter. The night he died I'd decided to weed the front garden. The streetlights were just coming on when I saw Ed round the corner. He slowed his pace and waved to me. I waved back, and that's when I noticed a car weaving down the road behind him. I called out, but not quickly enough. The car hit him square in the back. The driver didn't stop, didn't even slow down." Caroline shook her head, a puzzled expression on her face. "To this day I can't describe the make or color of the car. I watched Ed go flying across the street, and then suddenly, it was all over."

"I hadn't realized you were there when it happened."

Caroline nodded and took a deep breath. "I went through the motions of a wake and funeral, but it felt more like a bad dream than reality. I couldn't believe Ed was gone. I thought I'd wake up and it would all be over. After Martin and Nikki and my daughters left, I sat around in that big empty house with nothing to do but think of my husband."

She glossed over the details of her plunge into despair. She'd eaten little, slept less, and gradually withdrawn completely into herself. Her sense of loss became so great that even her children meant nothing to her. She'd shut them out, refusing to answer their calls and letters. Caught in the web of depression, she preferred the dark solitude of her memories to the comfort of her family.

"I guess I feared being alone," she told Carl ruefully. "I self-destructed to the point where my kids had to step in. They admitted me to a psychiatric hospital for treatment."

Carl pursed his lips but said nothing. Watching him watching her, Caroline realized she'd said much more than she'd originally intended. A woman who relished her privacy, she didn't easily or often reveal her innermost thoughts to others. For some reason, though, she felt compelled to tell Carl the rest of the story.

"I could have accepted death. But to be locked away, handed over to a keeper..." She shook her head. How could she explain the terror she'd felt once enrolled in the ranks of the emotionally lost? "Fear can be a powerful incentive for recovery. I forced myself back into life."

"That couldn't have been easy."

A whisper of a smile crossed Caroline's lips. "It's amazing what you can do when the adrenaline starts flowing. I felt like a trapped animal fighting the cage. I had to get out of that hospital!"

She didn't mention how she'd done it. She'd suppressed all thoughts except those of escape and concentrated solely on appeasing her doctors. Her nursing experience had taught her the rules; she played the game to perfection. The first step had involved abandoning the safety of sleep. She got out of bed and put on makeup. She forced herself to eat the bland meals set before her, remembering to compliment the staff when they came to pick up her empty trays. She began walking the halls, smiling and nodding at the nurses she met. When the doctors made their rounds, she hid her trembling hands in her pockets and answered their questions with contrived eloquence. She watched them nod in satisfaction, fooling them all until the day came when they could no longer find a reason to keep her.

"Martin told me some of this," said the professor. "I must say, the rapidity of your recovery surprised me. In my experience, emotions take longer to heal."

Caroline avoided Carl's eyes. Deluding her children hadn't been difficult; they'd wanted to believe the doctors. But Professor Atwater was a different kettle of fish. He didn't seem the type one could easily hoodwink.

"I can't say I totally overcame my depression by the

time I left the hospital," she admitted. "But I'm winning the battle now. I'm glad I moved to Rhineburg. Here I can put the past behind and get on with my life."

At least she hoped she could.

"Hmm. I've heard that said before and I've always wondered if it's possible to do. Putting the past behind can be an excuse for not dealing with one's problems."

"I don't think that's the case with me," Caroline said archly, denying the fact she'd wrestled with the same thought several times since leaving Chicago. "My temporary job as housemother is ideal for the time being. And I like being in the float pool at St. Anne's. It allows me a way to ease back into nursing." She smiled to take the sting out of her next words. "Ed didn't leave me a wealthy woman. I still have to work for a living."

The professor nodded. "Life presents us with hard choices. Sometimes it's difficult to make the right ones."

Caroline recalled the Mary Engelbreit card a friend had sent her. A banner at the top of the card proclaimed "Don't Look Back." Beneath it, a little girl carrying a suitcase strode purposefully down one of two forks in a path. A signpost pointing her way read "Your Life." The other fork was labeled "No Longer an Option." Caroline had framed the card. It hung on a wall in her apartment, a daily reminder of what she must do.

She thought of it now as she replied, "Sometimes your choices are limited. For now, I think I'm where I should be. As for the future, who knows?"

ATWATER HAD GONE OFF to talk to one of the waiters, giving Caroline a chance to compose herself. She didn't know why she'd been so frank with him concerning her illness. True, she hadn't told him everything. But she'd withheld things from her children, too. Only her two best friends were privy to the complete story. Perhaps she'd confided in Carl because they were no longer around. Maybe her present loneliness had less to do with missing Ed and more to do with missing companionship in general. The thought disturbed her.

"Feeling better?"

Caroline looked up to see Professor Atwater maneuvering his massive body onto the too small chair across from her. He plunked two bottles of beer down on the table.

"Sorry, but hot chocolate does very little for me. Care for one?"

Caroline shook her head. "It's late, Carl. We should be going."

"Soon, I promise. First, though, we have to discuss the bombing at St. Anne's."

Caroline leaned back in her chair. She felt totally betrayed.

"You're unbelievable," she said bitterly. "First you kidnap me off the street. Then you try to soften me up with music, hot chocolate, and a sympathetic ear. You worm your way into my confidence. Then, when I'm beginning to trust you, bingo! 'Would you please tell me what it's like to watch seven people blown to bits, Mrs. Rhodes?' Well, you listen to me, Carl Atwater. I have no intention of satisfying your morbid curiosity. If you want information about the bombing, go ask the police."

She stood up and strode angrily toward the exit.

"It's pretty cold out there. Are you sure you don't want your coat?"

Caroline stalked back to the table. She glowered at Carl, grabbed her parka from the chair, and shoved her arms into the sleeves.

"It's a mighty long walk back to the dormitory. You

could try hitchhiking, but the road is usually deserted at this time of night."

"I'll catch a ride with one of the waiters."

Carl shook his head. "Sorry to tell you this, but they're long gone. I agreed to lock up the place tonight."

Caroline looked around her. Sure enough, the lounge was deserted except for the two of them. Furious, she shrugged off her coat and sat down.

"I can understand why you think I'm driven by curiosity," said the professor. "Your presence at the party tonight caused quite a stir."

"So you noticed."

Atwater ignored the sarcasm. "I notice a lot of things, which is precisely why I want to talk to you about the explosion. There's something very wrong going on in Rhineburg."

"It doesn't take a genius to see that. Blowing up a hospital ward is hardly a socially acceptable act."

"I'm not talking about the bombing," said Carl with a hint of exasperation in his voice. "I'm referring to the way the police are handling this case."

"It seems to me they're being very thorough," replied Caroline. "They practically invaded St. Anne's. You can't turn a corner without running into some kind of cop."

"I know what you mean. The same thing's happening at the university."

"What are they doing over there?"

"Looking for a killer, of course. Apparently they think one of our students might have built the bomb."

Despite her initial aversion to the subject, Caroline found this latest piece of information intriguing. She couldn't help but speculate on it.

"I suppose the science majors have come under scrutiny. It's possible one of them is talented enough to build a bomb."

"That's ridiculous," said Carl with a dismissive wave of his hand. "Our students are interested in only one thing: a college education. We don't attract bombers to Bruck."

"Well, well! Aren't you the elitist." Caroline leaned forward and fixed Carl with a hard stare. "What are you saying? Is Bruck so removed from the outside world that it's immune to the problems of society? Troubled kids pop up everywhere today. Why shouldn't one land in your lap?"

"I'm not denying reality, Caroline, but you don't know our students. Think about what I told you earlier tonight. These kids have to agree to shovel snow and pick up garbage if they misbehave. If we had a truly disturbed student attending Bruck, he'd have rebelled at that rule long before he reached the bomber stage. The faculty met two days ago to discuss this very matter. Not a single teacher could name a student capable of committing this crime."

Caroline relented. "I agree it's improbable, Carl, simply because I don't see what the motive would be. But it's not impossible. The police have to examine every possible lead. I'm sure they're also checking out some of the townspeople."

"Oh, sure. But they'll get nowhere fast with that part of the investigation."

"Why not?"

"Rhineburgers don't easily open up about their neighbors. It's a close community where people are protective of each other."

"That's a laugh," exclaimed Caroline. "I've overheard plenty of gossip at the hospital. It seems to me there's a flourishing grapevine in Rhineburg."

"The operative word in your last sentence is *over-heard*. I'll bet no one at work has directly confided in you yet."

"No, but I'm a newcomer at St. Anne's."

"Exactly! And you'll be considered a newcomer for at least a year or two, if not more. That's the way it is in small towns. Unless you're born here…"

"I get the picture, Carl."

"But what you don't get," insisted Carl, "is that those FBI agents and state cops are even worse than newcomers. They don't belong to this town at all. I tell you, Caroline, it'll be like pulling teeth getting Rhineburgers to talk to them. The cops are going to need some help if they hope to solve this case. They're going to need us."

A hundred tiny flash bulbs exploded simultaneously in Caroline's brain. Finally, she understood.

"I CAN'T BELIEVE what I'm hearing. You want to play Sherlock Holmes, and you want me to be your Watson. Well, no, thank you, Professor. You're not dragging me into this."

"Come on, Caroline. Think how perfect it would be. I'm the insider who can plug into the grapevine, and you're the outsider with a direct link to the hospital. Not only can you go anywhere you want in the building, but you're also a reliable witness to the bombing."

Caroline's anger boiled over. "Who the hell do you think you are asking this of me? I came to Rhineburg to start a new life, to put a lot of unhappiness behind me. I'm here only a few months when I get mixed up in the bloodiest affair in the history of this town. Do you think it was a picnic that day on the ward? Do you imagine

I enjoyed the sight of seven bodies blown to bits? That I relished seeing Christmas tree branches sticking out of bloody chests and severed limbs?"

"Of course not. And I didn't mean to imply that. But you were there, Caroline, which means you're involved, like it or not. You have a stake in the outcome of this case. You must want to see the killer brought to justice."

"Listen to me, Professor." Caroline's voice shook with emotion. "I told the police everything I know about that day. I have no intention of getting involved. I've had enough grief to last me a lifetime, and all I want now is a little peace."

Atwater said nothing, but his eyes narrowed as he watched Caroline twist the silver band on her left ring finger. She appeared mesmerized, her eyes locked on the symbol of her past. When she spoke again, her words came out in a strangled whisper.

"I can't help you, don't you understand? I can't!"

Carl pushed back his chair and stood up.

"History is a compilation of man's misery," he said quietly, his voice devoid of any warmth. "No one born on this earth has ever escaped sorrow or suffering. Why should you be any different from the rest of us?"

He picked up his coat and walked out of the lounge. Alone in the shadow-filled room, Caroline stared numbly at her wedding ring.

TWO

December 20

CAROLINE AWOKE TO THE clamor of the telephone. Eyes still heavy with sleep, she groped for the receiver and cradled it between her ear and the pillow.

"Hello."

"Mother?" Martin sounded his usual brisk self. "Is that you?"

Feeling anything but brisk, Caroline counted to three slowly before mumbling, "No. This is the cleaning lady. Your mother's asleep, but I'll tell her you called."

"Wait a minute," hollered Martin. "I thought Mom did her own housework."

Caroline yawned and rolled onto her back. She forced her eyes open and glanced at the alarm clock. "Marty, it's nine-fifteen on my day off. Give me a break, will you?"

"Oh. Okay." Martin cleared his throat. "I called because...because I..."

"It's your nickel, Martin. Spit it out."

"Because I was worried about you."

Martin's words came out in a rush. Caroline suspected she knew why.

"What's the matter, dear?" she asked patiently.

"Professor Atwater is in a stinking mood this morning. When I asked what the problem was, he looked at me sadly and said, 'Your mother.' Then he told me to go home, he didn't feel like teaching classes today. Mom, he never takes a day off! It's unheard of for him to skip work. Something's wrong here."

Caroline closed her eyes again. "Martin, nothing's wrong with me, or with Professor Atwater. We both like an occasional day off, that's all."

"Oh, I get it. You're spending the day together."

"In your dreams, my boy. In your dreams. Good-bye, Martin."

"Hold on, Mom!"

But Caroline hit the "off" button, dropped the receiver on the bedside table, and pulled the blanket over her head. Unfortunately, she'd come wide-awake. After ten minutes of tossing and turning, she accepted the inevitable and climbed out of bed.

She'd had a rotten night. An old recurrent dream had jolted her awake at 2:00 a.m. She'd sat up in bed, sweaty and trembling, waiting for her childhood bogeyman to recede into the shadows of her subconscious. An ancient sea monster, it pursued her through a redbrick schoolhouse exactly as it had when she was seven. But now the monster had modernized itself with the addition of a white beard and mustache. Instead of the throaty growl she'd feared as a child, it shrieked the word *History!* over and over again. When her heart had finally stopped its wild beating, she'd leaned back against her pillows and chided herself for succumbing to such silliness.

"I wish I'd never met you, Carl Atwater," she'd moaned. Expelling the professor from her thoughts, she'd snuggled down under the comforter and awaited sleep. It didn't come until dawn when further dark dreams accompanied it.

Four hours of fitful sleep did nothing to improve Caroline's mood of the previous evening. She padded to the kitchen, poured a glass of orange juice, and swallowed two aspirin. Her head pounded and every inch of her body ached. Aggravated now not only with Carl but also with her son, she turned the shower on full blast and let the hot water pelt her skin. The steam slowly cleared her head while the water massaged her sore muscles.

By the time she toweled off and pulled on jeans and a flannel shirt, the heat and aspirin were taking effect. She returned to the kitchen, mixed a packet of instant oatmeal with water and a dollop of peach jam, and set it to cook in the microwave. Together with a second glass of orange juice, the hot cereal completed what the shower had begun. Caroline felt almost human again as she cleared the table.

With the breakfast dishes out of the way, she considered doing a thorough cleaning of the apartment she lived in at the far end of the nursing dorm. Lord knew it needed it. For some unknown reason, Caroline's neatness quotient had dipped dramatically since her arrival in Rhineburg. Perhaps she could blame it on sharing a building with dozens of sloppy teenagers. Or maybe the fault lay in her solitary lifestyle, a condition that discouraged visitors other than Martin and Nikki. Whatever had caused her to change habits of a lifetime, Caroline realized she no longer cared if she made her bed or let newspapers pile up on the end table like playing cards in a deck. She'd lost her zest for housework months ago and certainly wasn't in the mood for it today.

The hell with it, she thought, and opted instead for a shopping spree. A drive into Rhineburg would distract her from thoughts of the men in her life. And, she reminded herself, Christmas was only a few days away. That gave her an excuse to do some serious shopping.

It was a perfect winter day with the sun shining high in a cloudless sky. The crisp December air invigorated Caroline and she perked up considerably during the walk to the hospital's garage. Her spirits rose even higher when her old Buick started on the first try. A good omen, she decided. She pulled away from St. Anne's, humming a Christmas carol.

She slowed to a crawl where the hospital property ended and Bruck University began. The campus stretched before her in pristine beauty. Fresh snow blanketed old mounds and rested undisturbed on the rolling lawns. Like newly stretched lengths of cotton batting, it spilled over into the deserted parking lots adjacent to the library and auditorium.

The five main university buildings glowed brightly in the sunlight, their rosy hue the result of nature rather than man. They'd been constructed of pink rhyolite from the quarry outside of Rhineburg. The stone bore a unique color and could be seen on the exteriors of many of the older homes in town, along with City Hall, the courthouse, and the police station. There were those who found it hard to take a pink police station seriously, but the early Rhineburgers were practical men. They used the material at hand and dared outsiders to laugh.

Unlike the buildings, which were somber unadorned rectangles, the grounds of Bruck U. belied the pragmatism of its founders. Here the farmer's natural love of the land prevailed. Ancient oaks towered over Circle Road and dominated the whitewashed landscape of Bruck Green. The tall trees glittered with ice, and crystallized puffs of snow nestled in their twisted arms like sleeping frost babies. Hyacinth, wild rose, and honeysuckle bushes lined the paths crisscrossing the campus and the Green. They, too, reflected the fury of last night's storm with spindly branches bowing low under the weight of the snow. Nearer to the buildings, raised flowerbeds curved in formal patterns beneath three-foot drifts. Caroline had seen them in October when russet and gold chrysanthemums filled their borders. She wondered how they'd look in spring when the daffodils emerged.

Dressed in winter white, the campus exuded picture-postcard prettiness. Caroline drove on, the Green to her left, the university to her right, admiring the peacefulness of the scene. She switched on the radio and fiddled with the dial until she found a station playing Christmas carols. Humming to the music, she made a sharp right off Circle and turned onto a road that merged with the highway leading to Rhineburg.

Melting ice made the intersection slick and the Buick's tires spun wickedly before grabbing the pavement. Caroline eased up on the accelerator. Gripping the steering wheel more firmly, she considered the need to buy new tires.

Soon, but certainly not today. Today was reserved for Christmas shopping. Caroline drew up a mental gift list as the Buick skimmed along the highway. Snow-covered fields stretched endlessly on both sides of the road. She took no notice of them, too busy imagining the perfect present for each of her children. Her mind barely registered the stand of stubby pines that signaled a break in the fields to her right. Beyond the pines, the road turned and dipped into a shaded hollow of mixed trees and scrub brush. She automatically guided the Buick into the curve, unaware the sun hadn't touched this section of shadowed pavement.

A layer of black ice covered the road. The Buick's

tires shifted to accommodate the turn, but the old car wasn't up to the challenge of the slippery surface. It plunged straight ahead, skidding across the highway's yellow centerline. Thoughts of Christmas evaporated from Caroline's mind. She slammed on the brake and steered frantically to the right.

Wrong, her brain screamed. She released the brake pedal and hauled the steering wheel to the left. The Buick bucked into a spin, its tires now completely off the road, before veering sideways across the pavement. Caroline pumped the brake in an effort to go with the slide. She depressed the pedal a second time, felt it flatten uselessly to the floor. Horrified, she clung to the steering wheel while the car fishtailed toward the far embankment.

The forested slope was a blur of brown and white rushing straight at her. Caroline threw up her hands in an instinctive gesture of self-protection. The Buick plowed into a wall of brush, lurched skyward where it hung motionless for the briefest of moments, then slammed violently back to earth. It rocked forward and sank into the snow, its front bumper crumpling against a jagged tree stump.

Caroline's forehead met the steering wheel with enough force to send shock waves down her spine. She felt rather than heard herself cry out in pain before she passed into unconsciousness.

SOMEONE WAS PLAYING basketball inside her head. It had to be Marty dribbling that damned ball again.

"Cut it out, Martin," Caroline mumbled. "You're giving me a headache."

"It's all right, Mrs. Rhodes. Hold still now."

She felt a sharp jab in her left arm and winced.

"That's not funny, Martin. Lemme go."

She struggled to sit up, but Martin had her pinioned to the ground. Her arms and legs were clamped to her sides, and he'd tied something across her forehead to hold her down. She wanted to scream at him but something hard constricted her throat.

"What are you doing?" she whispered in confusion.

A large fuzzy form loomed over her. It bent close to her face, murmuring soft noises. She strained to focus her eyes on the semihuman shape.

"You're not Martin. Who are you?"

"Take it easy, Cari. They're only trying to help you."

The voice sounded vaguely familiar. Could it be Ed? He'd always called her Cari, never Caroline. *But Ed's gone,* she reasoned disjointedly. *Maybe I'm dead, too. But then I wouldn't be hurting like this, would I?*

Caroline blinked once, then again, to clear her misted vision. Shapes slowly sharpened in detail until she was able to make out a bunched hand dangling above her head. She concentrated on the hand. Fingers. Yes, she could make out fingers. Long ones with short nails. Squeezing something clear and shiny. Rectangular with black lettering. Long tubing extending from one end. A wave of nausea swept over her and she closed her eyes.

"I'm going to be sick," she said through clenched teeth.

"You'll be all right, Cari. Take a deep breath."

That voice again. Definitely not Ed's, but someone she knew. She just couldn't place where she'd heard it before.

"This oxygen will help, Mrs. Rhodes. Hang on now. We'll have you at St. Anne's in no time flat."

St. Anne's? Well, why not? She worked there, didn't she? Martin better hurry or she'd be late for her shift.

"Okay, Bob. We're ready to roll."

Bob? She didn't know any Bob. Oh, dear. Mother always said, never take a ride from a stranger. Mother wouldn't approve of this. Not one little bit.

Caroline focused on the hand again. "Are you a stranger?"

Through a fog of pain she heard male laughter. *How impolite,* she thought before closing her eyes and drifting off to sleep.

CAROLINE AWOKE WHILE being lifted from the ambulance. Her head throbbed, but her vision had cleared.

"How are you feeling, Mrs. Rhodes?" A slim man with a windburned face smiled down on her.

"You're a paramedic," she said slowly. She searched his face for confirmation.

"Absolutely right! You're coming around okay now. Pretty soon you'll remember everything."

The medic wheeled her through a double door and into the ER. More alert now, she realized she was strapped to a backboard with a plastic brace supporting her neck. Tape and blocks secured her head to the board and intravenous fluids dripped into her left arm.

"Caroline! What have you been up to?"

She smiled at the sandy-haired fellow bending over her. Paul Wakely held the title of newest doc in the department. He'd done his residency in Chicago, but preferred rural Rhineburg to the big city. Paul was not only capable but also kind. Caroline felt secure in his hands.

"I went for a spin," she answered wryly. It came back to her in a rush: the car refusing to take the curve, the headlong plunge into the snowbank. "I think I have a concussion."

Paul laughed and patted her hand reassuringly. "I'd

say that's a good diagnosis. The paramedics said you were out of it for a while."

"I must have bumped my head."

"Well, you know the routine here. First an X-ray of the C-spine, then a brain scan to rule out bleeding." He probed the back of her neck with his fingers. "Any pain or numbness?"

"I feel like death warmed over. Every inch of me hurts."

"You can't be in very bad shape if you're able to joke about it." Paul motioned to the paramedics and they transferred Caroline, backboard and all, to an ER cart. A nurse began the triage process with a quick check of Caroline's blood pressure.

"This will earn you a few days off," the nurse said with a smile. "The next time you want a break, though, pretend you have the flu."

Caroline relaxed as she traded barbs with her co-worker. Triage went quickly, and afterwards, a tech wheeled her to X-ray and CT. Martin and Nikki were waiting for her when she returned.

"Are you okay?" Martin asked. The look of anxiety on his face both comforted and saddened Caroline. She reached out and took his hand.

"I'm fine, Marty. Just a bit shaken up."

"More than a bit," remarked Nikki, "judging by that lump on your head. Thank God for Professor Atwater. You might have been trapped in your car for hours if he hadn't found you."

"Carl was there?" Caroline frowned. She tried to recall seeing the professor, but her mind drew a blank.

"Apparently he arrived soon after it happened," said Martin. "He said he saw steaming pouring out from under the Buick's hood. You must have blown the radiator."

"I blew a little more than that, I'll bet."

The Buick had been old; now it was old and crumpled.

"Don't worry about the car," said Nikki. "Marty called the garage. They'll tow it in."

Caroline smiled her thanks at her daughter-in-law. While Martin might have made the phone call, she bet Nikki had suggested it. She'd always been the practical one in that marriage.

"Good news, Caroline." Dr. Wakely covered the distance from the desk to Caroline's side in long easy strides. "Your cervical spine's intact and the brain scan is clean." He removed the head restraints and hard collar and began a systematic exam of his patient, poking and prodding until satisfied that she required no further testing. "You're going to be sore for a few days. I'll have to patch up that gash…"

"What gash?" Caroline looked at Paul with worried eyes. He laughed and touched the side of her head.

"Nothing that'll mar your natural beauty. Still, it'll require six, maybe seven stitches. And you'll be staying in the hospital overnight."

Caroline protested, but Paul wouldn't relent. "Forget it, lady. You're ours for twenty-four hours. Loss of consciousness, remember? Can't release you until we're sure all your working parts are working right." He motioned to Martin and Nikki. "You two can wait outside while I sew her up."

Never a fan of blood, Martin took one look at the laceration and willingly fled the room. Nikki gave Caroline's hand a quick squeeze before following.

"Nice young couple." Paul pulled the curtain closed,

shutting off the cubicle. "They're worried about you, you know."

He spoke a bit too nonchalantly for Caroline's liking.

"Why should they worry? They heard you say I'm fine."

His eyes downcast, Paul didn't answer. He appeared unusually preoccupied with his work, first fumbling to open a suture set, then struggling to remove a ring securing the lid on a bottle of lidocaine. "Damn things," he muttered. "Can't they make them any easier to open?"

"Let me do it." Caroline reached for the bottle and pulled on the tab. The lid flipped off easily. "You need a nurse, Paul. You're all thumbs today."

Paul grunted as he pulled on sterile gloves. He reached for a syringe and drew up the lidocaine, all the time avoiding eye contact with Caroline. This only made her more suspicious.

"Spit it out, Doc. What's on your mind?"

Paul hesitated briefly before placing the syringe back on the tray. He turned to Caroline and soberly gazed down at her.

"They would have kept their mouths shut, but they were frightened for you. I'm sure there's a perfectly good explanation for what happened out there today. But since they brought it up…" His voice dropped an octave. "Should I call this an accident or a suicide attempt?"

Too shocked to even speak, Caroline stared open-mouthed at the doctor. Did her children really believe her capable of taking her own life?

"Martin told me about your recent hospitalization," Paul continued. "Don't worry, I didn't chart what he said. This is strictly between you and me, but I do need to know the truth."

Caroline pulled herself together and met the doctor's steady gaze. "I did not attempt suicide, Paul. I slid on a patch of ice, panicked, and hit the brakes. The car went into a skid and crashed. If I wanted to kill myself," she added angrily, "I'd do it less painfully. Pills, probably. Not as messy as having body parts all over the highway."

Paul raised both hands. "I believe you. But it's my job to ask. I'd be a lousy doctor if I didn't."

"I know." Caroline closed her eyes rather than let Paul see her tears. Neither of them spoke while he scrubbed the wound. Suddenly he chuckled.

"Strange, isn't it? Parents worry about their kids and kids worry about their parents. It's a never-ending circle of concern." He placed several sutures in quick succession. "I meant what I said about our conversation being confidential. I hope you won't feel uncomfortable the next time we work together."

"Thank you, Paul. I know depression is nothing to be ashamed of. Still, it's not the kind of illness you can easily discuss with your employer."

"Human Resources won't hear about it from me." He tied off the last stitch and wiped the wound clean with saline. "That about does it. We'll get you up to a room as soon as we hear from the admitting office. Want something for your headache?"

Caroline nodded. Paul pulled back the curtain and walked off, leaving her alone to contemplate her sorrow and humiliation. How could Martin have betrayed her? Would it never end?

"Cari?"

Carl stood at the foot of the cart, concern written on his face. Caroline suddenly realized whose voice she'd heard when the paramedics were working on her.

"You were there. At the accident."

"I was coming from the other direction and saw you hit the snowbank. You scared the life out of me, Cari. I thought you were dead when I first reached the car."

"Martin says you saved my life."

"Martin is overly dramatic." Carl took her hand and held it close. Caroline looked away but left her hand in his.

"I didn't do it on purpose."

Atwater frowned. "Do what on purpose?"

"Try to kill myself. I'm sure Martin told you something to that effect."

Carl grasped her hand more tightly. "Look at me, Caroline Rhodes. Your son said no such thing. And if he had, I'd have called him a fool."

"You would?"

"Of course!" Carl shook his head. "I'm not a mechanic, but even I could tell someone tampered with your car. Someone wants you dead, but I certainly don't think it's you!"

AT EIGHT-THIRTY in the evening visiting hours ended. Tucked up in a private room on the east wing of St. Anne's, Caroline felt exhausted but relatively pain free. Muscle relaxants had worked magic on her sore neck and shoulders. Unfortunately, they'd done nothing for her mental distress.

Martin and Nikki had left, but not before Caroline confronted them with Paul Wakely's suspicions. Unable to hide how betrayed she felt, she tackled the subject as soon as they were alone in the room.

"You must think I'm some kind of nutcase," she said bitterly. "Why did you tell Dr. Wakely about my depression? Did I lose my right to privacy when I moved to Rhineburg?"

Martin's face reddened with embarrassment. He'd spoken with Professor Atwater and now knew the brakes had failed. "I'm sorry, Mom. We were worried sick when we heard what happened. I was afraid you'd gone and done something stupid."

"Like try to kill myself? Martin, you should know me better than that."

"Why, Mom?" Nikki inquired softly. "What makes you think Marty knows what's going on in your head?"

"Leave it alone, Nik," pleaded her husband. "Let's not discuss it now."

Nikki's dark eyes flashed. "Why not? Your mother may be angry, but so are you. Why not tell her the truth?" She turned to Caroline. "It's about time you heard it."

Flabbergasted, Caroline stared at the pair. Why were Martin and Nikki so upset? They weren't the victims here. She was!

"What are you talking about? I've done nothing to hurt Marty."

"You've done nothing to make him feel better either," retorted Nikki. "You've worried him for months, and you don't even seem to notice. Don't you ever think of anyone but yourself?"

Nikki's passionate attack threw Caroline off balance. She'd never seen her daughter-in-law this angry.

"I don't understand." She turned to her son. "What's going on here? Tell me the truth."

Martin leaned forward on his chair and took his mother's hand. He had difficulty meeting her unflinching gaze, but Nikki's eyes were boring into his back, willing him to be honest.

"It's true Nik and I have been concerned about…your state of mind. Krista and Kerry are worried, too. We don't know what you're thinking anymore. We feel cut off, like we're only communicating in the shallowest of ways." He took a deep breath. "How can I explain it? We all miss Dad a lot. He was our best friend besides being our father. When he died, we wanted to tell you how we felt about him. But you were so wrapped up in your own grief…"

Caroline tightened her fingers around her son's as his voice trailed off. She'd seen the pain etched on his face when he spoke of Ed. Why hadn't she noticed it before?

Because I didn't want to, she thought bitterly. *I was too busy thinking of myself.*

"I'm sorry, Martin. I never meant to hurt you and your sisters."

"Of course not."

"I was totally absorbed by my own loss. I regret that I didn't recognize yours."

She dropped Marty's hand and picked absently at the blanket while searching for the right words to explain her behavior. Her son had a right to answers, but could she bare her soul to him? Had she healed enough to do that?

"For me, your father's wake became a grotesque circus where I had to perform for the crowd. Everyone wanted to know the details of the accident. Some of the mourners, if you could call them that, were overly curious. I resented having to repeat the story over and over again." She shuddered, remembering the ghoulish look in the eyes of some of Ed's fire department pals. She guessed they were used to death, having seen enough of it in the line of duty. Maybe that's why they'd prodded her for answers.

"Then there were you two and the girls. You kept asking me if I was all right, and I thought I had to say yes so you wouldn't worry. But I wasn't all right. I wanted to scream at all those people in the funeral parlor. I wanted to tell them, 'Get out of here! Leave me alone so I can say good-bye to my husband!'" Caroline looked at her son. If only she could make him understand. "I never got that chance, Martin. Before I knew it, the funeral had ended and Ed was in his grave."

She saw the tears in Martin's eyes, but she had to go on. "I felt furious with your father for leaving me. I couldn't express that to any of you. I didn't think you'd understand. What started as grief turned into enough self-pity to last a lifetime. It wasn't until my hospitalization that I realized how engrossed I'd become in my sorrow, how destructive it was for all of us. I thought I'd gotten beyond my selfishness, but it appears I'm still thinking only of myself. All I can say is, I'm sorry. I'm truly very sorry."

Martin leaned over the bed and without a word gathered her into his arms. For several minutes they clung to each other, their sorrow binding them as one. Caroline recovered first. She reached up with one finger and wiped a tear from her son's cheek.

"You're a good man, Martin. There's a whole lot of your father in you." She smiled at Nikki. "And you're a better daughter-in-law than I deserve. Thanks for having the courage to tell me the truth."

"We both love you," Nikki said solemnly. "We want you to be happy again."

Caroline nodded. If wanting could make it so, she should be feeling glorious. She wanted to get on with her life, put the past behind her. Unfortunately, in trying to make the want in her heart a reality, she'd cut off the very people she loved the most: her family.

"I haven't coped very well the past few months. Deep inside I know that, and it scares me to death. I go into a cold sweat when I remember the psych hospital and what I went through there. I'm afraid if I think of your father too often, if I talk about him with you, I'll sink back into that awful depression and wind up as a patient again."

"That won't happen, Mom. Not if you let us share what you're feeling. We have to be open and honest about our pain. It's the only way to make it end."

And so they'd talked, their conversation lasting for hours. Now Caroline was alone again with only her memories. They were less threatening than before, but still, she wasn't totally at peace. Guilt tugged at her. She moodily considered its source. She'd driven a wedge in the family by denying her children the right to grieve with her. Could she undo the harm her selfishness had caused? Could she find a way to right all the wrongs?

She was staring out the window, brooding over her failures as a mother, when Carl Atwater appeared at the door, poinsettia in hand.

"Are you up for some company?"

Caroline smiled wanly. How could she refuse the man who'd saved her life?

"That's a beautiful plant you're holding."

"Thought you'd like it. Marty told me you're a Christmas nut. He said you have dozens of holiday CDs and you start playing them in June."

"Is there anything about me Martin hasn't told you?"

"Now, Cari. Let's not get snippy. Personal privacy is all well and good, but it's knowing the little things about people—what gives them pleasure, what causes pain—

that allows friendships to grow. Take Mrs. Ferguson, for example." Carl placed the poinsettia on the bedside table, stripped off his coat, and collapsed on a vinyl chair that sagged dangerously low beneath his three-hundred-plus pounds. "Your nurse is a connoisseur of confections. I know because I've seen her at the Fudge Shoppe agonizing over the unlimited choices displayed therein. Visiting hours having ended, she wanted me to leave—until I presented her with a box of fine chocolates. One look at that box and she decided my visit would do you a world of good. Those chocolates were meant for you," he added. "I'll bring you another box tomorrow."

"Save your money. I'll be out of here tomorrow."

"Then you're feeling better?"

"Occasional aches and pains. But I can't complain. At least I'm still in one piece."

"Thank God for that," Carl exclaimed. "I saw your car fly up the embankment and I figured you were a goner for sure."

"You actually witnessed the accident."

"Yes. I was driving home from a funeral when your Buick came careening across the road. I braked so quickly I nearly ended up in a snowdrift myself. Luckily, I had my cell phone along. The paramedics arrived within minutes."

Caroline, who usually forgot to carry her cell phone, silently blessed Carl for being better prepared than she.

"I stopped by the garage tonight to check on your car. You'll be needing a new one."

"I suspected that. Do you know what caused the brakes to fail? I slid turning off Circle Road, but I assumed the tires were at fault."

"You couldn't have prevented what happened. The truth is, someone tampered with your car."

"Wait a minute!" Caroline sat up straighter in bed. "You said something to that effect back in the ER. What do you mean, somebody tampered with it? How could that be?"

"It's not difficult to do. Someone simply cut the hoses to the wheel cylinders."

Caroline rolled her eyes. She had no idea what wheel cylinders were, much less what kind of hoses were attached to them. "You'll have to explain it better than that. I know next to nothing about cars."

Carl drew a pad of paper and a pen from his pocket and began scribbling.

"This is a diagram of your brake system. You've got a master cylinder under the hood, a reservoir holding brake fluid. The fluid passes down a tube to the metering valve. From there it flows through two other tubes to the wheel cylinders stationed behind your back tires. The tubes are made of aluminum, but they're connected to the wheel cylinders with flexible rubber hoses. If there's damage to the system, the fluid will leak out. You'll lose a little each time you put on the brakes until it's all gone. No more brake fluid, no more brakes. In your case, the hoses were slashed. Anyone could have done it."

"Anyone who knew something about cars," Caroline retorted. "Until now, I hadn't a clue those hoses even existed."

"But you're a woman," Carl said with a shrug. "You're not expected to understand cars. Most men, though, have tinkered with an automobile at one time or another. I'm sure Martin knows all about brake systems."

Caroline doubted it. Her husband had been the mechanical wizard in the family. Somehow the gene was lost on their son.

"I'm not sure I approve of your sexist attitude, Carl. But it's comforting to know it wasn't a fellow female who tried to kill me. I wonder who did. And why."

"Do you really want answers to those questions?"

Carl leaned forward, eyebrows raised. Caroline saw the challenge in his eyes.

"What's that supposed to mean?" she snapped. "Why wouldn't I want answers?"

"Because you couldn't do what you did last night. You couldn't say, 'Gee whiz, that's awful! But if I don't think about it, it'll go away.'"

Carl's words stung worse than a slap in the face. Caroline sank back against the pillows, furious with herself and the professor. Perhaps she deserved the blow, but did it have to come so soon after the one delivered by Martin?

"You don't think highly of me, do you?"

"On the contrary. I believe you're quite a woman. You've survived a lot of pain in the past year. But survival alone isn't enough. You have to come fully back to life. You have to start caring again."

"I care," Caroline retorted. "I care about my children, my patients…"

"But not about yourself. At least, not yet."

"I don't know what you mean," Caroline said impatiently. "If there's one thing I've been guilty of lately, it's caring too much about myself."

"Humbug," declared Carl. "You've been preoccupied with your problems. That's not the same as caring about yourself." He shook his head in exasperation. "You're a stubborn woman, Caroline Rhodes. I refuse to give up on you, though, so I'm going to say some things you probably won't like to hear."

"Go right ahead. I'm getting used to hearing about my faults."

"Then let's start with that line you fed me last night about moving here to start a new life. That was a bunch of bull, wasn't it?"

"Why don't you tell me," Caroline said sarcastically. "You seem to be the one with all the answers."

Carl ignored the taunt. "You came to Rhineburg because Martin told you to come. He gave you a song and dance about not wanting you to live alone, about how much he worried and how they'd move back to Chicago if you stayed there. Marty read me the letter. I told him to leave you be, but he's as bullheaded as you."

"I wasn't exactly the Rock of Gibraltar back then. I acted depressed and irrational most of the time. They had a right to be concerned."

"Concern is one thing. Blackmail is another."

"My son didn't blackmail me," Caroline insisted. "*I* decided to sell the house, not Martin. It was too big for one person."

"Bah! You loved that old place and you know it." Carl stood up and paced back and forth across the room. "You were on a guilt trip, ashamed of your depression, desperate to fool everyone into thinking you were fine. Moving to Rhineburg proved you loved your son. You were making the ultimate motherly sacrifice."

Caroline slammed her fist into the bedcovers. "Who the hell do you think you are? What gives you the right to judge me?"

"I'm not judging you," Carl said sadly. "I'm trying to open your eyes to who and what you are. Your husband died suddenly. In an instant, your world changed. You weren't prepared to live alone, to give up that one special person with whom you'd shared so much."

They stared at each other in silence. It seemed to Caroline like an eternity passed before she could summon the strength to reply.

"Ed made me laugh." She collapsed against the pillows, the fight gone out of her. "That may seem trivial to you, but to me, it made all the difference in the world."

"I hear what you're saying, Cari. I was married once also."

Caroline didn't know why that startled her, but it did. "I'm sorry, Carl. I didn't know."

The professor waved off her apology. "How could you? I never talk about it. I still remember her, though, and I understand what you mean about Ed. It's hard to let go of a special relationship, hard to say good-bye to a person you love." He sat down on the edge of the bed. "Everyone has a right to grieve, Cari. But there comes a time when you have to accept that the pain, in some degree, will be with you forever."

"I've accepted it. I'm living from day to day the best I can."

"Take my word for it: what you've been doing is surviving, not living. You isolated that one big pain of losing Ed and told yourself, 'That's enough. That's all I can take.' That's why you never noticed how badly Ed's death affected Martin. That's also why you refused to help me last night. You've decided never to risk being hurt again. You'll stay uninvolved, untouched by the tragedy of life. Of course, you'll miss out on life's pleasures, but never mind that. At least you'll survive."

"You make it sound awful," whispered Caroline. "I feel like a total disaster. I've failed Martin and my daughters the same as I failed Ed."

Carl cocked his head to one side. "Now we're finally

getting down to the truth. What's really holding you back is the knowledge that you're not Superwoman."

"Carl!"

"Don't 'Carl' me," the professor exclaimed. "Come clean, Cari. You're punishing yourself because you couldn't save Ed. There you were, the mother, the nurse, the problem solver in the family. But you couldn't solve the biggest problem of your life: the hit-and-run death of your husband."

"Stop it!"

"Not until you admit the truth." Carl took Caroline's hand and held it tightly. "You saw Ed run down. You couldn't prevent it and you couldn't save him. That's what really troubles you. You're a natural-born fixer, the kind of person who doesn't mind cleaning up other people's messes. Ed's death was one mess you couldn't fix. Not for yourself or your children."

"I'm a nurse," Caroline murmured. "An ER nurse! I should have been able to do something."

"Stop trying to make amends for being human. Only God can save some people."

Caroline pulled her hand away and stared at the ring on her fourth finger. Every instinct told her Carl spoke the truth. Ed had died almost instantly from massive brain damage. The autopsy explicitly detailed the wounds he'd received, wounds so extensive the best medical care in the world couldn't have saved him.

"You're beating yourself up for no good reason," continued Carl. "Talk it out with your kids. Let them know what you've been going through. Let them tell you their feelings. You're lucky to have a family, Caroline. Don't lose them because of foolishness on your part."

He stood up, reached for his coat, and shrugged it on.

"I'd better leave before Mrs. Ferguson finishes those chocolates or she'll be after me to buy her another box."

Caroline raised a hand in farewell. She waited until he reached the door, then she called out to Carl.

"I don't know how to thank you enough. It seems you've saved my life twice today."

Atwater stroked his beard self-consciously. "I only want to be your friend, Cari. It would be a shame to see an intelligent woman like yourself tied to a ghost for the rest of her days."

"I promise you, I won't be."

The professor nodded. "I'll hold you to that promise. And remember: life starts today. Give it a chance."

He turned and walked out of the room. Caroline watched him go, her vision blurred by salty tears.

THREE

December 21

A RELUCTANT RESIDENT doctor cleared Caroline for discharge at 7:00 a.m. Adamantly refusing any further excursions into the realm of diagnostic medicine, she slipped into her clothes, thanked the nursing staff, and fled the halls of the hospital. Her headache had vanished, and outside of a few stiff muscles, she felt fairly normal again.

She found her way to the underground tunnel connecting the hospital to the nursing dormitory. Minutes later, she passed through the dorm's green-tiled lobby. As a concession to her bruised body, she chose the ancient grillwork elevator over the stairs and ascended at a snail's pace to the third floor.

The building had originally been erected in the late 1930s as a rectangular three-story structure. Classrooms and offices occupied the ground floor. The students' living quarters were situated east and west of a central staircase on the upper two levels. The west wing of the third floor had been heavily damaged in a fire in the '70s. Faced with declining enrollment in its diploma program and tight economic conditions, St. Anne's had chosen to forgo extensive repairs to the ravaged area. The third floor had been sealed off and the second floor of the wing converted to storage space.

Despite the loss of the west wing, the building could

still house a good number of students due to the addition of a south wing in 1952. The school had been bursting at the seams with future nurses in the years following World War II. An auditorium, an up-to-date chemistry lab, and modern living quarters had been seen as a necessity. The south wing, named Stromberg after the family who'd financed its construction, had become the exclusive domain of students in their senior year of school. With its large dorm rooms, lounge, kitchen, and laundry facilities, Stromberg was the wing freshmen dreamed of and juniors lusted after.

Caroline lived on the top floor of the Stromberg wing. Her apartment at the far end of the hall formed an L shape and consisted of two rooms on one side of the corridor joined to a room on the other side. The resultant suite was comfortably spacious for a single woman. From her doorway Caroline could look the length of the hallway and catch seniors slipping in after curfew. The fact that she seldom did this earned her a five-star rating from the upperclassmen.

Like the rest of the dorm, Stromberg was deserted due to the holiday break. Caroline walked down the silent corridor planning the day ahead. Once inside the apartment, she headed straight for the phone.

"Nikki, it's Mom. I'm back home, and yes, I'm fine. I wanted to thank you again for all you did yesterday. Also, if you have it handy, I need Carl Atwater's phone number."

Nikki supplied her with the information, and after further assurances concerning her health, Caroline hung up and called Carl.

"It's Caroline Rhodes. Did I wake you?"

"Nope," Carl responded cheerfully. "I normally rise at five and do a little writing before school. By evening my brain is so crammed with trivia that I have trouble getting the creative juices flowing."

Caroline laughed. "And here I thought trivia mattered greatly to historians. After all, it fills in the blanks between important dates."

"Whoa! That's a low blow. What did I do to deserve such disrespect?"

"You gave my chocolates to Mrs. Ferguson. Just kidding, Carl. Actually, I called to say I've been thinking about our conversation last night, and…" Caroline hesitated, suddenly embarrassed by what she'd been about to say.

"And what, Cari?"

"And…and I need a car," she blurted out. "A new one, I mean."

Caroline heard strangled laughter on the other end of the line. She held the phone away from her ear, cursing herself for her cowardice. Why couldn't she just admit her indebtedness to this man?

"Are you done?" she asked impatiently. Carl's continued chortling was like a knife stabbing at her ego.

"You know what, Cari? You are something else!"

"What do you mean by that?" The chuckling noises had deepened into belly laughs. Caroline grew more irritated with each guffaw. "It's not all that funny, Carl," she said darkly. "If you're waiting for me to say you'd make a great psychiatrist…"

"Never that," scoffed Carl. "I'm satisfied simply seeing you take my advice. You needn't thank me," he added self-righteously.

"Thank you," Caroline muttered.

"What did you say? You're speaking so quietly, I didn't catch it."

"Will you or won't you help me buy a car?" Caroline asked through clenched teeth.

"Sure. It'll be fun checking out the new models. We'll do it as soon as you're released from the hospital."

"I've already been discharged. Give me thirty minutes to shower and dress. I'll meet you in front of the dorm."

"Sounds good to me. Oh, and Cari?" The professor allowed himself one last burst of laughter. "Congratulations!"

Once again, words failed Caroline. She hung up without answering.

"A JEEP? ARE YOU SURE you want a Jeep?"

"Definitely," said Caroline. "I'd love yours, but I'm sure you don't want to part with it. So, take me to wherever you bought it and I'll pick out one like it."

Carl stared at her in disbelief. "Don't you think you ought to test-drive an SUV before you decide to buy one?"

"Why? It seems to be the perfect automobile for these country roads. I've made up my mind, Carl, so don't argue with me. Now, drive!"

Carl mumbled something about stubborn women as he pulled away from the nursing dorm. Caroline ignored the remark and said, "Anyway, we have more important things to talk about than Jeeps. I want to find out who cut my brake lines."

"Are you sure?" Carl asked in surprise. "Yesterday…"

"Was yesterday. Today I want to know what's going on."

"Okay. I'm only checking to see if you mean it."

"I figure it happened during the faculty party. Or

maybe even later that night. The car ran perfectly that afternoon, and at five o'clock I parked it in the hospital garage. Whoever did the job probably waited until after visiting hours. If he'd entered the garage earlier than that, visitors looking for their cars might have seen him."

"It's dark in the garage at night, even with the overhead lights on. Lots of shadows to hide in."

"I suppose he used a flashlight to see under the car."

Carl nodded. "It wouldn't take long to slash the hoses. All our man had to do was get past the guard."

"That wouldn't be hard. The guard on duty mans an office near the entrance where he can watch who's coming and going. Every hour or so, he jumps in his van and patrols the garage. Our friend could have slipped in the main entrance then, or he might have entered through the back door near the ER parking lot. People use that shortcut all the time."

"Who knows you park there?"

"Anyone with half a brain," said Caroline. "There's no other place for employee cars. But you're assuming whoever did it was after me specifically. Couldn't it have been a random act of vandalism?"

"I doubt it. I've lived in this town most of my life. The Rhineburg version of vandalism is a few high school kids climbing to the top of the water tower to spray paint their team's logo on it. A beer brawl out at the Decatur Inn is our idea of rampant crime."

Caroline frowned. "I suppose you're right. Vandals usually toss eggs at cars or break their windows. They don't try to kill people by cutting their brake lines."

"And if it had been vandalism, you'd think other people would have been affected, too. Why stop at one car when you have a garage full of vehicles you can vandalize?"

"What you say makes sense. But why did he pick on me? I haven't any enemies in Rhineburg. At least, none that I know of."

"Perhaps you represent a threat to someone," Carl said carefully.

"Me? A threat?" Caroline almost laughed, the implication was so ludicrous. Then she glanced at the professor. The look on his face sobered her. "You're frightening me, Carl. What are you thinking?"

"Consider this," Atwater responded. "You're present on the psych ward the day of the bombing. Afterwards, you're interviewed by a host of policemen, all of whom ask you the same question: Mrs. Rhodes, did you see anything unusual that might help us in our investigation? You insist you didn't, but are you absolutely sure? Maybe you spotted some small inconsistency, something so insignificant you've already forgotten it. You answer the police truthfully. Still, the killer knows better. He's worried you might remember what you saw, so he decides to get rid of you. What better way than an accident? After all, it's winter, and you're unfamiliar with the roads around here. You go into an uncontrolled slide on the ice, hit a tree, and bingo! One less problem to contend with."

Caroline was more shocked than she wanted to admit. Vandalism she could handle. A deliberate attempt on her life was something else entirely.

"You think it's the same person behind both acts?"

"I do," Carl said emphatically. "Look at the way you evaded questions at the faculty party. You repeatedly said that the police asked you not to discuss the explosion. The more you said it, the more you aroused everyone's curiosity. By the end of the evening, half the faculty considered you a major witness in the case."

"Martin told me he'd heard a comment to that effect. I thought it funny at the time. The truth is, I made up that line. I did it to avoid having to recall the bombing."

"I understand how you must have disliked being the center of attention. Unfortunately, what you said added an aura of mystery to you. That phrase may have reached the wrong ears. You may have made someone nervous."

"Are you suggesting the bomber attended the party at Bruck Hall? That he's a faculty member?" The thought of Martin being acquainted with a killer sent a shiver of fear down Caroline's spine. What if Martin and Nikki were in danger, too?

"I'd hate to think that, but nothing is impossible," said Carl. "Of course, if you've been using that line around the hospital, it could be someone from St. Anne's. Any way you look at it, this was an inside job."

"Not according to Charles Paine," said Caroline, referring to the administrator of St. Anne's.

Carl wrinkled his nose. "Your Mr. Paine is a fool. He keeps spouting nonsense about a 'mad bomber' being responsible for the explosion. As if some nut would walk into town, plant a bomb in a Christmas tree, and then go off on his merry way. Bah!"

"Better that than having to explain why anyone would hate the hospital enough to blow it up."

A memory pushed forward in Caroline's mind, then slipped away as quickly as it had come. Annoyed, she tried unsuccessfully to force it to the surface.

"Why waste a bomb on a little town like Rhineburg?" continued Carl. "Why not make a big splash by blowing up an important Chicago hospital? Paine is dead wrong on this one. Psychos gravitate to big cities where they can get the publicity they crave. Whoever did this is no stranger to Rhineburg."

"Sounds like you've changed your mind. A minute ago you implied Rhineburg is immune to crime."

"Nothing of this proportion has ever happened before," Carl said as he drove past a sign welcoming them to Rhineburg. "The bombing sent shock waves through this community. People here depend on St. Anne's for healthcare and for jobs. You don't bite the hand that feeds you. Besides, several of the victims were from Rhineburg. The whole town's in mourning."

"Can you say that with absolute certainty? Are you sure someone isn't cheering a job well done?"

"If you'd lived here as long as I, you'd realize Rhine-burgers are not like..."

Carl caught himself and clamped his mouth shut. Caroline glared at him.

"Not like Chicagoans? Thanks a lot, professor. For your information, I can't recall a hospital back home ever being bombed. We aren't the gangsters you hicks picture us to be."

"I'm sorry. I didn't mean it that way. But these people are my friends, Cari. I'm compelled to defend them."

"I understand how you feel, but you're not thinking straight. You're leading with your heart instead of your head."

Carl refused to answer. He drove through the center of town and turned west on a road bordered by old Victorians converted to bed-and-breakfasts. Occupied with other thoughts, Caroline glanced at the buildings without truly seeing them.

"All right," she said with a sigh. "If our killer isn't

a local, what did you mean when you said he's 'no stranger to Rhineburg'? Who else fits the profile?"

"Someone like you," the professor said calmly.

"Like me? What the hell do you mean by that?"

Carl hushed her with a wave of his hand. "Don't get your dander up, Caroline. I wasn't implying you placed the bomb in the tree. I said, someone like you. Someone who knows the town, the campus, and the hospital well enough to get around on his own. Not a longtime resident, but a person with a working knowledge of the area."

"So you hesitate to blame a Rhineburger, but a casual visitor will do nicely."

"I'm not looking at this crime through rose-colored glasses," Carl insisted. "I'm convinced whoever did this had a definite reason for bombing the psych ward, but it wasn't to harm the hospital. I'm equally convinced you're an important link in a chain of deadly events."

While Caroline disliked being compared to the bomber, she knew Carl's analogy made sense. The killer, like she, might be a newcomer to Rhineburg, or even a relative of someone living in town. Either way, though, he had to be familiar with the hospital and the psych ward. How else would he have known about the tree? She was about to voice that thought when Carl pulled over to the curb and cut the engine.

"Here we are. Stromberg and Morgan, Purveyors of Fine Automobiles. The sign is pretty fancy, but you'll find the owner to be a down-to-earth guy."

Caroline stared at the wording on the dealership's plate-glass window. Her discussion with Carl had pushed all other thoughts aside. She no longer felt in the mood to look at cars, but as long as they were here…

She pulled herself together and climbed out of the Jeep thinking she might as well get it over with.

"HEY THERE, PROFESSOR. How you doin'?"

A tall blond fellow in an open-necked blue denim shirt and khaki pants hurried toward them, his hand outstretched. Atwater grasped it and winced.

"I see you're still lifting weights, James." Carl flexed his fingers in mock pain. "As for me, I'm still breathing. So, how's business? You're doing well I presume?"

The younger man flashed a grin, his dark blue eyes sparkling mischievously. "Couldn't be better. I sold that red Jag you were so fond of."

"You didn't!" Carl gazed ruefully out the window at the lot next to the dealership. "You knew I wanted that car."

James punched him playfully in the stomach. "You couldn't fit into that car and you know it. The Jeep suits you fine."

Carl sighed and shook his head. "Cari, this is James Morgan, car salesman extraordinaire, but certainly no gentleman. Jim, may I introduce Mrs. Caroline Rhodes, a prospective buyer and a true lady."

"At your service, madam." James executed a neat bow. A lock of curly hair tumbled over his forehead and he brushed it back with a muscular forearm. "I heard about your accident, Mrs. Rhodes. Glad to see you're okay. Your car's pretty banged up, though."

"It's a goner," said Caroline with a smile. She'd taken an immediate liking to the genial salesman with his easygoing manner and cheerful grin. "I want a Jeep," she said as James led her to a chair next to his desk. "Something similar to the professor's."

She outlined her wishes and James jotted down

options and prices. They discussed horsepower, multi-port injection systems, and gas mileage while Carl sat nearby fuming.

"I can't believe this," he sputtered when the conversation momentarily lagged. "You haven't even looked at the cars on the lot, much less test-driven one. How can you buy an automobile that way?"

"I told you," Caroline said sweetly, "I know what I want. I'm sure Mr. Morgan can offer me a suitable deal on a Jeep. By the way, Jim, it doesn't have to be new. I'd settle for a late-model used car."

"Ah. Then I may have exactly what you're looking for. Come with me." James led them through a side door to a multibay garage at the rear of the lot. "That arrived this morning," he said, pointing to a forest-green Jeep Cherokee parked in a service bay. "Mayor Schoen brought it in. It belonged to his wife."

Caroline circled the Jeep, examining it for dents and scratches. "Seems to be in good shape."

"The mayor takes excellent care of his cars. Brings them in for service right on schedule." James slapped the hood. "This baby is a beaut. Two years old, low mileage, and fully loaded with options. A reasonable price, to boot." He mentioned a number and Caroline's eyebrows rose.

"That's pretty expensive for a used car."

James shrugged. "Not for one of this caliber. Martha Schoen enjoyed her comfort. She special ordered this Jeep, got every possible luxury installed. This SUV will last you a lifetime. It'll get you wherever you want to go, and you'll go there in style."

Caroline glanced at Carl, who nodded his approval. She circled the Jeep again, climbed inside to check out its appointments, then made up her mind. "Let's go sign the papers."

Twenty minutes later they were shaking hands on the deal.

"It's been a pleasure doing business with you, Mrs. Rhodes. Some of our customers—" he grinned at the professor "—take forever to make a decision. By the time they do, the car they want is gone. I only wish my dad had been here to meet you."

"Where is your father?" Carl inquired grumpily. "Doesn't he know better than to leave the place in your hands?"

"He's at a car auction in Indianapolis. I told him to pick up a new Santa suit for you while he's there. The old one looked a bit tight on you last Christmas."

Carl blew out a hard sigh that lifted the ends of his mustache. "What have I done to deserve such treatment? I gave this boy an A in history, Cari, and look how he repays me!"

"That A came twenty-five years ago, Mrs. Rhodes," said James. "Professor Atwater never lets me forget it."

It surprised Caroline to learn Morgan was in his late forties. His youthful face and muscular body made him look ten years younger.

"I want my mechanic to go over the Jeep before you take possession," James continued. "I'll call you tomorrow to set up a delivery time."

"The sooner, the better, Mr. Morgan. I have lots of Christmas shopping to do."

"By the way," said Carl, "who bought the Jaguar?"

"Some new doctor from St. Anne's. The man walked in, pointed to the car, and said 'I'll take it.' Never even haggled over the price like you would have done. And," James added gleefully, "he paid for it in cash!"

THEY STOPPED FOR LUNCH in Rhineburg at a restaurant specializing in German cuisine and hometown atmosphere. Carl recommended the potato pancakes and Caroline concurred. She recalled aloud how, when she was a child, her mother had grated potatoes by hand to make this favorite Lenten dish.

"It was hard work. Then one year my brother and I saved our pennies and bought her a blender for Christmas. We had potato pancakes twice a week after that."

Carl took a sip of his beer. "You'll love the way they serve them here. Lots of sour cream along with a side dish of hot homemade applesauce. I'm getting hungry thinking about it!"

"Do you eat here often?"

"Too often, can't you tell?" Carl wiped foam from his mustache with a red-checkered napkin. "I'll bet James has been coming here, too. He's beginning to develop a paunch."

Now, that's the pot calling the kettle black, thought Caroline with amusement. The professor's girth tripled Jim Morgan's, but she politely refrained from mentioning it. Instead, she inquired as to the age of the jovial salesman.

"Jim turned forty-seven in March. He looks younger, but then, all the Morgans age gracefully. His dad could pass for fifty, although he's past retirement age. And his grandmother—well, you wouldn't believe she's ninety. She celebrated her birthday last month and she's healthier than the two of us combined. Alexsa Stromberg Morgan. Now, there's someone you should meet."

"There must be good genes in the family." Caroline suddenly frowned. "Did you say Stromberg Morgan? That's the name of the dealership, but it's also the name of the dormitory wing in which I live. The Stromberg wing."

Carl nodded. "Alexsa Stromberg's marriage to Thomas Morgan consolidated not only two of the oldest families in the county, but also most of the wealth in Rhineburg. The Brucks run a close second, but I'd say the Stromberg-Morgan fortune edges out theirs by a million or so."

"Amazing. I'd never guess that kind of wealth existed out here in the country."

"Old money, earned long ago and invested wisely. But that's another story. Let's get back to our present dilemma."

"Right," Caroline replied soberly. "If we're going to solve this mystery, we'd better put our heads together and come up with a plan. I think you're correct in saying the bomber is no stranger to Rhineburg. He had to be aware of events at the hospital or he'd never have sent the tree."

Carl was so pleased with Caroline's decision to help him that he missed the implication of her last words. "So you're going to join forces with me after all."

"I have no other choice. I've never been the target of a murderer before. I don't exactly like the feeling. One thing, though," she added. "Not a word of this to Martin or Nikki. They'd throw a fit if they knew what we were up to."

"Mum's the word," Carl said, making a zipper movement across his lips. "I'm not above engaging in a conspiracy of silence if the cause is worthy. Martin would quit the department if he thought I'd put you in danger. He's very good at research. I can't afford to lose him."

The waitress arrived with their lunch and they both dug into the food with gusto. Carl was right. The pancakes were delicious, and the cinnamon-laced applesauce complemented them perfectly. Maybe it was the clear country air or the stimulation of a thousand brain cells pondering a mystery that gave Caroline such a hearty appetite. Whatever the cause, she downed her stack of potato pancakes in record time.

"Seconds, Professor?" The waitress smiled her question as she gathered up their empty plates. "Or how about a piece of Black Forest cake, baked fresh this morning?"

Carl looked torn by the invitation. He glanced hopefully at Caroline, but she shook her head. "I guess not, Jenni," he said wistfully. "Another time maybe. Right now, I'm off to visit the Archangels."

"Say hi to the guys for me." The girl tore a sheet from her order pad and handed it to Carl. "Have a nice day, miss." She waved at Caroline and moved on to the next table.

"I must be the only one in town who doesn't know the Archangels," complained Caroline. "You said the Bruck brothers provide security for the university, but you never explained their nickname. Why do you insist on calling them the Archangels?"

Carl wrenched his frame out of the wooden chair, stretched his back muscles, and headed for the cashier's desk. "You'll find out soon enough," he called over his shoulder. "I want you to come along and meet them. Nothing gets by the Archangels. We may get a better handle on last week's events if they're willing to talk with us."

Outside the restaurant, Carl placed a hand on Caroline's arm. "There's one thing I have to know before we go any farther. How in the world did a woman who claimed to know nothing about cars suddenly turn into an expert on Jeeps?"

Caroline laughed mischievously. "Do you remember that brother I mentioned earlier? Alan's been in love with automobiles since he was five years old. I phoned him this morning. He advised me on Jeeps and told me exactly what to ask the salesman."

"I should have known." Carl shook his head in exasperation. "I'll never again underestimate your abilities."

"That, my friend, would be a big mistake," Caroline said with a wink. "I may not be Superwoman, but, like the Brucks, I run a close second!"

CARL PARKED NEXT TO the campus security building and glanced at his watch. "Perfect! We should be able to catch two of the boys. The shift changes at three, and it's 2:45 now."

Caroline followed him into the one-story pink-stone structure. Fashioned of the same fine-grained rhyolite as the surrounding university buildings, it appeared more modern in design than the others. She guessed it was a recent addition to the campus, built to accommodate a force that took its business seriously. Inside, the utilitarian nature of the facility was starkly apparent. State-of-the-art computers and television monitors occupied most of the visible space while electronic gadgets sprouted from the walls like acne on a teenager's face. The only evidence of frugality lay in the two scarred and battered desks placed back to back in the center of the room.

Two men stood near one of the TV monitors. They were sipping coffee and observing the black-and-white pictures on the small screen. First one, then the other, turned as Caroline and Professor Atwater approached.

"Afternoon, Carl," they said simultaneously.

Caroline blinked. Either she'd just experienced double vision or she was staring at the most perfect set of identical twins ever born to woman. Deeply tanned with hair the color of stone-ground mustard, the Bruck brothers matched each other in height, weight, and attitude. Each one topped out at over six feet, possessed the physique of a boxer in training, and wore a lopsided smile that felt welcoming to Caroline. She guessed them to be in their early thirties.

"Hello, Mike. Gabe." Carl shook hands with the brothers, then introduced Caroline.

"You're Martin's mother," said Gabe

"And the new housemom at the nursing dorm," said Michael.

"Plus, you were the victim of a suspicious accident," his brother added.

"Which we're glad to see you made it through alive," finished Michael.

Dumbfounded, Caroline turned to Carl. "You told them all that, right?"

"Oh, no," he said, shaking his shaggy head in delight. "I said these guys were special. If there's news to be heard, it reaches their ears."

"Most of the time." Michael pulled two chairs up to his desk. "Have a seat, Professor. You, too, Mrs. Rhodes. We were hoping you'd come visit us."

"Yeah," agreed Gabe. "Since we're not supposed to be involved in this mess, we couldn't quite go knocking on your door."

"President Hurst wouldn't approve," Michael said with a grin.

"But we've got a lot of questions only you can answer. We hope you'll cooperate with us."

Gabe flashed a dazzling smile meant to win Caroline's heart. It did exactly that. Captivated by the pair, she said, "Fire away. Anything you want to know..."

"Hold on a minute," interrupted Carl. "Are you saying Hurst put a muzzle on you fellows? Why?"

"Not just a muzzle," Michael retorted. "He practically chained us to our desks. We're to cooperate fully with all police agencies. But investigate on our own? No way."

"As for why," said Gabe, "we couldn't say for sure. There are a number of answers to your question, Professor. The problem is coming up with the right one."

"Garrison is obsessed with the university's public image," said Carl. "He's probably terrified the school will be crucified by the press."

"That'll only happen if the bomber turns out to be a student or university employee."

"Carl's convinced there are no real misfits enrolled at Bruck," said Caroline. "And it would take a misfit, an extremely disturbed young person, to commit this sort of crime."

"We agree, it's highly improbable. But the police think otherwise. They're going over the student records with a fine-toothed comb looking for anyone with a troubled history."

"They'd like to pin this on a local," added Michael. "Either a student terrorist or someone holding a grudge against the hospital. A nonlocal person would be harder to catch. Look at the Unabomber. He got away with murder for over a decade because he wasn't physically associated with his crimes."

"If an outsider—some psycho craving attention— planted the bomb, he's probably long gone by now,"

Gabe said grimly. "The bad news is, he was an efficient son of a gun. The cops have very little to go on."

"But you would know if we had troublemakers at Bruck." Carl reverted to his previous argument concerning the likelihood of the bomber being a student. "Angry kids take out their frustrations in class or at the dorm. Not a single professor could point his finger at a student. What about the campus grapevine? Have you heard anything?"

"Not a whisper," said Michael. "Of course, most of the kids have gone home for the holidays. I don't expect to hear much now."

"Which is exactly the point," said Caroline. "Everyone seems to have forgotten the holidays."

The three men looked at her as if she'd sprouted a second head. She hurried to explain.

"The bomb was in the artificial tree."

Gabe nodded. "Our killer packed the trunk with plastic explosives. The tree was one of those fancy jobs where each string of lights plugs into a multi-outlet fixture on the trunk. An electric cord extends from the fixture."

"The fixture was rigged with an electrically activated detonator," said his brother. "The bomb exploded when a patient plugged the cord into the wall outlet."

"Would it take long to assemble this type of bomb?"

"Not if you knew what you were doing," said Michael. "And where to get your hands on plastic explosives."

"Finding the material wouldn't be easy, would it?" Caroline persisted.

"You'd be amazed at what's available for the right price," said Gabe. "The ATF, the Bureau of Alcohol, Tobacco and Firearms, recovers loads of stolen military explosives every year. There's one called Composition C-4. A half pound of it would level this building."

"You won't find it floating around Rhineburg. But it's definitely on the market," added Michael. "Go to any large city and you can connect with a source. It might take time and effort..."

"But time is precisely what the bomber didn't have," insisted Caroline. "The ward's original tree was found damaged only three days before the explosion."

"What are you talking about?" Carl said sharply. "What's this about an original tree?"

Caroline realized the others hadn't heard the story behind the famous gift tree. She wondered if, like her, other ward personnel had failed to mention it to the police, assuming they already had the information.

"Every unit has its own box of holiday decorations," she began. "They're stored in the hospital basement, and in December, the maintenance men deliver the boxes to the various wards. This year the psych nurses got off to a slow start decorating because the rec room was being repainted. They didn't unpack their box until December 11th. What they found caused a minor commotion. Rodents had chewed through the box and gnawed whole chunks out of the tree's wooden trunk. The branches wouldn't stay in place."

"They needed a new tree," Carl said slowly.

"Yes," said Caroline. "But the hospital administrator refused to sanction funds for a new one. He based his decision on the unit's limited budget."

"Cheapskate," muttered Gabe. "I bet the nurses were up in arms."

"They sure were. The holidays are tough enough on psychiatric patients. The last thing they need is a dreary ward lacking any sort of Christmas cheer. The nurses made no secret of their little disaster. Within hours, everyone at St. Anne's knew they were collecting for a new tree. A lot of employees from other units donated to the cause."

"But the staff never bought a tree."

"They didn't have to, Michael. Three days after the discovery of the damage, a box arrived on the ward containing the most beautiful artificial tree I've even seen."

"No sender's name, though. No return address."

"That's true, Carl. But everyone assumed a doctor had donated it anonymously. The staff was thrilled. They put the tree together that very day, and then… Well, you know what happened after the patients decorated it."

Michael strolled over to the coffeemaker and poured four cups of the thick brew.

"So our killer only had three days to put his plan in motion," he said as he handed each of them a mug. "And if the ruined tree was discovered on December 11th, our students are home free."

"Of course," exclaimed Carl. "The semester break started that day. Most of the kids were on their way out of town by noon."

"I suppose the police could try to tie the bombing to a local student," Caroline suggested. "But that's pretty far-fetched. There are a lot more likely suspects inside the walls of St. Anne's."

"I agree." Gabe looked thoughtful as he added, "The bomber had to have inside knowledge of the situation on the ward. Only then could he be sure that the nurses would assemble the rigged tree."

"Three days," said Michael. "Not much time in which to build a bomb unless you're an expert with a ready supply of explosives. Tell me, Mrs. Rhodes, does the FBI know about the ruined tree? They're in charge of the case since the tree, and thus the bomb, was sent by mail."

"Was it posted in Rhineburg?" asked Carl.

Michael shook his head. "That's one of the few things they're sure of. The package originated in Chicago." He turned to Caroline. "The time element changes everything. Did you tell the authorities what you told us?"

"I never even thought about it until today," said Caroline with a shrug. "I can't speak for the other nurses. I haven't seen most of them since the explosion, and that day we were all in a state of shock."

"I wonder if that's why he tried to kill you, Cari," said Carl. He turned to the Bruck brothers. "I believe our bomber engineered Caroline's accident. She's a threat to him somehow. Maybe it's because of the time frame."

"I doubt it," said Michael. He added two teaspoons of sugar to his coffee, then flashed Caroline a smile as brilliant as his brother's. "I hate coffee, but they won't let us install a pop machine in here. Sugar helps to hide the taste."

Caroline felt herself melting like sun-warmed snow under the weight of the Bruck brothers' charm. Both seemed to know instinctively how to put her at ease. *No wonder they're good with students,* she thought. *They avoid the heavy-handed approach to authority.*

"Why do you doubt it?" Carl asked, referring to the attack on Caroline.

"Because Mrs. Rhodes isn't the only person who knows about this," Michael replied reasonably. "Everyone who worked on the ward is privy to the same knowledge: only three days elapsed between finding the damaged tree and receiving the rigged one. Eventually, someone besides your friend is bound to remember and tell the police."

"He would have to kill all of us to keep that a secret."

"That's right, Mrs. Rhodes," said Gabe. "Our man isn't worried about this particular piece of information. It may narrow the field of suspects, but only as far as the students are concerned. It still leaves almost everyone at St. Anne's open to questioning."

"And we'll make sure the FBI are informed," added Michael. "They'll probably want to talk to you again."

"We're back to square one," grumbled Carl. "Cari must know something, but I'll be damned if I can figure out what it is."

"We agree with Professor Atwater," said Michael. "What happened to you yesterday was no accident, Mrs. Rhodes. Until you recall whatever it is you've forgotten, you're in grave danger of another attempt on your life."

Caroline shivered involuntarily. One look at Michael's face told her he meant what he said. Suddenly she felt very afraid.

THAT EVENING CAROLINE had dinner with Martin and Nikki in their apartment above Kelly's Hardware Store. The building faced the town square on Wilhelm Street, and while Nikki busied herself in the kitchen, Caroline and her son admired the panorama below.

"I'm beginning to understand why you love this place," Caroline said. "You have a great view of the square."

"It's pretty, isn't it?"

"*Pretty* isn't the word. Between all the snow and the miniature lights sparkling in the trees, it resembles a winter fairyland."

"Nikki says it reminds her of a picture by Currier and Ives."

"An apt description, but I was thinking more along the lines of *It's A Wonderful Life.* Any minute now I expect to see Jimmy Stewart stroll through that doorway."

The words were barely out of her mouth when the doorbell rang.

Martin grinned mischievously. "Well, Mother," he said in his best imitation of the famous actor, "it sounds like another angel just got his wings." He opened the door with a flourish. "Professor Atwater!"

"Hello, Marty. I hope I'm not disturbing you." Carl staggered in, his arms piled high with books that he transferred to a bewildered Martin. "Can't you find a first-floor apartment? Those stairs will be the death of me yet."

"Hi, Carl." Caroline relieved her son of part of his load. She glanced at the top title. "What are these? Reference books?"

The professor brushed past Martin. "I didn't expect to find you here. You were all tuckered out when I dropped you off at the dorm."

"I napped," Caroline said with a smile. "I'm feeling much better now."

"Would anyone like to fill me in on what's happening?" grumbled Martin. He peered at the books as if he had a pretty good idea what they meant and didn't like it one bit. When his gaze then traveled to the professor and his mother, it was obvious he hadn't a clue as to why they'd been together earlier.

"I'm sorry, Martin," Carl said apologetically. "My publisher called. He wants the first draft of my new book by January 4th. Unfortunately, there are a few facts that still need to be referenced. I figured you could do it between now and then." He pulled a folded sheet of paper from his pocket and handed it to Martin. "They're minor details, but important nonetheless. It wouldn't do to have mistakes show up in print."

Martin looked at the list and groaned. "How many 'details' are you talking about? I had hoped to relax a bit over the holidays."

"It won't take you long," Atwater assured him. "A few hours a day and you'll be done in no time."

Martin glowered at the professor but held his tongue. It wouldn't do to antagonize his boss; he'd only come up with a longer list of demands. His eyes flicked to Caroline. "I'll see if dinner's ready."

Carl watched his protégé stalk glumly toward the kitchen, then he winked at Caroline. "That should keep him out of our hair for a while. He'll be so busy he'll never notice we're investigating the bombing."

"Oh, Carl, that's cruel!" Caroline suppressed a smile, but she couldn't hide the amusement in her voice. "But I must tell you, Nikki will not be pleased with this."

At that very moment the subject of her warning came flying out of the kitchen, a bowl of greens clutched to her chest.

"What's all this about Martin working during the holidays?" The salad bobbed in the air as Nikki gestured her exasperation with both hands. "It's Mom's first Christmas in Rhineburg. We wanted to spend some time with her, do some fun things."

Lettuce leaves and shredded carrots sailed past Nikki's shoulder and floated to the carpet. She looked perilously close to dumping the entire bowl on Carl's head.

"I think that's sufficiently tossed, dear."

Caroline rescued the salad and placed it on the table

while Carl stammered a surprised apology. Nikki would have none of it. Chin up and hands on hips, she glared defiantly at Atwater. Sensing a standoff in the making, Caroline decided to intervene.

"I for one am absolutely famished. Don't you think the lasagna's done?" She propelled Nikki toward the kitchen, throwing an *I told you so* look at Carl before adding, "I'm sure Professor Atwater will reconsider his decision after a good hot meal."

Thus forced into staying for dinner, Carl did his best to mollify his hostess. Caroline aided and abetted him by refilling Nikki's wineglass each time she took a sip. Before long, Martin's wife grew mellow with food and drink.

"I suppose it won't be all that bad," she mused. "We could go shopping while Marty works on the book."

"There goes the bank balance," Marty grumbled. He was a harder nut to crack than Nikki.

"Cheer up, lad," Carl said heartily. "Think of the extra money you'll make."

Martin laid down his fork and stared at the professor. "You're going to pay me for my time?"

"Of course," Atwater bellowed. "Didn't I mention that earlier? I could hardly expect you to work during semester break without compensation."

The atmosphere in the room immediately lightened. Like other struggling couples at Christmastime, the Rhodeses' bank account had taken a beating in December. This unexpected windfall would keep the hounds at bay for a while longer. Martin and Nikki practically fell over each other trying to make amends for their earlier behavior.

Carl waved off their apologies. "Enough already. Let's talk about something else."

Caroline happily complied by introducing the subject of her new car. The purchase came as a surprise to her son and daughter-in-law, who listened avidly as she touted the Jeep's many features.

"It was previously owned by Martha Schoen, the mayor's wife."

"She's one of the people who died in the explosion," Marty exclaimed. "I read about her burial yesterday."

Caroline's eyebrows rose. "Her husband sure didn't waste any time disposing of her belongings."

"Well, the two of them weren't exactly on friendly terms. At least not lately," confided Martin.

"Oh?"

"I doubt you heard about it," Nikki said. "It started before you arrived in Rhineburg."

"Actually, the trouble began years ago," said Carl. "It only came to a head in late summer."

Intrigued, Caroline asked to hear more.

"Mrs. Schoen attacked the mayor right in the middle of a City Council meeting," said Martin. "That's why he had her committed to St. Anne's."

"You could hardly call it an attack." Nikki grinned at her husband. "Tell your mother the truth."

Martin hovered between good taste and accurate reporting before falling victim to Nikki's affectionate chiding. He turned to Caroline, the shadow of a smile softening his usually proper expression. "Actually," he admitted, "she pelted him with a couple of cream pies."

"Right before a packed audience," Carl added. "The local rag captured the event for posterity and plastered the picture smack-dab on the front page. Teddy Schoen was a sight to behold with whipped cream covering his face."

"And the headline read, 'Coco-Nut Creams Mayor,'"

exclaimed Nikki. "You can guess what kind of pies they were, can't you?"

Caroline bubbled over with laughter. She saw the entire incident in her imagination and couldn't help but admire a woman with guts enough to attempt what Martha Schoen had done. "Did the good mayor deserve such a shellacking, or had Mrs. Schoen gone over the edge?"

"A bit of both," replied Marty.

"Oh, come on! He got exactly what was coming to him," said Nikki. "If you paraded around with another woman on your arm, I'd do more than throw a few pies at you."

Martin backpedaled, but managed to tease his wife at the same time. "Martha Schoen was one weird woman. But you're right. If I ever act like the abominable Teddy Schoen, you have permission to shoot me where it hurts the most."

"Let's hope it never comes to that," Nikki remarked dryly.

"I take it the mayor is a ladies' man."

"I've known Teddy for years, Caroline. He's a good businessman and an excellent mayor. Unfortunately, his proclivity for philandering wreaked havoc with his marriage and alienated many female voters. Martha was only reacting to his latest adventures in the Land of Lust when she heaved those pies at him." Carl tugged at his beard, his great white eyebrows drawn together in concentration. "You know, her death may prove beneficial to Schoen."

"How so?"

"For one thing, almost all the women in town were on Martha's side at the time of the council meeting incident. They became even more sympathetic toward her after Teddy had her committed. He usually doesn't make political mistakes, but he did that time. He almost lost reelection when the women in town voted en masse against him. It was the closest race of his life."

"He won't have to worry about her effect on the next election, will he?" said Caroline.

"No, he won't," Carl agreed. "Martha proved to be an embarrassment to Teddy's political aspirations. She had a passion for oddball movements. Once she led a campaign to protect the rights of the ring-tailed raccoon. She said the little critters were so adorable, they ought to be named the official town mascot."

"During my junior year at Bruck, she spearheaded a drive to outlaw tattoos in Rhineburg," said Martin. "Anyone wearing one would be fined fifty dollars. Boy! Did the students get riled up over that!"

"Nobody, least of all Teddy, knew what she'd do next," added Carl. "I thought her antics were meant to keep her husband in line. As long as he kept faithful to her, she behaved herself. But if she got wind of an affair in progress, she was off to the races. Politically speaking, Teddy's better off without her."

"I'm surprised they didn't divorce," said Caroline.

Carl shrugged. "Believe it or not, Martha loved Teddy. As for the mayor, I'd say he loved Martha's money. Along with stocks and bonds, she inherited a considerable holding in the Rhineburg quarry when her father died. The Schoen wealth was settled in Martha, not her husband, although no one would have guessed it. Teddy kept the fortune secure. He also grew it with smart investments."

"So Martha Schoen was a wealthy woman," Caroline mused. "I suppose the mayor benefited from her will."

"I imagine so. Teddy's often talked of running for

county commissioner. Now that he's rich, he's a shoo-in for the party nomination."

"And he'll make a nice profit from the rehab of the high school stadium," added Nikki. "With Martha alive, he couldn't negotiate a deal with the college. All that's changed now."

"What did Martha have to do with the stadium?" asked Martin. "And where'd you get the info?"

"I have my sources," Nikki responded archly. She gave her husband a wink, then relented when she saw the expression on his face. "Oh, all right. I'll confess if I must. I had a haircut yesterday at the Dip-N-Do. The usual preholiday bedlam reigned with women waiting in line to have their hair done. I couldn't help but over-hear the conversations taking place around me. Every-one seemed to have an opinion on the bombing, but the ball really got rolling when someone mentioned Mrs. Schoen's funeral. First there was speculation as to the identity of the mayor's current girlfriend."

"Anyone we know?" asked Martin with a grin.

Nikki threw him a withering glance. "After exhaust-ing that topic, they discussed the issue of the inheri-tance. According to a woman who teaches at the high school, Martha Schoen attended a PTA meeting back in September. She made a speech opposing renovation of the stadium based on the cost, saying the money could be better spent on educational needs within the school. A lot of people agreed with her. She pledged that, as the company's major stockholder, she'd fight any attempt by the quarry to take part in rehabbing the stadium."

"I'll bet President Hurst reacted poorly when he heard the news," said Carl.

"The mayor wasn't pleased either," said Nikki. "One of the hairdressers said Teddy Schoen was gung ho for the improvements because of his ties to the quarry. He would have made a bundle on the deal. With Martha dead, he's now free to pursue the plan in the City Council. He'll push it through, and you'll see: by September, Rhineburg will have a spanking-new stadium."

"We're talking big money here," Caroline commented. She glanced at Carl to see if he was thinking the same thing as she. Money could be a powerful motivator. Could the mayor be behind the bombing? Or the mayor and President Hurst together? Now there was a bloodcurdling thought. "What else did you hear at the beauty shop, Nikki? Any ideas about the identity of the bomber?"

"Oh, come on, Mother," Martin complained. "You can't be serious."

"I'm very serious, Marty. A beauty salon is a storehouse of knowledge. If you want to know what's happening in a town, that's the place to go."

"You've got to be kidding. The Dip-N-Do is nothing but a hothouse of gossip. The beauticians probably vote each morning on a new 'Victim of the Day,' some unlucky soul whose life they can dissect between haircuts."

Caroline smiled. "Seems fair to me, Martin. An hour under the hairdryer can be deadly boring without someone to talk about."

Her remark capped it for Martin. He suggested they continue the discussion some other time, then stood up, and started gathering plates from the table. Caroline winked at an amused Nikki before asking Carl for a lift back to the dorm. Within minutes the two of them were bundled into their coats and headed out the door.

"You enjoy goading your son, don't you?"

Caroline grinned. "Martin's a good man. But he

tends to be pompous at times. When he is, I consider it my duty to take him down a notch or two."

"He's very bright."

"And he knows it. Don't get me wrong, Carl. I thank God my son is intelligent. Occasionally, though, he forgets that not all knowledge resides in the university setting. Nikki's hairdresser probably has a greater appreciation of human nature than many of your colleagues at Bruck. I wouldn't take her opinions lightly."

"I confess I never imagined Teddy Schoen as a murderer before tonight. He certainly had a lot to gain from his wife's death, though."

"I'd say so. Not only will he inherit her money, but he may also end up with a juicy political job." Caroline frowned. "I wonder who gained from the deaths of the other bombing victims."

Carl swung off the highway and took the road leading to Bruck. "I'll bet the FBI is asking the same question."

"I suppose so. But they may be looking for answers in the wrong places. I doubt their agents have visited the town's beauty parlors."

"I see what you mean," Carl said slowly. "There's a gold mine of information out there, but if you're not plugged into the local grapevine, you might overlook an important clue."

"Exactly. The authorities have so much ground to cover that they'll never have time to check out the gossip flying around town."

"But we could do it." Carl pulled up in front of the dormitory and shifted into Park. He turned in his seat to face Caroline. "If you're still committed to finding the killer, that is."

"I wish you'd believe me when I say I mean to go

through with this. I won't pretend I'm not afraid, especially after Michael Bruck's warning this afternoon. But I refuse to be a sitting duck for a murderer."

Carl grinned broadly. "That's my girl. I knew you had it in you, Cari. Now let's decide where to start this investigation."

"We don't have the resources of the FBI, so it's useless to copy what they're doing," Caroline said firmly. "Let's leave the physical evidence to their lab people. We can rely on the Archangels to keep tabs on any progress in that direction."

"Agreed."

"Since we've discounted the 'mad bomber' theory, we have to assume there's a logical motive for the murders. As far as I can see, there are only two reasons, the first being that someone wants to ruin St. Anne's. An explosion not only destroys property, but it also frightens off potential patients. The hospital census has fallen considerably since the bombing. Folks are driving south to Newberry for everything but emergency care."

"Has it reached the crisis point yet?"

Caroline shook her head. "No, but it will if this keeps up much longer. My shifts have been cancelled twice since the explosion. The hospital doesn't need floaters when their patient-nurse ration is four to one."

"I can't see St. Anne's as the target. It doesn't make sense to me."

Caroline didn't argue the point. Privately, she thought anything was possible. But she knew Carl's thoughts on the issue. She wasn't going to sway him with logic.

"Of course, the motive may be a personal one. The murderer could have been out to kill someone on the ward. Whether or not he accomplished his mission is still unknown."

"Seven people died that day, Cari. I'd say his plan succeeded."

"Not necessarily," said Caroline. "He didn't manage to destroy the entire ward, only the rec room. His intended victim may have escaped unharmed."

"You're saying he may strike again."

"If needs be. We can't be sure of anything, but I believe our best chance of catching him is to investigate the people who were on the ward. We should work on the premise that someone wants one of them dead, and then look for the reason why."

Carl thought about it for a few seconds, then nodded. "It's a sensible approach to the problem. All right. Let's concentrate on the victims first. We can tackle the survivors later."

"I'll speak to Jane Gardner, the unit manager. She may be able to help us with background information."

"And I'll put out some feelers in town. I'm more or less a fixture in Rhineburg, so folks are apt to be open with me."

They left it at that. Caroline promised to call if she learned anything. Carl agreed to do the same. Neither of them mentioned the danger they were courting, but Caroline watched with a certain sense of dread when the professor pulled away from the dorm. Two days ago she'd sneered at his Holmesian attempts. Tonight she'd joined him as an active participant in the game. But this game had no rules. And someone was playing for keeps. It scared her to think they might easily lose. She shivered as she unlocked the lobby door. When it closed behind her, she made doubly sure she pushed the deadbolt home.

FOUR

AT 1:00 A.M. CAROLINE glanced at the clock and groaned. Exhausted and still sore from the accident, she'd gone to bed soon after arriving home, sleeping soundly until midnight when she awoke with a start from yet another disturbing nightmare. This time she was roving a deserted hospital, searching aimlessly for her coworkers and calling their names. Walking down one corridor after another, she came to a dead end at a door marked "RECREATION." She flung open the door and chunks of sharp-edged plaster and stone tumbled out from a room that stretched endlessly toward a horizon of falling snow. The rubble kept spilling into the corridor, threatening to bury her as she stood rooted to the floor. She panicked, her throat tightening and her breath coming in strangled gasps. She tried to lift her feet, tried to move, but couldn't drag herself from under the growing pile of debris. Then she saw the Buick racing toward her from the other end of the hallway. It was almost upon her when she jerked awake.

Wrapping herself in a terry-cloth robe, Caroline headed for the apartment's tiny kitchen, where she poured two fingers of crème de menthe into a glass, added a dash of cold milk, and downed it in two gulps. Now, an hour later, she sat staring out the bedroom window, slowly sipping a second drink. She'd stopped shivering, but her mind raced with memories of the explosion at St. Anne's.

She could recall every detail of that day. It had begun at 6:55 a.m. when she'd arrived on the psychiatric floor.

Jane Gardner waved at her.

"Hey, Caroline. Glad to see you again." The unit manager wore her chestnut hair in a casual cut that curled softly around her oval face, causing her to look younger than her thirty years. Slim yet muscular, she possessed the build of an athlete and the temperament of a Zen enthusiast: quick to smile, she appeared totally undisturbed by the emotional hotbed in which she worked. "You didn't seem enthralled with us the last time you were here, so it surprised me when Samantha called from the staffing office to say you were coming."

Caroline blushed. "I confess, this isn't my favorite place to work. But when you commit to the float pool, you go where you're needed."

Actually, Caroline had almost turned down the assignment. Her first tour of duty on the ward had been a disaster. She'd been tense with the patients, whose problems she related to, and wary of the doctors, whose methods she abhorred. She didn't catch on to the source of her discomfort until late in the shift. *There but for the grace of God go I,* she'd thought. She'd decided then and there that she couldn't risk another day on the unit. But when Sam had called, practically begging her to fill in for an absent nurse, Caroline had relented and agreed to work.

"We appreciate your help. We're shorthanded with two nurses out sick. I promise we'll give you the easier patients."

Caroline smiled her thanks, then followed Jane into the lounge where the night shift nurse reported an uneventful evening. Caroline hoped her eight hours would be equally quiet.

Breakfast had been cleared away and morning exercises begun when the intercom suddenly crackled into life summoning all staff to report to the manager's office.

"What's up?" Caroline asked when she saw the glee on the faces of her coworkers.

"Look what just arrived," one of the nurses said excitedly. She stepped aside and pointed to a large rectangular box leaning against Jane's desk. "Someone's sent us a tree. We're going to have one after all!"

Seeing the blank look on Caroline's face, another nurse explained how the mice had damaged the unit's original tree.

"Our cheapskate administrator refused to buy us a new one. He said it wasn't in our budget."

"But some kind soul donated this," Jane gloated. "I can't find any message, so I assume one of our docs is playing Santa. Let's put it together now. The patients can decorate it this afternoon."

"We should have a party," an orderly suggested. "I've got a great recipe for punch."

"Sure you do," Jane retorted. "One-fourth lemonade and three-fourths Jack Daniels."

"We could invite Charles Paine," a third nurse joked. "I say we slip a little arsenic in his drink and be done with him."

The discussion dissolved into a series of ribald remarks aimed at the unpopular administrator. Jane had some difficulty regaining control.

"Okay, everybody. Let's get back to the subject of the party. I think it's a great idea. I don't see why we couldn't take the money we collected and spend it on a cake and ice cream now that we have a Christmas tree."

With the plan approved, Jane assigned Caroline to be their shopper.

"If you call Meyer's Bakery, I'm sure they can whip up some kind of cake by one o'clock. And we'll need candy and cookies and maybe some cider, too. I'll get you the money, Caroline. You others, divvy up her patients."

Cash in hand, Caroline happily set off for Rhineburg. Not only was she relieved to be off the ward, but she also appreciated the staff's concern for their patients. No one enjoyed being stuck in a hospital at Christmas. Psychiatric patients, though, were especially prone to holiday-induced depression. They needed a little fun in their lives and would certainly benefit from the party.

Caroline made it to town in less than ten minutes due to light traffic on the highway. She stopped first at Pregenzer's, the local grocery store, where she picked up ice cream, cider and cinnamon sticks. A quick trip to the Fudge Shoppe then netted her two pounds of chocolate creams. Next on the list came Meyer's Bakery. The owner smiled broadly when she entered the shop.

"Ah, Mrs. Rhodes! I have finished the last flower." The old baker held up a sheet cake for Caroline to examine. "You will agree it is a work of art?"

"It's perfect, Mr. Meyer," she exclaimed, and it was. Shiny red poinsettias filled the corners of the cake, their green leaves pointing to the center where tiny chocolate reindeer pulled a miniature Santa in an ebony sleigh. Above and below this scene the words *Merry Christmas* were inscribed in peppermint-pink on the white buttercream frosting. Caroline grinned like a kid in a candy shop; it looked exactly like she'd imagined when she ordered it.

She purchased five pounds of cookies before leaving the bakery, then nosed the Buick out of its parking spot and headed back toward the hospital. Once outside of town, she accelerated past the speed limit.

What the heck, she thought as the speedometer inched toward sixty. *If I get a ticket, at least it will be for a good cause.*

CAROLINE RINSED THE LAST of the crème de menthe down the sink and wandered back to the bedroom, memories of the explosion continuing to plague her. So far she hadn't remembered anything unusual that would account for the attempt on her life. Disgruntled at her lack of progress, she returned to the window and gazed at the stars glistening above Bruck Green. Their number and brilliance never failed to amaze her. In Chicago they competed with the city lights and only the brightest stars could be seen summer or winter. Ed had loved the stars. He'd tried to teach her the names of the constellations, pointing out Orion the Hunter and Lyra spread across the northern sky. She remembered Vega, the brightest of the night stars, but the rest had been lost on her. Not that she didn't appreciate them—was there a soul alive who hadn't at least once gazed in wonder at the Milky Way?—but she rebelled at placing the stars in tidy groupings. The supreme need for order in man's life impelled him to organize everything he saw, to name it as if it belonged to him. The stars belonged to no one. She preferred it that way, claiming no other link to the heavens than a common Creator.

Thinking of Ed had caused pain in the past. Tonight as she stared up at the stars she felt only a fondness for his memory. Perhaps she'd turned a corner in her life when she met Carl Atwater. His objectivity allowed him to be brutally honest, whereas her family and friends had been all too ready to coddle her. She'd needed a good kick in the butt to jumpstart her back into life. Figuratively speaking, Carl had done exactly that with his blunt assessment of her behavior. He could do no more; it was up to her now to move on.

With that thought in mind, Caroline picked up the list of names she and Carl had drawn up. The victims of the explosion were virtual strangers to her. Fortunately, she had access to someone familiar with all seven. Jane Gardner, the unit manager, would of necessity know the histories of the patients. Plus, she'd had a working relationship with the student nurse who'd been killed.

The youth of the last victim particularly disturbed Caroline. The girl had looked to be in her early to mid twenties. Now she was dead, murdered by someone who probably didn't even know her name. Caroline recalled how impressed she'd been by the young woman as she watched her move about the ward that fateful day. She'd been in the rec room when Caroline entered it around one-thirty.

"The food's ready," Caroline told Marina, one of the ward's staff nurses. "It's set up on carts in the kitchen."

"Thank goodness! Things are getting out of control in here." Marina nodded toward the people clustered around the tree. "They've been at each other's throats ever since Gail brought in the decorations."

"Getting their feelings out in the open?" Caroline joked. "Where are the rest of the patients?"

"They'll show up when the cake is served. These are the only ones we could coerce into decorating the tree. Of course, Mr. Canty was no help at all. He's really out of it. But then," Marina remarked with a grin, "as the Cheshire cat said, 'We're all mad here!'" She motioned to the tree. "Looks pretty good, doesn't it?"

Caroline surveyed the splendid balsam in the corner. It was a graceful tree, soft to the touch and perfectly proportioned for the size of the room.

"I think it's great. Although," she said as she cocked her head to one side, "that angel on top is a bit crooked."

Marina laid a restraining hand on Caroline's arm. "Please don't mention it to Martha Schoen. She'll bite your head off if you criticize her masterpiece."

Caroline laughed. "I'll watch my tongue." She drew Marina's attention to Gail Garvy. "Our student is doing a good job, don't you think?" She watched the young woman deftly interpose herself between two male patients who were glaring at each other. The girl said something to one of the men. His reply brought a gasp from a matronly woman standing near the tree.

"Now what?" Marina grumbled. An argument had erupted over who should light the tree. Voices were raised, then someone called out a name and Gail moved away from the group. She walked toward a solitary figure standing near the fake fireplace.

Caroline frowned. The student tried to coax a thin, gray-haired man into joining the group around the tree. His reluctance was obvious. He raised a closed fist, bringing it close to the young nurse's face. Caroline took a step forward, but the man made no attempt to hit Gail. Instead, he uncurled first his index finger, then one by one three others. The gesture reminded Caroline of a child's counting game. She watched with growing interest as the man leaned forward to whisper something in Gail's ear. Unfortunately, she stood too far away to catch the words.

Marina nudged her on the arm. "Let's go get the goodies."

"Hum? Oh, sure. I'll be with you in a minute." Caroline continued to observe the scene unfolding before her. The patients were now gathering around the Christmas tree. Gail Garvy began to sing "Silent Night" and slowly the others joined in. The man Gail had guided across the room stood forlornly by her side. He said nothing when she placed the tree's electrical cord in his hand.

Caroline turned to leave and promptly collided with a man walking briskly toward the doorway.

"Sorry," she said apologetically. "Didn't mean to run you down."

The patient glared at her without stopping. Caroline followed him, her attention focused on the empty corridor down which he strode. The man headed for the exit, then hesitated as if he knew he was being watched. He made a sudden about-face and slipped into a classroom across the hall from Jane's office.

"That's right, my friend," Caroline muttered. "There'll be no patients escaping the ward today."

"Are you coming?" Marina wheeled a cart out of the tiny area that served as a kitchen for the staff. She pushed it in the direction of the rec room. "Once we're set up in there…"

Then the explosion occurred with its deafening noise and disastrous results. Caroline instinctively fell to her knees. She crouched against the nearest wall, ducking her head and covering her ears. She felt the wall shake as debris erupted from the rec room. Chunks of plaster flew across the corridor, slammed into the chart desk, and careened off the ceiling. Thick gray dust filled the air. Caroline fought for breath in the suddenly darkened hallway. Burying her face in her scrub shirt, she crawled backward until her foot touched an open doorway. She twisted around and fell into the room, then struggled to her feet, coughing convulsively.

It took several seconds before her lungs cleared and she could breathe with any ease. Shouts came to her from the hallway, a person screaming in pain, someone else calling out in answer. The frightened voices roused her nursing instincts. She plunged back into the corridor where dust still whirled and confusion reigned. Caroline could see shapes beyond the desk area moving toward the staircase. She heard Jane shouting orders to her nurses as they hustled patients to safety. Then suddenly the unit manager was at her side.

"Marina's hurt," she yelled. "Help me!"

Caroline and Jane hurried back to the ruined rec room. Marina lay on the floor, conscious but groaning in pain. Her left leg twisted at an unnatural angle. Blood ran from an ugly gash above her knee. Together, the two nurses half dragged, half carried her down the hall. Staff from the floor below arrived to help. They assisted Marina down the stairs, leaving Jane and Caroline free to return to the rec room. What they saw there caused them to retreat in horror.

"Are you two okay?"

The first firemen to reach the hospital emerged at a trot from the staircase. One of them saw the two women huddled together in the corridor, the older one comforting the younger, and ran to their side. Standing next to them in the silence of the deserted psych ward, he repeated his question.

"Are you all right? Is there anyone left in there?"

Caroline continued to hold the sobbing Jane in her arms. She looked up into the eyes of their rescuer and slowly shook her head.

"Not alive," she murmured. "Not alive."

CAROLINE CRAWLED BACK into bed at 2:00 a.m. and willed herself to sleep. Recalling the explosion hadn't helped one bit. She continued to be puzzled over the attempt on her life. She set the alarm for seven and when it rang, she awoke with a fierce headache.

Aspirin wouldn't help this time. What Caroline needed was eight hours of undisturbed sleep. She'd made plans for the day, though, and refused to change them. She used the phone, then showered, dressed, and left the apartment by 7:45. Minutes later she entered the hospital cafeteria where she found Jane Gardner waiting at a table.

"Sorry to call so early," Caroline said as she slid into a chair. "But the only time I can catch you is over breakfast."

Jane grinned. "My life is not my own anymore. Since the bombing, I seem to spend more time with the police than with my staff." She took a sip of her coffee. "Glad to see you're in one piece. I heard about your accident."

"It wasn't an accident." Caroline gave the other nurse an edited version of the past days' events, omitting only Carl's part in them. It wouldn't do to give the hospital grapevine any more business, she reasoned. Jane listened silently, her chin cupped in one hand, her brows furrowed, while Caroline explained her theory of the killer's familiarity with the hospital and the victims.

"You know, if your theory's correct, you're playing with fire."

Caroline rolled her neck to expel the tension in her

shoulders. "Somebody's out to kill me," she said with a grimace. "I don't know why, but I figure I better do something about it."

Jane nodded but made no comment.

"I need your help. You knew those patients better than anyone on the unit. If the motive for the bombing lies with one of them, you could help me to discover it."

"Clients," Jane murmured absently.

Caroline frowned. "What did you say?"

"Clients," Jane repeated heatedly. "We don't call them patients any longer. They're known as clients."

"Sounds very businesslike."

"Why shouldn't it? Medicine has become big business. You'd better use correct terminology if you want to be in sync with the times."

"Like 'unit manager' instead of 'head nurse.'"

"You've got it," Jane exclaimed. "We're big on techno-talk since Charles Paine became administrator. Before his arrival nurses were allowed to concentrate on patient care. Now we have to endure endless policy meetings and quality improvement seminars."

"If it's any consolation to you," Caroline said mildly, "the same thing is happening all across the country. Some people call it progress."

"Bull! Don't get me started, Caroline." Jane crushed her empty coffee cup angrily. "Let me tell you something. You've reached your own conclusions concerning the explosion, but I have a different theory. I think someone became sick and tired of being manipulated by the bigwigs here. He planted the bomb as revenge for all the havoc wrought by Charles Paine."

Caroline was taken aback. "I don't know much about the new administrator. He may be a villain to some..."

"Oh, he is," Jane responded vehemently. "He's a

tightfisted businessman brought in by the Board to boost St. Anne's financial standing. He's done that, but at the expense of every worker in this hospital. He's cut the number of staff so drastically we can hardly handle the patient load."

Caroline hadn't anticipated this twist to the conversation. Still, Jane's view of the situation at St. Anne's merited attention. She wondered if the unit manager had vented her spleen to the authorities. If so, the FBI was searching for a malcontent among the hospital employees. No wonder the investigation had advanced so slowly.

"Tell me more about Charles Paine. Exactly what has he done to make everyone so angry?"

Jane settled back in her chair and stared at the ceiling. "Number one, he took the place of a very popular administrator. Sister Ambrose cared about people first and finances second. That's not to say she wasn't sharp when it came to money. She kept us out of the red, but she didn't push St. Anne's far enough into the future to suit the Board. They had dreams of glory; she was more down-to-earth."

"How do you mean?"

"She understood the limitations we face. St. Anne's isn't a big-city hospital. This community can't support a wing for open-heart surgery or a dialysis center for kidney patients. Sure, there are some wealthy families in Rhineburg, but ordinary working people make up the bulk of the population. They're not the kind of folks who leave bequests to hospitals in their wills."

"So Sister Ambrose ran the hospital on a shoestring."

"The budget was tight," Jane admitted. "But the practice of medicine remained excellent. Health care is a community thing here. Half the town works at

St. Anne's, making us more than just a hospital. We're part of the lifeblood of Rhineburg."

"And Charles Paine is a threat to the role St. Anne's plays."

Jane wiped an invisible speck of dust off the table before answering.

"We had to send some patients to other hospitals when we couldn't treat their conditions here. Like I said, we couldn't afford to do some of the services offered at larger facilities. Unfortunately, the Board of Directors didn't share Sister Ambrose's vision of a small-town hospital. I don't know if it was an ego thing or if the Board simple didn't understand the high cost of modern medicine, but they felt Sister's presence prevented St. Anne's from growing. They voted her out as administrator and hired Charles Paine to replace her."

"Could they do that? I thought a religious order owned this place."

"Oh, no. The town built St. Anne's a little over eighty years ago. But the powers-that-be back then made a deal with a German order of nuns to run it. They figured the sisters were old hands at operating hospitals, so they gave them a free rein in decision making. The board of directors put in place by the mayor served mainly as a rubber stamp. Since the initial funding for the hospital came from the town, it only seemed right that the City Council be kept aware of its financial standing."

"But somewhere along the line all that changed."

"Different times call for different approaches, according to the Board." Jane shifted in her chair. "To be honest, I can understand their concern. Government involvement had turned health care upside down. Medical advances have added to the confusion."

"We're doing procedures never thought possible fifty

years ago," Caroline said. "People are living longer and requiring a different kind of health care system."

"In a way, Sister Ambrose represented the past."

Jane's voice trailed off. She stared at her now cold coffee as if seeing in the dregs a swirling outline of an earlier life. Caroline didn't press her.

"I started here fresh out of nursing school," Jane said after a moment's silence. "Back then, the hospital sponsored picnics on the back lawn in summer and a party for the staff at Christmas. Everyone here knew and loved Sister Ambrose. She was a nurse long before she became administrator. She never lost her love of the profession. She visited each ward on a daily basis to see how we were doing."

"A personable woman," Caroline remarked.

Jane looked her straight in the eye. She had a hard wedge to her voice when she said, "A caring administrator, unlike Mr. Paine. He sits locked away in his office all day, handing out memos and thinking up new ways to cut staff. The Board thinks he's a financial wizard, but the nurses hate him. He laid off a lot of people the month he arrived. He called it the 'economics of medicine.' Then he decided to consolidate some units and form new ones to increase hospital revenue. The psych ward was his brainchild."

"I heard it was a new addition to the hospital."

"Relatively speaking, yes. Paine came from Chicago and still has financial connections there. Soon after becoming administrator, he returned to the city and convinced some people to financially support his plans for St. Anne's. Shortly afterwards, he closed down a medical ward, refurbished it completely, then reopened it as a psychiatric unit. During its brief existence, it hasn't done a booming business, but it seems to pay for itself."

"Your administrator sounds like the consummate businessman. But I still don't understand why you consider him a target for a bomb."

Jane leaned forward and stared hard at Caroline. "I told you, Paine fired a lot of people here. I saw which way the wind was blowing, so I updated my education at the university. When the position opened, I qualified for hire as the psych unit manager. But most of the nurses from the closed unit weren't able to return to school. Some had families to support. Others couldn't afford the tuition. They were great at their former jobs, but they didn't know beans about psych nursing."

"So they were out on their ears."

"Without any place to go. Paine had promised to shuffle them onto other medical floors. But with the general layoffs, there weren't any positions open. A lot of careers went straight down the drain."

"You think a former employee planted the bomb in the Christmas tree."

"It's possible," said Jane.

"But the ward opened last summer," said Caroline. "If there was going to be trouble, it should have happened back then, not now. Six months is a long time to hold a grudge."

"You never know, do you?" Jane replied. "Working in psych has taught me that people can explode long after the precipitating event. Who's to say one of our displaced staff members didn't go over the edge? Not that I want to be right about this, but I'd say my theory is more believable than yours."

THE LIGHT BLINKED RED on Caroline's answering machine when she returned to the apartment.

"Mrs. Rhodes? My name is Tom Evans. I'm with

the FBI and I'd like to talk to you about your auto accident. Apparently there are some…suspicious aspects to the crash that need to be discussed. I understand you also have something to add to your statement about the bombing at St. Anne's. I suggest we meet this morning at the hospital. I'll be there by nine-thirty. You can reach me through the operator."

The message ended abruptly and another one began. This time the voice belonged to a woman. Unlike the FBI agent, she seemed to lack both confidence and sophistication.

"Mrs. Rhodes? Mrs. Caroline Rhodes? The police… they said you're the dormitory housemother and I should call you. About Gail's things. They said you've got the keys and can let me in. I guess you're not home now, so I'll call again later today. Umm…I'd like to come over tomorrow. To pick up Gail's…to pick up…everything. Well…I…I guess that's all."

The answering machine beeped twice and then rewound the tape. Caroline paid no attention to the slight whirring noise as she considered the two very different messages. Something in the first one disturbed her. Agent Evans had sounded cynical. He'd hesitated before uttering the word *suspicious* and clearly emphasized it. He'd also sounded demanding, almost egotistical, as he'd instructed her to meet with him. *A man used to getting his way,* she thought.

The second message elicited a stronger emotion in Caroline. The woman's voice had broken several times before she'd managed to finish the message. She'd been so upset, she'd failed even to leave a name. Caroline knew what sorrow could do to a person. She suddenly felt incredibly sad. Her sympathy went out to this unnamed woman.

Caroline opened a desk drawer and rummaged through it until she found her student resident file. She scanned the two-page list for the name of the dead student. There it was: Gail Garvy, room 206, Stromberg, Elvira Harding identified as next of kin. The last names were different, nothing too unusual these days. The mother may have remarried after widowhood or divorce, and Gail had retained her father's name. At least she now knew who had called her.

She sat down at the desk and considered what to do next. She wanted to talk with Carl, tell him what she'd learned from Jane Gardner, but her report would be incomplete without information on Gail Garvy. She'd forgotten to mention the girl when talking with Jane.

But now I know the police have unsealed the dorm room, she thought. *I'll have a look in there before I call Carl.*

She rummaged in her pants pocket and found the master key to the dorm rooms. It was hard to imagine a young nursing student as anything other than an innocent victim of the explosion. Still, it never paid to be sloppy. Excluding Gail from the investigation might be a grave mistake. With that in mind, Caroline left the apartment and took the stairs down to the second floor.

Just as she'd been told, the police tape had been removed from the door of 206. Caroline slipped her key in the lock and stepped inside. The room looked much as she expected. Posters covered the walls, mainly colorful ones of rock bands with strange names like Grapevine Homage and Battle Me Back. The twin beds were made, but sloppily. Various articles of clothing were scattered over both of them. Because these were two-student rooms, she made a cursory exam of both desks before deciding Gail's was the neater of the two. She sat down and pulled out the drawers. The FBI had probably removed anything of interest from the room days ago. Nevertheless, she hoped something in the desk would shed light on Gail's character and background.

"Bingo!"

Caroline found a stack of rubber-banded letters in the bottom drawer. She took them out and placed them on the desktop, then swept the empty drawer with her fingertips, aware that something wasn't quite right with it. The drawer looked about ten inches deep on the outside, but the inside appeared much smaller. She ran a fingernail along the edge of the plywood base and found a groove separating the back of it from the drawer wall. Inserting the tip of her nail into the groove, Caroline pried up the false bottom.

"Now, what have we got here?" she muttered. She placed the plywood base on the floor and reached into the drawer, withdrawing a slim leather notebook from its depths. It appeared to be Gail's diary. Caroline flipped through the book. She was tempted to read it right then and there, but in the end opted to take it back to her apartment where she could examine the pages more closely. She replaced the false bottom and closed the drawer.

A stack of spiral-bound notebooks occupied the center of the desk. Caroline leafed through them but found only classroom notes. She left them on the desk and glanced at Gail's dresser. Surely that contained some clues to the student nurse's brief life.

The top of the dresser was bare except for a photograph in a carved wooden frame and a small jewelry box half-hidden behind it. Caroline picked up the photo first. It showed a young woman, probably in her early twenties, seated on a porch swing and smiling. Wearing a plaid flannel shirt and jeans, she cradled a baby in her arms. It was impossible to date the picture. The clothes were timeless, the woman's haircut neat and simple. Caroline turned the photo over but found no writing on the back.

Placing the photograph back on the dresser, she picked up the jewelry box and opened it. Two antique cameos rested on the velvet lining along with a gold wedding band. The ring looked almost new. Inscribed on the inside were the letters *MGH.* Caroline guessed that the *G* stood for *Garvy,* but it couldn't be Gail's since the first initial didn't fit. Her mother's then? But wasn't Elvira Harding her mother? Maybe it had belonged to her grandmother. No, Caroline decided. It would have been thin and worn from wear. Another little mystery to solve.

Caroline replaced the ring and closed the jewelry box. To be thorough, she checked the closet, then took a quick peek under the bed and beneath the pillow. She slid her hand between the mattress and springs and came up empty-handed. She wasn't sure what she was looking for, but the desk's false drawer bothered her. If Gail had gone to such lengths to conceal her diary, she might have hidden other personal items as well. The question was, what and where were they?

This is silly, Caroline thought, suddenly embarrassed by her own curiosity. She dusted her hands on the legs of her jeans. *What would Martin think if he saw me rummaging through this room like some nosy old biddy?* She pictured her son shaking his head in disgust. He would certainly disapprove of her attempts at detection. But then Carl's face replaced Marty's in her imagination. *Why do you care what Martin thinks of you?* he asked.

"Why, indeed," Caroline grumbled, annoyed now with herself and her son. She scooped up the items on the desk before taking one last look around. On the surface, the room appeared no different than when she'd arrived. No one would ever know she'd been there. As for the diary and letters, she'd return them before Mrs. Harding's visit. Content that she'd investigated as best she could, she left the room, locking the door behind her.

The phone rang as she entered her apartment. Hoping it was Carl, she dumped Gail's belongings on the coffee table and grabbed the receiver.

"Hello, Carl?"

"Sorry, Mrs. Rhodes. Wrong man. This is Jim Morgan." Pause. "From Stromberg and Morgan." Another pause. "The car dealership, remember?"

"Oh! I'm so sorry, Mr. Morgan." Totally flustered, Caroline babbled on brightly. "I'd almost forgotten about you. I mean to say, I'd forgotten about the car! Not actually forgotten I'd bought it, but…"

"Oh, dear," Morgan broke in with a roguish laugh. "And here I thought I'd swept you away with my charm. Must be losing my touch if you've dismissed me from memory so easily."

Caroline relaxed. The man's wry sense of humor swept away her embarrassment. "I haven't exactly dismissed you, Mr. Morgan."

"Please. Call me Jim. Or James, if you prefer to be formal like Professor Atwater."

"Jim," Caroline continued, "my mind's been elsewhere this morning. I do apologize. I hope you're calling with good news."

"Definitely," the salesman responded. "Your Jeep is ready to go. My mechanic pronounced it fit for any and all action, and knowing how badly you need it…"

"Oh, I certainly do," Caroline assured him. "But I probably can't pick it up until later this afternoon." She'd have to call Carl and ask him to drive her to town.

"No problem, Mrs. Rhodes. I'll be here all day until six o'clock."

Caroline thanked him again and hung up, a happy woman. Having her own car meant independence and not having to beg rides from Carl. Not that she minded his company, especially since they had much to discuss. She picked up the phone and dialed the professor's number.

"Hi, Carl. It's Caroline. Are you free to meet me sometime today? I have news to report."

"Did something else happen?"

"Relax," she said soothingly. "No more attempts on my life, at least not yet. I had breakfast with Jane Gardner this morning. I thought you'd be interested in her take on the bombing."

"I have some news for you, too. How about I pick you up in ten minutes? We can grab a light lunch at McGinty's."

Caroline surmised that any working relationship with Professor Atwater would involve food. No wonder he and Martin got along so well. Her son was also a devotee of restaurants. She only hoped that Marty had the good sense to curb his appetite more firmly than Carl did his. Nikki might not appreciate a roly-poly husband eating them out of house and home.

"I'm not hungry," she said tentatively. "But if you are…"

"Woman," the professor roared. "You're practically skin and bones! I'll bet you didn't even eat breakfast today."

Caroline briefly considered her 140-pound frame

and her lame attempts at dieting, but decided not to argue with Carl. "I'll be in front of the dorm in ten minutes," she said with a sigh. "I don't intend to freeze out there, so be on time." She hung up the phone before he could reply.

CAROLINE STARED AT the plate the waitress placed before her. A three-inch-thick Reuben sandwich sat center stage flanked by a mound of French fries on one side and three giant pickles on the other. A pint-sized stein of Rhineburg's hometown brew completed the meal.

"You call this a light lunch?" she asked, her eyebrows arched in disbelief. "This is enough to last me all day."

Professor Atwater dismissed her complaint with a wave of his hand. "You city types are bent out of shape over food. You think bean sprouts and wheat germ constitute a well-rounded meal."

Caroline grimaced. "They're not high on my list," she replied archly. "But an occasional vegetable wouldn't hurt your cholesterol level, would it?"

"I ate my veggies yesterday," Carl protested. "You tell me, what are potato pancakes made from?"

"Lots of starch deep-fried in oil!" Caroline shook her head. The man was simply impossible. The Reuben sandwich, on the other hand, grew more attractive by the minute as the aroma of fresh corned beef and sauerkraut tickled her nostrils. A few bites wouldn't hurt, she reasoned. After all, breakfast had been over three hours ago.

Twenty minutes later Caroline polished off the last French fry and sat back contentedly. Carl politely refrained from commenting on the speed with which she'd devoured her sandwich. Instead, he simply ordered apple pie and ice cream for the two of them.

"So what were you up to this morning?" Caroline kept her tone light. She'd seen the twinkle in Carl's eyes when he'd ordered dessert, but she'd be damned if she allowed him the satisfaction of knowing how much she'd enjoyed the meal.

"I made a few phone calls. Then I went over the obituaries of all the victims of the bombing. Thought I might get a clue as to motive, but no such luck."

Mention of the murders sobered them both.

"James Belding was born in Rhineburg, but buried in Chicago. Private funeral, family only," Carl added. "His was the last of the services."

"You were at a funeral the day of my accident."

"Yes. Everyone knew May Eberle. She and her sister, April, were the unofficial town criers of Rhineburg. They made sure we were aware of each other's sins."

"Puritans at heart? Or busybodies?"

"More like Victorians, I'd say. Full of self-righteous indignation, although I suspect they secretly enjoyed exposing their neighbors' faults. They certainly spread some scandalous tales."

"Could be a motive there," Caroline suggested. "Perhaps May put her nose in the wrong place one too many times."

Carl frowned. "I don't know about that. April took a fall back in August and died of a brain hemorrhage. Then in September, May's father became ill and died. She didn't tell a soul, just kept his body in the house for weeks after his death."

"How macabre," remarked Caroline. "I assume she eventually buried him."

"He's safely tucked away in the Rhineburg Cemetery, but no thanks to May. Old habits and the root of all evil led to the discovery of his body."

"Old habits and…money?"

"Yep, good old money. You see, Mr. Eberle lived his life on a schedule. He had a time for everything and did everything on time. He was so regular, in fact, that you could set your watch by his comings and goings."

"Then one day he didn't show up somewhere."

Carl nodded. "He visited the bank every Monday morning to withdraw cash for the week's shopping. When he missed two Mondays in a row, the teller reported it to the bank president. He in turn mentioned it to the chief of police. Chief Moeller thought it strange enough to warrant a visit to the old man's house. When he got there, Jake found May in an upstairs bedroom chattering away to her dead father. He took Mr. Eberle to the morgue and May to St. Anne's. She was committed to the psychiatric ward that very day."

"How sad," commented Caroline. "She lost both her father and her sister within a matter of weeks. It must have been too much for her to handle." She fell silent, remembering her own weakness in dealing with death. "Didn't May have any other family?"

Carl shook his head. "She was the last of her line. Because of her tendency to gossip, she had no real friends. I guess that's why I went to her funeral. It seems wrong to be buried without any mourners present."

The apple pie and ice cream arrived. Carl dug in with gusto.

"Tell me about your meeting with Jane Gardner," he said between mouthfuls. Caroline pulled herself back to the present and related her discussion with Jane. She emphasized the manager's concern that an ex-employee might be the bomber. Carl considered the idea but discarded it as improbable.

"Do you really think the average nurse has the skills to build such a complicated device?"

"No," Caroline answered truthfully. "Bomb Making 101 wasn't offered in the curriculum back when I attended college. But not everyone laid off was a nurse. Some male orderlies lost jobs also."

"And you think one of them waited this long to strike back at the hospital."

"I said practically the same thing to Jane. But she pointed out that people sometimes explode long after what she called 'the precipitating event.' I'm sure the police went over the personnel records of employees fired or laid off. That only makes sense, doesn't it? And I suppose one of those orderlies could have found work at the quarry. If so, his job may have involved explosives. Maybe he used what he learned to take revenge on the hospital."

"Remember, Cari, that tree was packed with plastic explosives. I'm not positive about this, but I think they only use dynamite at the quarry. I could ask the Archangels to look into it if you like."

"Would you?" Caroline asked. "Jane would be relieved if we could prove that none of her old friends is the bomber."

Carl swallowed his last piece of pie before answering. "I'll call Michael this afternoon. It won't take him long to hunt down the answer."

"Oh, one more thing. Jim Morgan called this morning. My Jeep is ready to be picked up. Could you give me a lift over there?"

Carl stroked his beard to hide his pleasure. "I'd be delighted. But first, will you come with me to visit Jim's grandmother? We're invited to her home at two o'clock."

Caroline's eyebrows shot up. "Alexsa Stromberg

Morgan? I don't think I'm dressed for the occasion." She glanced ruefully at her jeans and hiking boots. Why hadn't Carl mentioned this when they talked on the phone? She would have worn something more appropriate. Honestly! The professor could be absolutely maddening.

Atwater reached across the table and picked up Caroline's plate. "You're not going to finish this, are you? Good," he said happily when she shook her head. He stabbed at the pie, raised a piece to his mouth, then lowered his fork when he saw the expression on his companion's face.

"What's wrong?" he asked in surprise. "You're not worried about your clothes, are you? Don't bother. Alexsa won't even notice what you're wearing. She's not that kind of person."

All women are "that kind of person," Caroline reflected, but she refrained from saying so. True to his gender, Carl possessed an abysmal lack of understanding of the opposite sex. She would be wise to remember that whenever they discussed the female victims of the explosion. Hopefully, Carl's observations about the men in the case would be more accurate.

"WHAT A LOVELY PULLOVER. A fisherman's knit, isn't it?" Alexsa Stromberg Morgan fingered the soft wool of Caroline's sweater. "From Ireland, of course."

Caroline murmured assent while glaring at Carl over the elderly woman's bent head. "I bought it in Chicago, but it's imported."

"How I'd like to go there again," Alexsa sighed. "Chicago, I mean. I've not been to Ireland. The continent, of course, but never to Ireland. Too much fighting going on. You never know what you might get caught up in." She beckoned with a bejeweled finger and they fell in step, following their hostess down a carpeted hallway toward the back of the house. "But Chicago... Of course, that's another story altogether. Quite safe now with Capone dead. I'd visit all the shops on Michigan Avenue and buy absolutely tons of clothing."

Stopping abruptly, Alexsa turned to Caroline, lowered her voice, and said confidentially, "Don't know where I'd wear them, of course. I hardly go out anymore since I broke my hip." She tapped her left leg with the ivory-handled cane she carried. "The doctors said it would be as good as new after the surgery, but you know how they are. Promise you anything as long as you pay the bill! They do try..."

"Of course," Caroline said, finishing the sentence for Alexsa. She was amused by the old lady's disingenuous behavior, yet doubted she was as scatterbrained as she made herself out to be.

A glimmer of annoyance flashed in the eyes of the Morgan matriarch. She recovered quickly, though, and signaled them toward a set of double doors with her cane.

"I thought we'd sit in there, Carl. Would you please lead the way?"

The professor strode past and swung open the heavy oak door. "After you, madam," he said with a bow.

He ushered Alexsa into the room and Caroline followed. Once inside, she stopped dead in her tracks. They'd entered what appeared to be a modern gymnasium. Exercise equipment lined the windowless walls like ranks of silent soldiers standing at attention. A square blue mat occupied the center of the floor under a maze of rings dangling from the ceiling. A balance beam stood off to the left next to a suspended punching bag. Beyond that at the far end of the room was a lounge area with soft chairs and end tables gathered in a semicircle around a large screen TV. A well-stocked wet bar flanked by a billiard table sat in the corner.

"Come along, dear. No need to gawk," Alexsa chirped. She reverted once more to a sort of rambling chatter, clearly meant to disarm her guest. "This is the boys' room, but I sneak in on occasion when I want privacy for my visitors. The servants tend to eavesdrop, you know. With this excellent soundproofing—" she gestured around the gym "—I can talk to my heart's content and not worry that my conversation will be repeated all over town."

Caroline grinned despite herself. *Clever old girl,* she thought. She followed her hostess to the lounge where Carl had drawn three chairs into a circle. The professor winked at her as she sank into the plush elegance of a brocaded recliner. *So this is how the rich live,* she silently marveled.

"Whiskey or beer?"

"Um…what?" Caroline looked up to find Alexsa standing over her. The old woman's eyes bore into her.

"I said, whiskey or beer? There's not much choice in here. The boys are rather limited in their tastes."

"Nothing for me, thank you." Caroline needed a clear head if she wanted to figure out Alexsa's little game. The granny act couldn't be for real. "How many children do you have, Mrs. Morgan?"

"Only one, dear. When I speak of the boys, I mean my son, Bill, and his son, James. They may be grown men, but they still enjoy boys' games, as you can see." She waved a hand languidly toward the exercise equipment. "They retreat to this room every evening on the pretext of 'shaping up.' In actuality, they sit in here drinking and watching whatever sport the TV has to offer. Carl! Take whatever you want, but bring me a whiskey, large and neat." She sank down on the middle chair, leaning her cane against the arm before commenting cheerfully, "I'm glad to see you're not dead, Mrs. Rhodes. It would have been a shame to have missed meeting you."

"Alexsa!" Carl's voice sounded heavy with disapproval.

"I feel the same way about you, Mrs. Morgan," Caroline replied with a wicked smile. Two could play this game, she decided.

"Cari!" Professor Atwater practically sputtered the name.

"Do be quiet, Carl. And please sit down. You're distracting me with all your bustling around." Alexsa accepted her drink, raised it in silent toast to Caroline, then downed half the whiskey in a single swallow.

For her part, Caroline did her best to maintain an expression of total disinterest. She mentally applauded Alexsa's display of showmanship. It didn't intimidate her a bit, though. In her mind, this was only the second inning, the score tied one to one.

"Let's get down to business," Alexsa said brusquely. "You've come to discuss this affair at St. Anne's, haven't you? What exactly do you want to know from me?"

"How did you guess?" asked Carl.

"Servants work both ways, don't they," Caroline said shrewdly. "They may repeat what they hear in this house—although I doubt it; you wouldn't put up with that, would you, Mrs. Morgan?—but I suspect it's mainly the other way around. How else would you have known about my accident?"

Casting off the appearance of a frail old lady, Alexsa

threw back her head and laughed the hearty laugh of a woman in firm control of her life. Alexsa Stromberg Morgan was nobody's fool and she wanted Caroline to know it.

"You'd make a worthy opponent if we were enemies," Mrs. Morgan stated. "Thank goodness we're not. You may call me Alexsa, and I shall call you Caroline. Cari is much too diminutive a name for a woman with your powers of perception."

Caroline nodded graciously. She was still puzzled by Alexsa's behavior, but obviously a truce had been granted. She would take advantage of it while it lasted.

"What in the world is going on here?" Carl looked from one woman to the other, clearly mystified by them both.

Alexsa patted his arm. "Nothing, dear Carl. I'm just being obnoxious today. Now that I'm ninety, people expect it of me."

"Not I," Carl responded heatedly. "I expect your help."

"And I'll try to give it, but you must tell me what you want. I'm not a mind reader, although I've been accused of that in the past."

"We were wondering about the people killed in the explosion. The professor—" Caroline smiled sweetly in his direction "—told me you know the folks in this town better than anyone else."

"And why shouldn't I?" Alexsa sniffed. "I've outlived practically everyone born in Rhineburg. I must also admit to an inquisitive nature. But," she added solemnly, "I know how to keep a confidence."

"Unlike May Eberle?"

Alexsa looked away momentarily. A trace of sadness stained her eyes when she faced Caroline again.

"Poor May. She didn't deserve to die that way, even if she did gossip. She and her sister, April, were like church mice, timid but troublesome. They clung to each other like the proverbial orphans in the storm, which, in fact, they were."

"What do you mean?" Caroline asked.

"Their mother died soon after May's birth. Their father, a brutish, strong-willed man who cared for no one but himself, raised the girls. He treated the girls like slaves, allowing them no friends, no pleasures, just a life of drudgery and devotion to his whims."

"He never remarried?"

"No woman in her right mind would take Albert Eberle for a husband. He was furious when his wife died leaving him without a son. He courted far and wide, but he never persuaded another girl to marry him."

"It's as I told you, Cari. May was the last Eberle."

"Not exactly, Carl." Alexsa's dim blue eyes twinkled mischievously. "Albert liked to, shall we say, dabble in the sexual arts. He left progeny scattered in his wake much like a child eating cookies leaves crumbs. There's many an inhabitant of this county with Albert's genes in his blood."

Carl stared at her dumbfounded. "I never knew that. We've discussed Albert Eberle before, but you never told me about his philandering."

"Of course not," Alexsa retorted. "You might have been tempted to mention it in one of your books. Even if you'd omitted his name, people would have known you were writing about Albert. Think how that would have hurt his daughters."

So Alexsa hadn't been boasting when she'd claimed she could keep a secret. Caroline wondered how many other scandals the old woman was aware of. Plenty, she bet.

Carl appeared put out by Alexsa's lack of confidence in him. He turned his back on her to address Caroline. "With May dead, someone stands to inherit a hefty piece of change. If he, or she, can prove paternity, that is."

"If it's a motive you're after," Caroline replied, "you'd do better to check out Albert's grandchildren. May's half-brothers-and-sisters must be at least as old as she."

Carl grunted. "Hadn't thought of that."

"The Eberle girls were odd little creatures," Alexsa continued. "They had no manners, no social graces. When they moved about in public, they were either ignored or ridiculed by the townspeople. I suppose that's why they took to spreading stories about their neighbors. It was their way of taking revenge on Rhineburg."

"Were their stories believed?"

Alexsa smiled sadly. "Small towns thrive on gossip, Caroline. While there were grains of truth in some of the tales, mostly they were pure fabrication. But the Eberles told their awful lies to anyone who'd listen, and the stories spread exactly as they wished. They did a great deal of damage in Rhineburg. They broke up marriages, destroyed friendships. There were those who lived in real fear of what the women would do or say next."

Alexsa gazed down at her blue-veined hands, her mood suddenly pensive. Caroline wondered if there'd been a time when the sisters' vicious gossip had touched her. Given the old woman's standing in the community, she'd be a prime target for talk.

"April died in August, didn't she? I suppose her death devastated May."

"Wouldn't you be devastated," Alexsa said softly, "if your father murdered your best friend and only companion?"

Carl bolted upright in his chair. "Are you accusing Albert of killing his own daughter? Come now, Alexsa!"

Alexsa met his frown with a steady gaze. "April didn't fall down those steps on her own, Carl." She turned to Caroline. "Albert said she slipped at the head of the staircase and tumbled headlong down the steps. But Elvira Harding cleaned house there that day. She told me Albert was in a terrible mood over some missing money. He accused both daughters of theft, then he stalked upstairs to search their rooms. April ran after him, begging him to stop. Elvira didn't see it happen, but she heard Albert slap her. Then April screamed. Elvira ran into the hallway as April came hurling down the stairs."

"Why didn't Elvira tell this to the police?" Carl groaned. "They would have arrested Albert Eberle."

"If they would have believed her. I told you, Elvira never actually saw what happened upstairs. She only heard what sounded like a loud slap. Then April fell to her death. Elvira couldn't prove murder, but I trust her account of that day. Albert killed his daughter as sure as I'm sitting here. And furthermore, May poisoned him in revenge."

Carl appeared stunned. And angry.

"I can't believe you'd say that," he roared. "May was a pest and a gossip, but she certainly wouldn't murder her father."

"She hated him all her life," Alexsa maintained. "April's death brought it all to a head."

"Nonsense! Everyone knows Albert bullied the two

girls. They didn't move out, though, did they? They stayed in that house and waited on him like servants."

"Bah! For an intelligent man, Carl, you're talking like a fool. Those two had no choice but to stay. Albert was a tyrant who kept them firmly under his thumb. Neither girl ever learned how live on her own."

"And how did May poison her father?" demanded Carl.

Alexsa shrugged. "I suppose she slipped something in his food. May gardened. She probably had lethal compounds at her disposal."

"You're reaching, Alexsa. You've absolutely no proof of what you're saying."

"Perhaps not. But Albert was a strong, healthy man until April died. Then suddenly he expired, too. The coroner didn't care why. He wrote Albert off as an old man and his death as a heart attack." Alexsa's spoke rapidly, her frustration showing. "No one else really cared either. May was clearly around the bend, so why pursue the matter? They carted her off to St. Anne's and buried him alongside his wife."

Carl slumped in his chair, silent as the walls surrounding him. Caroline suspected his ego was badly bruised. The professor considered himself an insider in Rhineburg, a man privy to all that happened there. He'd suddenly been shown how little he knew of his neighbors' lives.

Caroline let the air settle a bit before she said, "May I remind you two that we're discussing the explosion at St. Anne's? May Eberle is important to us only if she was the bomber's target. Alexsa, I'd like to ask you again if anyone hated May enough to plant that bomb in the Christmas tree."

Alexsa pursed her lips and stared up at the ceiling.

"Certainly people are greatly relieved that May is no longer around to spread her ugly rumors," she said after a moment's thought. "But of course, you can hardly blame them. It's only natural to rejoice over the defeat of one's enemies."

The old woman's comment sent shivers down Caroline's spine. More chilling, though, was the thought Alexsa failed to put into words: the ultimate defeat for anyone was death. Of course.

CARL AND CAROLINE were alone in the gymnasium. Alexsa had been called away to the phone, leaving the two of them free to discuss her odd behavior.

"I don't know what's gotten into her today," Carl said. A troubled frown darkened his usually jovial features. "Her manners are usually impeccable. And I've never seen her drink whiskey. Something strange is going on."

"I knew that the minute the maid took our coats."

"What do you mean?" Carl's expression had changed to utter bemusement.

"You were speaking to her as she hung up our things," Caroline explained. "You said something about her brother in the Army, I think. Anyway, while the two of you were talking, I happened to glance in the mirror hanging in the hallway. I caught a glimpse of Alexsa standing at the head of the staircase watching us. Actually, it was almost like she was sizing us up. Then she started down the staircase, moving very spryly for a woman her age. But she stopped halfway down the stairs. Suddenly, her entire demeanor changed. She shrunk right before my eyes, became old and bent over and her hands began to tremble. She gripped her cane like she couldn't take another step without it. When I first saw her, she resembled a healthy seventy-five-year-old woman. By the time she reached the hallway, she'd become a frail ninety-year-old grandma."

Carl snorted. "There's certainly nothing frail about Alexsa. She broke her hip three years ago, but hasn't used her cane since coming home from the hospital. I attended her birthday party in September. She danced with every man in the room."

"There has to be a reason for the act. Perhaps Alexsa knows something about the bombing that she'd rather not tell."

"Impossible," Carl retorted. "If anything, she'd want to get to the bottom of this business. After all, Martha Schoen was her cousin."

"I knew she was a Stromberg before her marriage, but I wasn't sure how closely related she was to Mrs. Morgan."

"Close enough for Alexsa to come to her defense after the pie-throwing incident."

"Then Alexsa didn't approve of Martha's hospitalization?"

"Certainly not," Carl replied. "The mayor got his cousin, a GP in Newberry, to sign the commitment papers. Martha Schoen annoyed a lot of people, including Alexsa from time to time. But Alexsa backed her cousin one hundred percent on the subject of Teddy's philandering. I'd say she hates that man with a passion."

Caroline recalled what Alexsa has said about rejoicing over the defeat of one's enemies. If she considered the mayor capable of bombing a hospital, she'd have surely made her feelings known.

A door clicked shut behind them. Caroline turned to see Alexsa crossing the room.

"I'm sorry to have kept you waiting," she called out.

"That was Jim on the phone. I told him you stopped by to visit." She smiled charmingly as she settled back in her chair. "Now where were we?"

"You said some people are relieved that May Eberle's dead," Caroline reminded her. "Would you care to say who's celebrating her passing?"

Alexsa cocked her head to one side. "You certainly are the curious one, aren't you? Perhaps you'd better explain first why it is you want to know all this."

Carl heaved himself out of his chair and walked over to the bar. "I'll answer that," he said as he pried the cap off another bottle of beer. "You heard that Cari wrecked her car."

"Actually, I was told someone fiddled with the brakes. You were fortunate to escape with so few injuries, dear."

Caroline marveled at Alexsa's wide network of informants. "I was very lucky. Carl thinks the attempt on my life could be tied to my presence on the psychiatric ward the day of the bombing. He believes the person who planted the bomb also tampered with my car."

"So the two of you have set out to unmask the killer." Alexsa made it sound like they were a couple of kids playing Clue. Caroline blushed, but Carl's anger flared. He strode over to Alexsa's chair and glared down at her.

"See here, Alexsa. Caroline could have been crippled or even killed in that accident. We have every right to try to find out who's behind these murders."

Alexsa remained unruffled. "Put that way, I suppose I agree with you. Sit down, Carl. I'm not attacking the two of you, but you're asking a great deal of me. If I revealed names, and you two mentioned them to the police, a lot of innocent people could be dragged into this case. You seem to believe the killer was after one of the patients. I'll tell you what I can about those I knew, but I won't point a finger at one of my neighbors and say, 'There he is! He's the murderer!' I can't do that."

"Fair enough," said Caroline. She dug a small note-book out of her pocket and flipped through the pages. "I think we can dismiss Richard Canty from our list of likely targets. The man's been in and out of psychiatric hospitals for the past ten years. He arrived at St. Anne's four weeks ago after being picked up by the state police. They found him wandering down the highway stark naked."

"*Brrr!* Maybe he belonged to the Polar Bear Club."

Alexsa referred to a group of Chicagoans who swam the icy waters of Lake Michigan each winter. Caroline smiled at her hostess, aware that she meant to ease the tension in the room. Carl's face, though, remained set in a scowl. He wasn't going to forgive the old lady that easily.

"Jane Gardner gave me what information she could without breaking the rules on patient-nurse confidentiality. Even though a lot of this was public knowledge, she saved me from having to scrounge through newspaper files for it. She said Richard Canty's body wasn't claimed after the explosion. Apparently he had no family."

"He wasn't from around here," Alexsa stated. "That's an English name. We have few Rhineburgers of British descent."

"The police traced his fingerprints when they picked him up. He had a minor record dating back several years ago. Between hospitalizations, he did some shoplifting in grocery stores. If it hadn't been for that, the cops might not have discovered his identity."

"He doesn't sound like a threat to anyone. It's safe to

cross him off the list." Carl motioned toward the note-book. "What else do you have in there?"

"Next comes Thomas Adrian. A man in his early seventies, he'd suffered from paranoia for years before admitting himself to St. Anne's. Jane felt he'd improved under treatment." ·

"I doubt it," Alexsa remarked dryly. "Thomas was a fine actor. I'll be he simply played the role of recovering patient to test his doctors. Probably wanted to see how smart they were."

"You knew him? He wasn't from Rhineburg."

"No, but my husband and I were acquainted with him. He stayed as a guest in this house several times."

"Of course," cried Caroline. "Now I know why his name is so familiar. He did Shakespearean theater, didn't he?"

Alexsa nodded in Caroline's direction. "You continue to amaze me, Mrs. Rhodes. Thomas's stage career was well before your time."

"Actually, my daughter told me about him. Kerry is a theater major. She studied his work." Caroline refrained from repeating Kerry's opinion of Adrian: she considered him a first-degree nutcase!

"Thomas was one of the best," Alexsa recalled. "Unfortunately, his career ended all too soon. You see, he couldn't get through a run without demanding that someone, either an actor or a member of the crew, be fired. He was convinced people were out to destroy him. He would fixate on someone, then imagine that person was plotting against him. His paranoia knew no limits."

"How did you meet him?" asked Carl.

"My late husband supported the arts. He backed several of Adrian's plays and liked the man. Thomas could be extremely unnerving, but brilliant in his interpretation of Shakespeare. He had a rare power about him, the ability to focus so completely on his role that he actually became the character he played. I sometimes thought his madness derived from too close an association with *Hamlet*." Alexsa allowed a smile to cross her lips. "If I had to describe Thomas, I'd say he was a combination of fire and ice, a most difficult man to comprehend. His paranoia and odd habits made for strained relationships both on and off stage. Directors became wary of hiring him. Over time, casting calls fell off and all the best parts went to others. Eventually he accepted retirement."

"What a pity," Caroline remarked. "I wonder how he ended up at St. Anne's."

"That was my doing," Alexsa admitted. "I recommended it to him, although I never imagined my advice would lead to his death."

"I'm confused," said Carl. "I thought you knew Adrian years ago, and only through your husband."

Alexsa smoothed the wrinkles in her skirt, avoiding Carl's eyes. "I had no contact with Thomas for years. Then last spring I came across an article about a home for retired actors in California. It mentioned he was living there but had been asked to leave due to his constant accusations involving other residents. I realized Thomas was still delusional. I wrote to him and suggested he come to St. Anne's. He didn't answer my letter, but I learned he'd checked himself into the hospital in October."

"You can't blame yourself for Adrian's death," Carl said gruffly. "You were trying to help the man."

"Are you sure these attempts on his life were all in his mind?" asked Caroline.

"Well…" Alexsa temporized as she stared off into

the distance. "I've wondered about that ever since the explosion. Thomas made many enemies in his heyday. People lost their jobs because of his demands. Some of them threatened to do him harm because of it."

"Those folks would have to be the same age as Adrian," Carl reminded them. "I can't see some septuagenarian building a bomb to knock off an old rival."

The professor's words rang true to Caroline. She turned to Alexsa. "Can you think of any other reason someone might want to see Adrian dead?"

Alexsa's eyebrows puckered in concentration. "The most likely motive is money. Thomas invested heavily in the stock market. Even though he retired at a relatively young age, he had no financial worries. He was a wealthy man."

"Any heirs?"

"I told you, Carl, I lost track of him years ago. He may have married. I don't know."

Carl grunted. "It doesn't sit well with me. I can visualize someone losing control and taking a knife to Adrian, but blowing him up with a bomb? No, it doesn't make sense."

"Unless you consider his mob connections."

"What?" Carl nearly jumped out of his chair. "Adrian got mixed up with them?"

"I heard some talk of it," said Alexsa. "Thomas knew the most unlikely people. He adored gambling and spent a good deal of time in Las Vegas. He said he had friends there, which is why he relocated to Vegas after retiring from the theater."

"That doesn't necessarily mean he became involved with the Mafia," Caroline said gently. She wondered why Alexsa had withheld this bombshell until now. The police would be interested in any possible ties between Adrian and organized crime. The mob wouldn't be above planting a bomb to rid itself of a troublesome character.

"My husband thought he did, and that's proof enough for me," Alexsa snapped. "You didn't know Thomas Adrian like we did."

Methinks the lady doth protest too much, Caroline decided. She let the matter drop when she caught sight of Carl's face. He looked ready to explode.

She consulted her notes. "William Chapell lived in Rhineburg before his commitment in late September. Jane told me he suffered a nervous breakdown after the deaths of his wife and brother in a house-trailer fire."

"I remember that case," said Carl. "Supposedly the brother romanced the wife behind Chapell's back. Her family claimed Chapell set the fire to punish them both. They wanted the police to press charges against him, but he cracked up before anything came of it."

"A guilty conscience," Alexsa stated.

"Perhaps. Chapell and his brother worked opposite shifts at the quarry. Pretty convenient timing for carrying on an affair. Chapell's father-in-law was employed there also." Carl shot Caroline a meaningful look. "There might be something in that, you know. Maybe the man is skilled in handling explosives."

Caroline wrinkled her nose. "I don't like it. If the father-in-law wanted revenge, he would have taken it immediately, not waited three months. Anyway, how would he have learned about the damaged tree? That seems to be the sticking point in this entire affair. Someone had to know about the tree."

"Teddy Schoen probably did," Carl remarked. He turned to Alexsa and explained about the ward's ruined

Christmas tree. It was the first she'd heard of it, which meant her spies had missed something.

"Teddy kept a close eye on Martha," Alexsa told them. "It's likely he heard about the tree. But much as I despise Teddy, I don't see him as a murderer. He hasn't got the guts for it."

Caroline didn't know what to say to that. She doubted Alexsa's objectivity when it came to the mayor. Despite what she said about hating him, the two were related by marriage. Alexsa might not be willing to point a finger at someone so closely tied to her family.

"That leaves James Belding," she said. "Do you know anything about him, Alexsa? He came from Rhineburg originally, but they buried him in Chicago."

Alexsa appeared deep in thought. She took her time answering. "I don't recall anyone by that name. He might have come from one of those transient families that work off and on at the quarry. Jobs are always changing hands there."

"There must be someone around town who remembers Belding. Carl, maybe you could…"

"It seems to me these were all quite ordinary people," Alexsa snapped as she rose from her chair. "It's true May Eberle was a thorn in the side of several people in town, and as I said before, Thomas Adrian had some dubious acquaintances. But I think the police are better equipped to carry out an investigation than you two. Why not leave the detecting to them?"

With that she picked up her cane and walked toward the door. Caroline and Carl had no choice but to follow. They weren't exactly being pushed out of the house, yet clearly the interview was over.

"Mrs. Morgan."

Alexsa stopped and slowly turned to face Caroline.

Her lips traced a polite smile devoid of any warmth. "What is it, dear?"

"Is there anything you can tell us about a student nurse named Gail Garvy? She also died in the explosion."

Alexsa looked at her queerly, her dim blue eyes reflecting no emotion at all. She hesitated, then replied quite firmly, "I'm afraid not, Mrs. Rhodes. Elvira Harding is an old and valued friend, but I hardly knew her niece." She shifted the cane to her right hand and, leaning heavily on it, walked away from them. When she reached the double doors, she looked back. "Elvira is in mourning," she told them. "I hope you have the decency to leave her alone."

Carl began to protest, but Caroline laid her hand gently on his arm. "Leave it be," she murmured. "She's upset enough."

Carl frowned but held his tongue. The two friends watched in silence as their hostess swung open the heavy door and, without another word, disappeared into the quiet emptiness of the old house.

CARL YANKED OPEN the car door and stood aside while Caroline climbed in. She'd barely settled into her seat when he slammed it shut and strode around to his side.

"My, aren't we in a fine mood."

Carl shot her a look of pure fury. "It's not funny, Cari. I don't appreciate Alexsa's rudeness."

"I wouldn't say she was rude, just cautious. After all, Alexsa doesn't know me from a hole in the wall. Perhaps she thinks I'm the one who planted the bomb."

"Come on," Carl sputtered. "Alexsa knows I'm a better judge of character than that. I'd hardly come waltzing into her house with a murderer on my arm."

Caroline gave him a lopsided smile. "You yourself said the murderer had to be someone like me. Someone with a little knowledge of the town and hospital. Alexsa's a pretty sharp woman. If she's fallen for that stuff about a 'mad bomber,' she might also suspect it's no coincidence that I arrived in Rhineburg around the time all those victims were admitted to St. Anne's."

The professor pounded the steering wheel with a closed fist.

"That's ridiculous," he exclaimed. "In fact, it's libelous. And if Alexsa dares to say even one word in public..." Carl shifted uncomfortably. A new thought had struck him. "I hope she doesn't share that theory with the police. They may be desperate enough to believe her."

"I wouldn't worry about the police," Caroline assured him. "After all, they know someone tried to kill me." She explained about the phone call from the FBI.

"You shouldn't be alone when you meet with that agent," Carl said grimly. "I'll go with you."

"Sure, if you want to. Say, who's that woman down by the fence?" Caroline pointed to a solitary figure standing several yards away. She had her back to them and was staring off into the distance, her arms wrapped about her and her long blond hair blowing loosely in the wind.

"That's James's wife, Elizabeth."

As he said it, the woman turned and began walking their way. Her head was bent, her wind-whipped hair covering her face. When she reached the driveway, she looked up. She stared at them for an instant, then changed course and vanished around the side of the house.

"I guess she didn't want to say hello."

Carl shook his head. "Elizabeth is a strange woman," he said. "Very withdrawn, very cool. She seems an odd match for James."

Caroline thought of the jovial salesman with his boyish good looks. Even from a distance she'd noticed that the woman appeared older than he.

"Do they have children?"

Carl nodded. "Two girls. Teenagers."

That could account for it. If Jim was like most men, Elizabeth did the lion's share of parenting. Kids at that age were known to cause gray hairs and age lines in mothers.

"We'd better get to the dealership." Carl switched on the ignition and threw the Jeep into gear. "There's one thing I don't understand. Why would someone who's been out of touch with a man for years suddenly up and write to him? And about something as personal as his mental condition?"

"You're talking about Adrian, right? That's a very good question, Carl, one I don't have an answer for. It could be Alexsa wasn't telling us the whole truth."

"What do you mean?"

"There may have been a romantic connection between the two. Not lately perhaps, but back when he was a dashing young actor and she a middle-aged matron lacking excitement in her life."

Carl huffed through his mustache. "You're jumping to conclusions again."

"Maybe I am. But think about it. Apparently her husband introduced Alexsa to the theater scene when he first backed Adrian's plays. If she traveled to Europe, she certainly spent time in New York. Consider her life there compared to here in Rhineburg. Much more attractive, I'd say."

"Perhaps," Carl agreed reluctantly.

"It wouldn't be the first time a bright, beautiful woman from a hick town—pardon me, but Rhineburg isn't the Hollywood of the Midwest—became entranced by the glitter of the big city. Under the circumstances, she could easily have fallen in love with a New York Romeo."

"She did use the word *unnerving* to describe Adrian."

Caroline nodded. Atwater's defenses were breaking down. "I suspect Alexsa was drawn to Adrian. Being a sensible woman, though, she opted for a comfortable marriage to a man she knew rather than a romantic interlude with an unstable thespian. All the same, memories have a way of deluding us."

Don't I know, she mused. Shaking off a sudden surge of melancholy, she continued. "Alexsa read about Adrian's predicament. Remembering the past, she probably felt compelled to renew their relationship. Now she genuinely regrets writing to him."

"Do you suppose he was the main target? Could there be a Mafia connection there?"

"I guess we should inform the FBI of the possibility. They'll probably want to look into it, maybe interview Alexsa. I'll call my daughter tonight. Kerry studied Adrian in acting class, and she's acquainted with all sorts of theater people in Chicago. Perhaps one of her friends will remember him. Better yet, maybe Kerry knows an old actor who worked with him on stage."

"Alexsa didn't have much to say about William Chapell," Carl noted. "Do you think she's hiding something there also?"

"I doubt it. Wealthy women generally don't hang around with quarry workers. Surely the same social rules apply in Rhineburg as in Chicago. I'm surprised she didn't know James Belding, though. He grew up in Rhineburg and attended school here."

"Yes, that's odd all right. If I remember correctly, a preacher in the area by the name of Belding died a few years back. The two were probably related."

"The Archangels would know, wouldn't they?"

"It's worth asking them. It struck me as queer that Alexsa didn't know Belding's sister. According to the newspapers, she's the CEO of a company in Chicago and one rich lady."

"Wealth generally knows wealth. Unless Alexsa no longer has a role in the family business, I'd guess she'd at least have heard of the woman. Jane told me the sister brought Belding to St. Anne's in September. He'd been with the Army in Vietnam and afterwards suffered a nervous breakdown. I understand he was pretty much out of it."

"Doesn't seem a likely candidate for murder, unless the bomber had something against the sister or her company."

"Wouldn't it be better to blow up the corporate headquarters if you hate the CEO? Unlikely as it is, I'm sure the FBI is investigating that scenario. I wish we had a little more background information on both of the Beldings. Alexsa's reference to the family was vague at best."

"We need a better local paper," said Carl. "*The Rhineburg Rag* hardly mentioned him at all."

"I haven't had time to read *The Tribune,* but I've kept all the copies printed since the explosion. I'll take a look at them tonight. Belding's obituary may be in one of them."

The conversation died as they reached Rhineburg. Carl slowed the Jeep and drove cautiously down busy

Wilhelm Avenue. Caroline stared out the window absently, her thoughts still on the victims of the bombing. They knew so little about any of them, least of all Gail Garvy, the student nurse Alexsa had refused to acknowledge. She suddenly remembered the diary and letters she's taken from Gail's dorm room. She'd better look them over as soon as she got back to the apartment.

"You seem to be a million miles away, Cari."

"Hmmm? Oh, we're here already."

"Yep. Stromberg and Morgan…"

"'Purveyors of Fine Automobiles.'" Caroline glanced at the sign above the doorway of the dealership and sighed. "I hope my new Jeep lives up to Jim Morgan's standards."

"It better," Carl growled. "Or I'll have that young squirt's head on a platter!"

"I'VE BEEN WAITING for you." James greeted them at the door with his boyish grin. "You're going to love her, Mrs. Rhodes."

Caroline wondered why men automatically genderized automobiles as female. Ed had named all his cars Annie. During his lifetime he'd owned Annie I, II, and III. She had no intention of carrying on the tradition. She'd start a new custom. She'd call her Jeep Clyde, or Abe, or Rudolph.

"We've just come from your grandmother's," Carl said as they followed Jim across the showroom.

"Oh? I'll bet she enjoyed your visit."

"Actually," Caroline replied, "I think we may have upset her."

Jim frowned, his blue eyes darkening with displeasure. "How so, Mrs. Rhodes?"

"We were discussing the people who died in the explosion at St. Anne's Hospital. Alexsa knew one of the victims quite well, a man named Thomas Adrian."

"Oh? I've never heard mention of him." Jim seemed genuinely surprised by Caroline's statement. She decided to spring another name on him. Maybe his reaction would be more revealing this time.

"There was another man, a James Belding." She hesitated as if reluctant to pursue an unpleasant subject, then shrugged and gave Jim a beguiling smile. "Your grandmother appeared somewhat distressed when his name came up. I got the distinct impression her memories of him weren't happy ones."

"I don't know why that would be," Jim responded cautiously. "Belding left town as a teenager. I doubt my grandmother even knew him."

"But you did, right?"

Jim walked over to the coffeemaker and poured himself a cup. He appeared distracted, so much so that he forgot to offer coffee to his customers. With his back still turned to them he said, "Not really. He was a year or two ahead of me in high school."

"What about his sister?" Carl persisted.

"His sister? I don't know… Yeah, I guess maybe she was in my class. Or maybe the one ahead of me. It's hard to remember that far back."

Caroline exchanged a puzzled glance with the professor. Jim was acting as reticent as Alexsa. Either evasiveness ran in the Morgan family, or they'd stumbled onto something important. She tried another tack.

"I take it Alexsa and Elvira Harding are close friends. Gail Garvy's death must have come as a shock."

"Elvira is my grandmother's housekeeper. Has been for years." Jim suddenly swung around. "Why all these questions, Mrs. Rhodes? What are you looking for?"

Caroline opted for honesty. She told him about the Buick's damaged break lines. She wasn't surprised by his calm acceptance of the story. Like his grandmother, Jim had already heard it. What astonished her was the way he brushed it off.

"Probably some college kid out to get his kicks. I wouldn't give it a second thought."

"You're kidding," roared the professor. "Attempted murder doesn't bother you?"

Jim's jaw jutted forward. "Mrs. Rhodes survived the crash, didn't she? No broken bones, no internal injuries. Just a cut on the head." He drew in a deep breath and turned to face Caroline. "Not at all like Gail Garvy. She had no chance at all, poor kid." He put down his coffee cup and checked his watch. "You'll have to excuse me, but Liz is waiting on dinner. The Jeep is around back." He pulled open a desk drawer and took out a set of keys. "I'll drive it up front and meet you there. If you have any problems with the car, Mrs. Rhodes, you know where to find me."

He escorted them out the door, locking it firmly behind them. Caroline saw the fury in Carl's eyes as he glared through the plate glass at Jim's retreating figure. The professor clamped down hard on his pipe.

"If you're not careful, you'll bite that stem in two."

Carl snatched the pipe from his mouth and grimaced. "That's twice today I've been thrown out of places by old friends. What the hell is going on?"

"Alexsa got to him," said Caroline. "Don't you remember, she took a call from Jim while we were at her house? I'll lay you odds she warned him not to talk to us. She probably shared her suspicions with him, and he took it from there."

"This is downright ridiculous," Carl fumed. "Jim practically accused you of sabotaging your own car."

"It would be a smart move if I were the bomber. I'd blame someone else and draw the attention away from myself."

At that moment Morgan pulled up to the curb in Caroline's Jeep. She ran her hand over the sparkling-clean forest-green Cherokee. It was perfect.

"Thank you, Mr. Morgan," she said as he handed her the keys. "It's exactly what I asked for."

"Remember to read the owner's manual. Give me a ring if there's anything you don't understand." Jim had slipped back into his salesman's persona. He smiled automatically before jogging off to his own car. He made a U-turn in front of them and drove rapidly away.

"In a real hurry, isn't he?"

"Probably rushing over to grandma's place to find out what she told us."

"I'd say you're right about that, especially since Jim's house is back that way." Carl jerked a thumb over his shoulder.

Caroline smiled at him grimly. "Well, Sherlock, we seem to have stirred up a hornet's nest in Rhineburg. It'll be interesting to see who gets stung next."

The professor kept his tone light, but his words cut to the quick. "Hopefully, my dear Watson, it won't be us!"

FIVE

December 23

CAROLINE PULLED HER Cherokee over to the curb and depressed the window switch. She waited until Carl stopped alongside and did the same.

"Call me in the morning," she shouted above the wind. It was snowing again, thick wet flakes whipping about the cars as the full fury of the latest blizzard hit Rhineburg. Caroline could barely see Professor Atwater through the curtain of whiteness separating the two Jeeps. Then he leaned across the passenger seat and gave her the thumbs-up. She waved back and signaled him to go ahead. With the four-wheel drive in gear, she followed as far as the hospital before he turned off for home.

The day had ended pleasantly. Caroline wanted to show Martin and Nikki her new car and Carl agreed to accompany her. They drove from the dealership to the apartment where Martin insisted on celebrating what he called his mother's "Christmas toy" with pizza ordered from a local eatery. Nikki then pulled out a box of ornaments and dragooned the pair into helping decorate the couple's Christmas tree. Carl bellowed his way through an assortment of carols, substituting bawdy limericks for the original lyrics while tossing tinsel over prickly green branches. Marty did his best to harmonize. His clear tenor blended nicely with the professor's deep bass, but Nikki and her mother-in-law shunned any attempt to match their boisterous singing. Content to be the audience, they cheered enthusiastically each new version of an old favorite.

It was nearly midnight when the party broke up. Now, as she turned into the parking garage, Caroline checked her watch one last time. 12:22 a.m. In fifteen minutes she'd be tucked in bed enjoying a well-earned rest. Just thinking about sleep made her yawn.

She left the Jeep in a slot on the third level and followed the snow-covered sidewalk to the ER entrance. Inside, she stamped the snow from her boots and loosened her scarf. She walked past the triage room and into the ER proper.

"Hi, Caroline. Quite a storm out there." Paul Wakely had pulled night shift duty. He waggled a chart at her, inviting her to join him at the desk. "How you feelin'? Any headaches?"

Caroline took a seat next to the man who'd sutured her after the crash. "I'm fine now except for these stitches. They tickle!"

"That means you're healing nicely. Come see me when it's time to take them out. And don't overdo it, okay?"

"Of course not. I'm getting my share of rest."

"That's not what I hear," Paul said jovially. "You've been running around town ever since you were released from the hospital. Even bought a new car."

Caroline hid her annoyance with difficulty. It didn't matter that Paul knew her every move, but if he could track her so easily, so too could her attacker. She shivered at the thought.

"What's wrong?" Paul leaned forward looking concerned. She waved him off.

"Nothing. I'm just surprised at how quickly news travels around here."

Paul grinned. "That's what you get for moving to Rhineburg. You ought to know there's no privacy in a small town."

Caroline forced a laugh as she rose from her chair. She left the ER by the back door, passing the X-ray department and the lab, and turned left into the hospital's south corridor. Her boots squeaked noisily on the polished floor.

Paul's words echoed uncomfortably in her mind as she walked toward the courtyard nestled in the center of the four-winged complex. A blast of wind and wet snow met her when she tugged open the plate-glass door and stepped outside.

Devoid of light and thick with drifting snow, the courtyard seemed a poor choice tonight as a shortcut to the dorm. Caroline almost retreated back to the corridor when suddenly the snow thinned to a flurry. She gripped the hood of her parka and plowed on, keeping as her goal the dimly lit windows on the other side of the yard.

Halfway to her destination a curious scene unfolded. She saw two figures outlined in a window. Locked in an embrace, they swayed in and out of view in the shadowy north corridor. Caroline slowed to a halt, her curiosity piqued by the strange movements. A sixth sense told her she wasn't watching the romantic scuffling of two employees. She knew she should go back for help, but instead she ran toward the north wing door. She was only a few steps away when a sudden gust sent snow swirling through the courtyard. Icy pellets slapped her cheeks and she ducked her head, shielding her eyes with an arm. When she looked up again, the couple had vanished from a now darkened north corridor.

Caroline stumbled through the last of the drifts and reentered the building. It was pitch black inside. She paused to get her bearings. An exit lamp glowed above the elevators at the far end of the corridor, but all the overhead lights were off. She turned to her right, her hand sliding along the wall as she moved cautiously down the passageway. Her eyes quickly accommodated to the darkness and she began to make out shadows ahead of her. One particular shadow thickened into a still gray mass on the floor. Steeling herself to recognize it for what she instinctively knew it to be, Caroline approached the body.

The man huddled beneath a window, his knees drawn up, his left shoulder propped against the wall. His head twisted crazily upward and to the right. A sudden burst of moonlight through the window captured a look of surprise in his open staring eyes. Caroline bent down for a closer look. A lock of silver hair covered the man's forehead. She gently smoothed it back into place alongside its copper brothers. Charles Paine had been fastidious about his appearance. Hopefully the undertaker would do him justice.

"Damn," she said, rising to her feet. She looked up and down the corridor but saw no one. The cafeteria was a few feet up the hallway. Caroline remembered the house phone hanging on the wall inside the entrance. She found it easily enough even in the dark.

"Code Blue," she told the operator. "Near the cafeteria. And call maintenance. There are no lights down here."

She disconnected, then hit 9-0 for an outside line. The operator announced the code over the loudspeaker as she dialed Carl's number. He picked up on the second ring.

"Thank God you're home."

"What's the matter, Cari? What's happened?"

"Can you come to St. Anne's right away? Charles Paine is dead. Murdered."

"Where are you?" Carl asked crisply.

Caroline told him. "Will you call the Archangels? I'd feel much better with one of them here."

"Right. Stay where you are and I'll be there soon."

Caroline hung up the phone with a feeling of relief. She didn't want to be alone when the police arrived with their endless questions. With Carl for support, she could face the coming unpleasantness.

"Where the hell are the lights?"

The code team had arrived. Caroline could hear the sound of running feet and the crash cart being trundled down the hallway.

"Down here," she called out. She swept the wall with her fingers, searching for a switch. She found it inches beyond the phone and flipped it up. Light spilled out from the cafeteria into the corridor.

"Be careful," she warned the newcomers. "He's been murdered. The police will want to see everything as it is."

"Not you again." Dr. Paul Wakely motioned the rest of the team back. He gave Caroline a quick smile that vanished when he bent over the body. He felt for a carotid pulse before placing his stethoscope on Paine's chest.

"You called the code?"

Caroline nodded. "I knew it was useless as soon as I saw him, but I didn't want security messing around with the body before the police arrived. It seemed best to call a code first."

"We'd better notify them now." Paul signaled to one of the nurses who nodded her understanding before walking briskly toward the elevator. The overhead lights came on as she passed an employee in a brown uniform hurrying their way.

"Who's been fooling with the lights down here?" The man glared at Paul and Caroline before catching sight of the body on the floor. His face went pale. "Oh, shit! Is that guy dead?"

Paul stepped in front of the corpse, blocking it from the man's view. "Don't worry about him. What's wrong with the overheads?"

The maintenance man took a step backward. He dragged his eyes from the body and addressed Dr. Wakely gruffly. "Somebody opened that panel." He pointed to a metal cover on the wall at the end of the corridor. "Whoever did it blacked out the entire hallway."

"Was the panel unlocked?" Caroline asked.

"Hell no," the man replied. "You think we leave it open so some damn fool can play games down here? Somebody jimmied it. Now we'll have to replace the entire panel."

"Did you touch the door when you turned the lights back on?"

"Look, lady, are you into dumb questions or what? Of course I touched the door. I had to swing it open to get at the switches inside."

Paul drew the fellow off to one side and cautioned him to stick around. Like it or not, he'd have to talk to the police. Left alone, Caroline found herself engrossed with the behavior of the code team. None of them were expressing regret for the administrator's sudden demise. Despite the circumstances, a couple of nurses were actually smiling.

Guess I can't blame them, she mused. Paine had been a hatchet man during his years at St. Anne's. All of these nurses knew someone affected by the cuts. She turned to Paul, about to ask him if the cause of death was what she suspected, when the elevator bell jingled.

"Okay, you all hold it right there!"

A tall, broad-shouldered man in a blue military-type uniform had emerged from the elevator. He strode toward them, a gun gripped dramatically in both hands and pointed squarely at the code team.

"Holy shit," Paul swore softly. "The cavalry has arrived."

"LET'S GO OVER THIS one more time."

Tom Evans, FBI, unlaced his stubby fingers and placed both palms flat on the table. Lips pursed and brow furrowed in concentration, he gazed solemnly at Caroline. She might have bought the act if she hadn't seen it coming.

"You know what?" she said. "You've got the Columbo bit down to a *T,* but it's beginning to get on my nerves. Why don't we stop playing these silly games? I don't intend to confess to murder, and you haven't any real evidence against me. So why don't we call it a night?" She stood up and stretched her muscles. After forty-five minutes on a straight-backed chair, her spine screamed in pain. What she wouldn't give for her own soft recliner.

"Please sit down, Mrs. Rhodes. This won't take much longer."

Angered by the agent's officious manner, Caroline

spat out her words with a vehemence she rarely felt. "No way, my friend! I've told you everything I know about what happened tonight. Why don't you question President Hurst? I told you I heard him arguing with Paine during the faculty party at Bruck Hall. Something was going on between those two."

"Mr. Hurst will be given an opportunity to explain that conversation," Evans replied smoothly. "I intend to speak with him next."

"Good! Then you won't need me any longer."

Caroline grabbed her coat and headed for the door. Evans waited until she'd stepped into the hallway, then he called out, "Don't leave town, Mrs. Rhodes."

Caroline turned on her heel, looked back at Evans, and shook her head in exasperation. "You should work on your lines. Your whole performance is outdated."

She restrained herself from slamming the door and instead crossed the corridor and entered the administrator's office suite. She found Carl in the waiting room deep in conversation with one of the Bruck brothers.

"Are they finished with you?" the professor asked. He pushed his rotund frame out of the thickly padded sofa and guided her to an easy chair, a sympathetic look in his eyes.

"It's more like I'm done with them," Caroline responded wearily. "I couldn't take it anymore. Evans went over and over the same things, trying to trip me up on my answers." She gestured toward Paine's office. "Is Hurst in there? He's next in line for a grilling."

"The president waits for no man." Carl grinned. "He bullied one of the officers into taking him downstairs for coffee. They should be back any minute now."

"Then let's get out of here. I don't think I can stomach any more of that man tonight." Caroline rose and headed for the door. "Are you hungry? Why don't you come up to my apartment, and I'll fix us some sandwiches."

The two men were quick to take her up on the offer. They followed her through the empty hospital corridors toward the tunnel connecting St. Anne's with the dormitory. Five minutes later they were walking through Stromberg.

"Welcome to my humble abode." Caroline ushered them into her apartment. "Make yourself at home while I check out the fridge."

"Let me help you," Carl insisted, making a beeline for the tiny kitchen. He opened a cabinet and took out three plates. Caroline pulled a chair up to the kitchen table before opening the refrigerator. "Have a seat, Mike," she said while searching the shelves for sandwich makings.

"I'm not Michael," the young many said sheepishly. He pushed a strand of blond hair off his forehead and smiled. Caroline straightened up in embarrassment.

"I'm sorry, Gabe. You two are so identical…"

"I'm not Gabe either." Another quirky grin lit his face. "My name is Rafael, Mrs. Rhodes, but you can call me Rafe. I'm the youngest and last of the Bruck brothers."

Speechless, Caroline stared at the security man before breaking into loud peels of laughter. "I should have known," she said, shaking her head. "There are three Archangels mentioned in the Bible: Michael, Gabriel, and Rafael. So you're the most junior of the Brucks. By how long, Rafe?"

"About a minute and a half," he answered with a chuckle. "Mom had a C-section."

Caroline didn't know what to say. She motioned to

the chair again, still shaking her head in amazement. The three brothers looked incredibly alike. Hopefully, they were equally intelligent.

"I was on duty when the professor called," Rafe said, getting back to the business at hand. "Unfortunately, we didn't get to talk to you before the FBI arrived. The hospital security people sealed off the ground and first floors. We had a heck of a time persuading them to let us in."

Caroline handed Rafe a package of sliced roast beef, a jar of mayo, and a loaf of rye bread. She turned back to the fridge for lettuce and cheese. "It looked more like a three ring circus than a crime scene after that gun-toting guard stepped off the elevator. He refused to holster the damned thing until his boss showed up."

"He'll be out of a job tomorrow," the youngest Bruck assured her. "Harns is a good security chief. He doesn't put up with stupidity."

"I hope not. Do you know, that fellow actually asked Dr. Wakely for his identification card? He wanted to search the code team for weapons."

"Damn fool," Carl grumbled. "When did Hurst show up?"

"He came trotting down the hall behind Chief Harns. He said he had an appointment with Paine. When the administrator didn't show up at his office, he notified security. They were searching the first floor when I phoned in the code." Caroline slapped bread on three plates and began making sandwiches. "Hurst swore he didn't suspect anything until he overheard the message on the guard's two-way radio. Harns had put out a general alarm after being paged by one of the ER nurses."

"Then he called the FBI," said Rafe.

Caroline nodded. "Mr. Harns seems to know his

business. He figured Paine's murder might be related to the bombing."

"That's a pretty good guess," replied the security officer. "Tell us about the interrogation, Mrs. Rhodes."

Caroline finished making the last sandwich and sat down. Carl handed her a bottle of beer. She took a swallow of the cold liquid before answering. "It was unnerving, to say the least. Evans seems to think I'm the murderer."

"What?" Carl almost dropped his sandwich. "Don't tell me…"

Caroline nodded. "Alexsa spoke to Agent Evans. He said she only wanted to share a few thoughts with him. He appeared quite grateful for her help."

"Dammit!"

"Now, Carl, don't get upset. I told you she didn't trust me. Anyway, Evans had already been digging into my past. He started investigating after the accident."

"And what did he come up with?"

Caroline glanced at Rafe and blushed. The professor knew of her past, but she wasn't happy discussing her emotional problems with relative strangers. She knew that anything she said would be repeated to Rafe's brothers.

"He knew about Ed's accident and my hospitalization," she finally admitted. "The Chicago police sent him the file on the hit-and-run. It contained a lot of background information on Ed, including the fact he'd served in the National Guard and was adept at judo and karate. Evans wanted to know if Ed taught me any special moves." She took another sip of beer, but she didn't miss the glance exchanged by her two guests. She slammed the bottle down angrily.

"Look, you two," she snapped. "I'll tell you exactly

what I told that damned fool FBI agent. Ed was the expert, not me. I was too busy taking care of three kids to fool around in a gym with a bunch of grown-up boys in white togas. My husband had that honor. He enjoyed the physical training and the company of the other guys in the class. You know—the male-bonding bit."

Rafe silently studied his sandwich while Carl huffed and puffed through his mustache. Caroline had embarrassed them both with her outburst, and she wasn't finished yet.

"If it's any comfort to you," she continued bitterly, "I swear that although I can recognize a broken neck when I see one, I have neither the ability nor the strength to twist someone's head until his spine snaps."

"No one suggested that," Rafe protested. "But you have the unfortunate habit of being in the wrong place at the wrong time. You were on the psychiatric ward the day of the explosion. Tonight you were the one who found Paine's body. Evans may be hard-nosed, but he's a street-smart cop. He doesn't believe in coincidences."

Carl allowed her a moment to calm down before asking, "What did Evans say about your accident?"

"He had one of his men check the Buick. He acknowledged that the brakes were tampered with. Then he pointed out that we are in the 21st century. As he put it, women do know something about cars today."

"He thinks you cut the hoses yourself?" Carl groaned. "I was afraid of that, Cari. The FBI is stuck, and Evans is looking for anyone to pin this bombing on."

"That anyone might be me if we don't come up with some answers pretty quickly. I told him about the argument I overheard between President Hurst and Charles Paine, but he didn't bat an eyelash. He kept returning to the fact that I arrived in town the same month that all the victims were admitted to St. Anne's. On top of that, my past history doesn't lend to my credibility."

Rafe frowned at her. "I guess I'm missing part of the story. What do you mean by your past history?"

Caroline pondered her current situation. If she was going to rely on the Brucks for help, she had no choice but to be honest with them. In for a dime, in for a dollar.

"I had a nervous breakdown several months ago." She told Rafe briefly about Ed's death and her plunge into despair. "Evans suggested that I never recovered my sanity. He thinks I'm a nutcase out to punish the world for the loss of my husband."

"That's ridiculous! Rafe, you said this man had brains!"

"He does, professor. Evans has one hell of a reputation when it comes to breaking big cases. That's why the big shots assigned him to this one. You have to remember he's under a lot of pressure from various sources. There's politics involved here as well as big money."

"You mean Mayor Schoen," Caroline said.

"For one," Rafe allowed. "Politically, this could ruin him. Folks won't forget he dumped his wife in St. Anne's shortly before the explosion. Already the gossips are suggesting he had a hand in it."

"His opponents must be jumping for joy."

"You bet, professor. There's nothing like a rumor of murder to drag down a potential candidate."

"And the fact that her death made him a wealthy man doesn't help his cause."

"There you're wrong, Mrs. Rhodes," said Rafe. "The mayor can only claim property they held in joint tenancy. Martha Schoen's personal fortune was tied up in a sort of tontine."

"A tontine? With whom?" Carl asked incredulously.

"Her blood relatives." Rafe chewed on his lip as he wrestled for the words to explain the convoluted dealings of the Stromberg family. "Mrs. Schoen's great-grandfather set up an arrangement by which only blood relatives could benefit from his wealth. In order to inherit, his children had to sign a binding agreement designating their own children as sole beneficiaries of their wills. His grandchildren were required to do the same and their children also. Marriage partners were not considered suitable to inherit. The money was meant to stay with the bloodline."

"So Teddy got nothing?"

Rafe shook his head. "Not a red cent, professor. This all came out at the reading of the will. Since Martha died childless, her share of the family fortune reverts to her closest living relative."

"That would be..."

"Alexsa Stromberg Morgan," Rafe concluded with a grin. "The old lady is rolling in money as it is. Now she'll get even more."

"What about Martha's shares in the quarry?" Caroline asked.

"She inherited them from her father. They'll go to Alexsa."

"Then the mayor will still have problems pushing through the stadium construction project." Caroline outlined what Nikki had told her about Martha's opposition to the plan. "If Alexsa truly despises Teddy, she'll follow her cousin's lead. It appears Schoen gained nothing but trouble from his wife's death."

"Maybe that's why he sold her Jeep so quickly," Carl mused. "Teddy may be looking for cash to invest on his own."

"Perhaps," agreed Caroline. "What's most important about this is that it rules out Martha as the target of the bomber. The only person to profit from her death is Alexsa Morgan. And Alexsa doesn't need Martha's money."

"That leaves us with Chapell, Adrian, Belding, and May Eberle. The motive for the bombing must be connected to one of them." Carl turned to Rafael. "Is there anything you can tell us that would indicate which of these people was the killer's intended victim?"

"I don't know anything about Thomas Adrian," Rafe said with a shrug. "Chapell's father-in-law blamed him for the fire that killed his daughter. He threatened to kill Chapell, but he had a stroke right after the funeral. He's been bedridden ever since. The girl had no other male relatives, and I can't think of anyone else in town who hated him enough to do this."

"Then we should cross him off the list also. How about May Eberle? Alexsa hinted that she'd caused trouble for a lot of people. Could there be a motive there, Rafe?"

"She and her sister spread some ugly rumors in their day. I know of at least two divorces they had a hand in. Now if May had been found dead with a knife in her chest, I could give you a whole list of potential suspects. But somebody bombing St. Anne's for revenge?" Rafe shook his head. "I doubt any of her victims would have gone to such extremes."

"Alexsa might disagree with you," said Caroline. "By the way, she accused May of murdering her father. Carl thinks that's a lot of nonsense."

Much to Carl's amazement, Rafe took Alexsa's accusation seriously. "She may be right. Old man Eberle was a real—pardon my language—bastard. He treated his daughters like trash, which may be why the sisters resorted to their gossipy ways. They couldn't lash back at their father, so they took out their frustrations on the town."

"To tell the truth, I always felt sorry for the Eberle girls," said Carl.

"You and me both," said Rafe. "Elvira Harding visited the office the day April died. She told Mike what she'd seen and heard, but it wasn't evidence of murder. It would have been her word against Eberle's as to what actually happened on that staircase. Personally, I wouldn't put it past the old guy to hit his daughter. When he died so suddenly, I figured May helped him along to the grave. She loved her sister. April's death was the straw that broke the camel's back."

"But no one investigated Mr. Eberle's death."

"Why should they? What good would it have done?"

Caroline had to agree with him. With May safely admitted to St. Anne's, what was the point in creating a scandal?

"Who inherits May's money?" Carl asked.

"There is no money," Rafe told them. "The house is a run-down monument to miserliness. Eberle pinched pennies when it came to upkeep on the place. The roof is falling in, the wiring is a fire hazard, and the foundation is crumbling. No one ever visited except for Elvira, who went there once a month to clean. No one else knew what a mess it was inside. May willed the place to the Historical Society, but they don't want it. I expect the town council will have it torn down."

"I knew Eberle was a skinflint," Carl said. "But I thought he'd leave enough for his daughters to live on."

"God only knows where his money went. He had only a few hundred in his bank account when he died."

"Alexsa told us that Albert Eberle had several children outside of marriage. Do you think it's possible one of them, or one of his grandchildren, might have thought there was something to be gained by getting rid of May?"

"Are you kidding?" Rafe grinned. "No decent Rhineburger would own up to being related to the Eberles!" The look on Caroline's face sobered him. "I'm sorry. I know you're worried about this, but I'd say Alexsa Stromberg exaggerated Eberle's sexual prowess. I've never heard the slightest hint of anyone other than his daughters being fathered by the man."

"Humph," grunted Carl. "So Alexsa was playing games with us."

Caroline glanced at her watch: 2:45 a.m. "You must be tired, Rafe, but could you please tell us what you know of James Belding before you go?"

"It's very little, I'm afraid." Rafe drained the rest of his beer. "A preacher by the name of Ty Belding had a house outside of town, but he died years ago in a hunting accident. He was James Belding's uncle. James and his sister, Janice, lived with him for a while outside of town. The Belding kids attended high school here, then dropped out of sight after graduation. We know Janice went to Chicago and married the son of a business tycoon. As for James, he entered the Army and served in Vietnam. That much we learned from the newspapers. Unfortunately, they haven't printed a whole lot on either one of their backgrounds. Mike's trying to find out more about them. He'll call you if he digs up anything." He pushed up from the table, shrugged on his coat, and started for the door. He stopped midway there. "By the way, what was that you said earlier about an argument between Hurst and Paine?"

Caroline related what she'd overheard at Bruck Hall the night of the faculty party. "I didn't realize Paine was talking to Hurst until tonight when the president introduced himself to Paul Wakely. He used his first name, Garrison. Then I remembered hearing Paine call the other man Gary. It had to be Hurst in that room."

"That's a good guess, Mrs. Rhodes. I don't know of any other Gary associated with Bruck U. It sure would help, though, if we knew what that conversation was about."

"They might have been arguing over university business," Carl suggested.

"I don't think so," said Caroline. "Charles Paine sounded very angry. He said something like 'a maniac did it.' I'm sure he meant the bombing."

"Well, if you remember anything else, give us a call." Rafe flashed the signature Bruck brothers smile and left. Carl hugged Caroline before also heading for the door.

"Don't worry, Cari. We'll figure this out sooner or later."

Caroline doubted it, but didn't voice her misgivings. After the two men were gone, she threw herself down on the bed, setting the alarm clock for five o'clock in case she fell asleep. Her eyes were burning from fatigue, but her mind was racing as she recalled her interrogation by the FBI agent. Evans had accused her of creating the story about Hurst and Paine, calling it a "convenient memory." She feared he had settled on her as his prime suspect.

"How in the hell did I get into this mess?" she muttered. Her life had taken a definite downhill slide since Ed's death. Now her future seemed more precarious

than ever. *It's all your doing, Ed,* she though irratio-
nally. *If you hadn't gone and left me...*

Cut it out, she told herself angrily. Tossing the blan-
kets aside, she stood up and began to pace the room. *It's
your own fault if Evans questions your mental stability.
You acted like a fool back in Chicago, so why expect
people to think you're sane now?*

"Thank goodness May Eberle's dead," she grumbled aloud. "I'd be in jail by now if she was alive and
spreading her gossip."

Reverting to typical ER black humor helped rouse
Caroline from her doldrums. She stretched out on the
bed, a smile tugging at her lips. She pictured herself in
prison blues begging for mercy from a tight-lipped May
Eberle. The absurdity of the scene brought perspective
to her problems. She closed her eyes and began making plans for the morning.

A VERITABLE FLEET of battleship-gray clouds crowded
the sky outside when Caroline made her first phone call
at 5:00 a.m. "Kerry? Hello, honey! I'm sorry to wake
you so early in the morning, but I wanted to catch you
before you left the apartment."

Her youngest daughter mumbled something incom-
prehensible before dropping the phone back in its cra-
dle. Caroline dialed again, and this time when Kerry
answered she shouted into the receiver. "Kerry! Don't
hang up on me. This is your mother." Afraid she'd hang
up a second time, Caroline placed two fingers to her
lips and whistled shrilly. That got the girl's attention.

"What the hell! Who is this?" Fully awake now,
Kerry sounded hopping mad.

"My goodness, dear! What was the noise? Are you
having trouble with your phone?"

"Is that you, Mother?" Kerry demanded grimly. "What in the...world...do you want at this time of day? Don't you know it's only... Wait a minute! Is something wrong? Are you okay?"

Caroline assured her that all was well in Rhineburg. Both Kerry and Krista knew of her accident because Martin had called them from the hospital. But they were as unaware as he of her latest troubles.

"I know it's an ungodly hour to be calling, but I need some information about an actor, and of course I immediately thought of you." Caroline's rapid-fire delivery was aimed at arousing her daughter's curiosity. She knew the girl well. Once intrigued by a problem, Kerry would go to hell and back to find a solution.

"This is important, dear, so listen carefully." She told her as much as she could about Thomas Adrian. The stun-gun approach worked well; she overwhelmed Kerry into silent attention. "I'm also looking for a connection between Adrian and a woman called Alexsa Stromberg Morgan. If you can dig up anything on the two of them, I'll be forever in your debt. And, Kerry," she added without a pause, "I need you to get back to me by eight o'clock."

She realized she was asking a lot, and her daughter confirmed that appraisal in no uncertain terms. After a bit of haggling, they settled on a more reasonable time frame. Caroline hung up with a smile, confident that Kerry would come up with some answers.

At six o'clock she placed another call to Chicago. Her brother answered on the third ring.

"Caroline! Hey there, how's the new Jeep?"

"I love it, Al. It handles as nicely as you said it would. With all the snow we've had, the four-wheel drive comes in handy."

"That's great," her brother said, "but you wouldn't be calling this early to talk cars. What's on your mind, sis?"

"I need your professional help, bro. I'm in trouble, big trouble!" Caroline didn't beat around the bush. She explained the situation as concisely as possible. Alan reacted angrily when told the accident had been engineered to permanently eliminate his sibling.

"Why didn't you tell me this before?" he demanded.

"I didn't want to worry you, Al. I'm fine, except that the FBI thinks I planted the bomb at St. Anne's. Agent Tom Evans also suspects me of Charles Paine's murder."

Alan indulged in several graphically colorful statements before regaining control of his temper. "Would you care to explain his reasoning on the matter?"

"The FBI heard about my nervous breakdown. Apparently I fit their profile of a 'mad bomber.'"

Alan swore again. "So this Evans guy figures you're a loose cannon traumatized by Ed's death. I suppose he thinks killing people is your way of handling grief."

"Something like that. I don't intend to sit by quietly, though, while they build a case against me." She told him about Professor Atwater and their joint effort to track down the murderer. That alarmed her brother even more.

"Holy shit, Caroline," he roared. "You could get killed playing that game."

"Listen to me," Caroline replied with equal vehemence. "This man has already tried to put me in my grave. I refuse to give him a second chance. I could use your help, Alan, but if you'd rather not get involved…"

"Don't be a fool," Alan said gruffly. "Of course I'll help you. Tell me what you need."

Caroline knew she could count on her brother. She

told him about James Belding and his sister, Janice. "According to the newspapers, her name is now Honeywell. She married the head of some company in Chicago."

"Honeywell Industries."

"That's the one. Do you happen to know her?" As the VP of a commercial bank, Alan's social circle ranged far beyond hers.

"Not personally, though I've met her at various functions. An attractive woman and bright, too. You know, Caroline, I read about her brother's death in the papers here, but I never suspected you were involved."

"Everything happened rather quickly," she said in apology. "Until last night, I had no idea the FBI suspected me of anything."

"Okay, sis. It's no use beating a dead horse. Now let me get this straight. You want background info on both Beldings, right?"

"And their uncle Ty Belding. He was a preacher here in town. James and Janice lived with him at one time, but he's dead now."

"We may have some difficulty with him, but I'll get my people on it right away. Anyone else on your list?"

"One more person," Caroline replied. "Alexsa Stromberg Morgan is a very rich woman who knows everything about everybody in Rhineburg. Strangely enough, she can't seem to remember the Belding family, even after all the newspaper coverage."

"That's odd," Alan admitted. "Money usually knows money. You'd think she'd keep tabs on a hometown girl who married a millionaire. So when do you want the results of this little investigation?"

"Would yesterday be too soon?"

"Of course not!" Alan laughed. "I'll shake a few bodies out of bed and call you back later this morning."

"Thanks a lot, Alan. I'll appreciate anything you can come up with.

"Listen up, doll," Alan drawled in his best Edward G. Robinson imitation. "Don't worry about a thing. The cops ain't got nothin' on us big-time bankers. We've got stool pigeons everywhere!"

"Don't I believe it!" Caroline laughed.

"Believe this, too," Alan said more seriously. "I love you and I'm concerned for your safety. Tell me you won't do anything rash."

"Of course not, Alan. I give you my word I'll be careful."

Little did she know that in a matter of hours she'd be breaking her promise.

"HI, JANE." Caroline placed her breakfast tray on the table opposite the unit manager and sank wearily into a chair. The effects of sleeplessness were evident in the dark circles under her eyes.

"You don't look so good," Jane commented between mouthfuls. "I suppose I wouldn't either if I'd stumbled over a dead man last night."

"So you've heard."

"Who hasn't? Word spreads quickly in these hallowed halls." Jane sipped her coffee and watched Caroline pick gingerly at her food. "Didn't anyone warn you to avoid the omelets? Half the ingredients are rejects from the lab."

Caroline grimaced and pushed her plate aside. "Now you've made me lose my appetite. Oh, well. I need to go on a diet anyway." She leaned back and grinned at the other nurse. "So tell me, what's the gossip on our late administrator? Any bets on who killed him?"

"I don't know about bets, but the staff is ready to crown you Employee of the Year."

"Keep your voice down," joked Caroline. "If the FBI hears you talking like that, they'll pull me in for further questioning. Speaking of questions, I have a few for you."

"As long as they're original, my friend. I'm sick of answering the same ones over and over again."

"I take it you've been worked over by the Feds, too."

"I've talked to more different police than I ever knew existed. Every time I think they're done with me, they come up with a new angle to explore."

"Have they questioned you about the tree the mice destroyed?"

"Funny you should ask. I forgot all about that when I made my first statement, but yesterday a very annoyed FBI agent visited me. He wanted to know why we put up a brand-new tree in the rec room, and more importantly, why I withheld that information from the police."

"What did you tell him?"

Jane shrugged. "I said it slipped my mind in all the excitement after the explosion. Since then, I've been too busy trying to get the ward back in order to worry about mice."

"How soon before you can reopen the unit?"

"God only knows," Jane answered grimly. "The rec room is sealed off for repairs, but Paine was adamant that we start admitting patients again right after Christmas. Now that he's dead, I'm not sure where we stand."

Caroline changed the subject. "What kind of a student was Gail Garvy?"

"Why are you interested in her?"

"Just curious, I guess," Caroline lied. "She seemed to work well with the patients."

"So she impressed you, huh?" Jane flashed her an amused smile. "I must be the only one who didn't like the girl."

"Why not?"

Jane hesitated, her expression turning sober. "I suppose I shouldn't speak ill of the dead, but something about Gail didn't ring true for me. She seemed to be faking her interest in medicine. I discovered early on that she didn't give a damn about the patients. Except for one, that is."

"Who?"

"James Belding."

"Belding." Caroline suddenly recalled the scene in the rec room prior to the explosion. Someone had called out Belding's name and Gail approached him, coaxing him into joining the others around the tree. He'd whispered something to her after raising four fingers.

"Why do you think she cared about him in particular?" she asked.

"I don't know. No matter who we assigned her to, she'd drift away from her patient and cozy up to Belding. I got the impression she was studying him, but not like a student studies an interesting case. Her fascination seemed more personal, more compelling." Jane paused to gather her thoughts. "I can't put my finger on it, but I swear she was after something. What that could be, I don't know. Belding arrived here in a catatonic state. He needed full care, never speaking, never interacting…"

Caroline interrupted her. "What do you mean he never spoke? I saw him talking to Gail right before the explosion."

"What!" Jane almost spilled her coffee in her excitement. "He actually said something to her?"

"I was too far away to hear his words, but I certainly saw his lips move. And Gail answered him. It looked like a perfectly normal exchange between patient and nurse."

Jane appeared stunned. She rocked back in her chair and slowly shook her head. "Do you know how hard we worked to communicate with that man? Everyone on the unit knew they were to report directly to me if he said even one word. Mr. Grove insisted on weekly summaries of his progress. He also wanted an instant update if Belding responded in any intelligible way to treatment."

"So you considered James Belding to be mute."

"Not just mute, but totally out of it." Jane drummed her fingertips on the table. "Why in the world would Gail keep this to herself? She should have reported his behavior to me at once. Unless," she said, hesitating, "what you saw was a first for Belding. In that case, she never had the chance to tell me."

"Who's this Mr. Grove?"

"He's a personal assistant to Mrs. Honeywell, James Belding's sister. He acted as a liaison between her and the hospital concerning Belding's care. He flew into town every other week to check up on things."

"That's a lot of checking up. Didn't the sister trust you?"

"Of course she did," Jane replied indignantly. "Mrs. Honeywell provided the money to establish the psych ward."

Caroline's eyebrows shot up. This was news to her. "You told me Charles Paine had financial backing from connections in Chicago, but I never guessed they were so impressive. According to the newspapers, Janice Honeywell is rolling in money."

"I believe she bankrolled the unit so she'd have a safe place to keep her brother. Safe from publicity, I mean."

But not from a killer, Caroline thought. She tactfully skirted the issue.

"Did you ever mention Gail's behavior to her instructor?"

"Sure. She talked to the girl twice. Both times Gail had an excuse for hanging around Belding. She seemed prepared for any objections I raised." Jane smiled wryly. "Gail was one smart cookie. She knew only qualified staff were assigned to work with Belding. Whenever Tony Grove appeared, she'd hurry back to her own patient. Between his visits, she gravitated to James like a bee to honey."

Like Jane, Caroline wished she knew the reason for Gail's behavior.

"Mrs. Honeywell intended to make another large donation to the hospital. I suppose she'll cancel it now."

"Hmm?"

"Sorry, Caroline, I'm thinking out loud." Jane took another sip of coffee. "Belding's death hurts St. Anne's in more ways than one. Paine persuaded Mrs. Honeywell to fund a major renovation project involving the outpatient department."

"And now the deal's off?"

Jane raised her shoulders in a *who knows?* gesture. "Grove's still hanging around, but Paine's murder certainly makes negotiations difficult."

Caroline considered that the understatement of the year.

"Then again, I may be wrong." Jane pointed to the doorway of the cafeteria. Caroline swung around in time to see two men carrying empty trays into line by the breakfast bar.

"Who are they?"

"The older man is Bill Bruck, grandfather of the Archangels and presiding officer of the Board of Directors. The short one in the thousand-dollar suit is Tony Grove."

The Honeywell representative looked to be in his early to mid fifties. A barrel-chested man with dark, slicked-back hair that hid his growing baldness, he carried himself with a confidence born of success. Caroline recognized his type immediately. He was the sort of man to whom winning meant everything, be it in business or at play. She suspected his cool demeanor concealed an ego of huge proportions.

"So that's…" Caroline stopped in midsentence as a stony-faced Grove turned in their direction. His eyes seemed to bore right through her.

"I've met that man before," she said slowly. "Only I can't remember where."

"Impossible," Jane countered. "If you'd ever dealt with Grove, you'd remember him. He's a tough customer, the kind who generally gets his way and never makes mistakes. Nevertheless," she said with a grin, "I think he made one today."

Caroline shifted her puzzled gaze to the other nurse. Jane winked and pointed to the tray Grove carried.

"He ordered the omelet," she laughed.

BACK AT THE APARTMENT, Caroline fielded a couple of calls from reporters who'd learned of her role in Charles Paine's murder. She dealt with them swiftly and in no uncertain terms. She wasn't so lucky handling her son's call.

"It's been on the news all morning," Martin exclaimed. "You should have called me, Mom. I would have come right over."

"Professor Atwater arrived with Rafael Bruck. I managed quite well with their help."

"So you met the third Archangel. Are you impressed?"

"Rafe seems as bright as his brothers. They're young, though, to be in charge of security at the university."

"I guess so," said Martin. "But they were trained by their father. He was the best chief of security Bruck ever had."

"He's not working any longer?"

"He had a heart attack a while back. His sons are in charge now. Did Nikki tell you about their wives?"

"No. Is there something special about them, too?"

"I'll let you judge for yourself. They're coming to our New Year's Eve party, so you'll meet them then. Speaking of parties, are you coming to the one in town tonight?"

"The Winter Festival? Nikki mentioned it to me. I'll try, dear, but I can't promise I'll make it." Caroline didn't mention that she might be busy hunting down a killer with Professor Atwater. The less Martin knew of their adventures, the better.

No sooner had she hung up on her son than Kerry called. "How you doin', Mom?"

"Fine, Kerry. What have you got for me?"

"My goodness! You're certainly businesslike this morning. Not even a 'Hi. How are you?' for your favorite daughter."

"Hello, dear. How are you?" Caroline answered automatically. "Now, what have you got for me?"

Kerry sighed in exasperation. "Whatever's going on

there better be good. I woke up a bunch of people to get this information."

"I do appreciate it, Kerry, but please! Tell me what you've uncovered. I don't have time to explain."

Kerry sighed again. "I expect a full account when I come to Rhineburg for Christmas. Okay, let's see what I have here." Papers rustled on her end of the line. "Ah, yes. Thomas Adrian was considered a rising star in the early fifties, mainly due to his roles as Hamlet and Macbeth. You know, Mom, Shakespeare wrote many fine plays, yet producers always seem to go for…"

"Kerry! Can we please stick to Mr. Adrian and his career?" Caroline pleaded. Discussions with her youngest daughter were often tricky, Kerry's thought processes tending to be erratic at best. Like a butterfly in a garden of wildflowers, the girl flitted from subject to subject, enamored by them all.

"Sorry about that. Sometimes I get carried away. As I was saying, Adrian knew how to act, but he had this thing about trusting people. He always thought his co-stars were out to steal the show."

"Is that so unusual in the theater?" Caroline asked. "I thought most actors were peculiar in one way or another."

Dead silence filled the line. Then, her voice dripping with sarcasm, Kerry said, "Thanks for the vote of confidence."

"I didn't mean you, dear," her mother replied hastily. It wouldn't do to ruffle the girl's feathers. Kerry had dug deep gathering this information. She deserved Caroline's thanks. "I meant some actors."

"Forget it, Mom. Actually, you're right in a way. There's a lot of ego involved in acting. But Adrian pushed ego to the limit. He was positively impossible, which is why directors stopped hiring him."

"I heard Adrian was so paranoid that he believed other actors were out to kill him. Is that true?"

"Well, I have a marvelous book written by Frederic Gordon, the theater historian. He lists Adrian as one of the finest interpreters of Shakespeare known to America. He also calls him erratic and temperamental. Gordon doesn't go so far as to call him paranoid, but I guess he couldn't write that about a live person. Defamation of character and all that rot. I wonder if he'll update the chapter now. I should call the publisher and get Gordon's address. I could…"

"Kerry, you're wandering again."

"Oh. Where was I?"

"Adrian made a lot of wild accusations against his coworkers. Was anyone really gunning for the man?" Caroline closed her eyes and forced herself to be patient.

"Anna's uncle would have gladly strangled him, but he's been dead for years. The uncle, I mean. Not Adrian. He's only been dead for a few days."

Count to ten and start over. "Who is Anna, dear?"

"Mother! How many times do I have to tell you? Anna is my inspiration in the theater, my mentor, my…"

"Professor. Now I remember. We met at Hamlet last year. So you're telling me her uncle knew Adrian, right?"

"Not only did he know him, he directed three plays in which Adrian had the lead. Mr. Karasov left his diaries to Anna. She let me look at them this morning. There were several references to Adrian's unstable mental condition. Apparently the guy was a real fruitcake."

"Fruitcake or not, Kerry, did anyone other than Mr.

Karasov want to kill him?" A long dead-director hardly seemed a likely suspect.

"Fruitcake. That's a traditional Christmas gift, isn't it? I can't think of anything for Anna, and I really should give her a present."

Caroline sighed. "It's a wonderful idea, dear. Now what about Alexsa Stromberg Morgan? By any chance did Mr. Karasov mention her name in his diary?"

"How'd you guess?" Kerry exclaimed. "Who is this mystery woman, Mom?"

"She lives here in Rhineburg," Caroline said shortly. "Tell me about her, Kerry."

"Well, according to Anna's uncle, the only reason Adrian got the lead in his last play was because Mrs. Morgan paid all the bills. She insisted he receive the role."

Caroline perked up. "You're positive it wasn't her husband who backed the play?"

"Definitely not. Mr. K. made a notation next to an entry concerning payments to the theater. He wrote 'Foolish woman!' then underneath that he scribbled her name."

Could this be confirmation of a romantic link between Alexsa and Adrian? Or had the director been referring to the woman's spending habits?

"Maybe it means Adrian talked her into bankrolling a bad play," Caroline thought aloud.

"Shakespeare didn't write bad plays," Kerry replied indignantly.

"Sorry, dear. You're right, of course. I meant to say, perhaps it was a poor production."

"Hard to tell since it never even made it to opening night. Evidently all kinds of things went wrong. A set collapsed, injuring a crew member. It had to be totally redesigned. Then there was a mix-up with keys. Somehow Adrian got locked in the wardrobe department. He suffered from claustrophobia and practically tore the place apart before they found him. The head seamstress walked out on the play after that little scene. Then Adrian claimed someone poisoned his tea. He insisted that all the previous accidents were aimed at him and were actually attempts on his life. The newspapers loved the story. This was front-page stuff."

"And that's when the production shut down?"

"Yep. Karasov couldn't stand any more bad publicity. He called Mrs. Morgan and told her to get a new director. She said forget it, the play's off. She withdrew her backing, which killed the play."

"Sounds like a disaster from the start."

"What could you expect?" her daughter replied matter-of-factly. "They were doing Macbeth."

Caroline recalled the old superstition concerning that play. Actors believed it to be bad luck to mention its name before opening night. Considering all the calamities that occurred, either someone had shouted "Macbeth" at each and every rehearsal, or Adrian wasn't quite as crazy as people thought.

As a likely target for murder, Thomas Adrian moved up to the top of the list.

"Mrs. Rhodes? Mrs. Caroline Rhodes?"

The female voice on the other end of the line sounded too unpolished to belong to a reporter. Still, Caroline responded cautiously.

"Yes, this is she. May I ask who's calling?"

"My name is Elvira Harding. I'm Gail Garvy's aunt. I left a message for you yesterday on your machine."

"Of course, Mrs. Harding. I'm sorry I didn't get back to you yesterday."

"That's all right, Mrs. Rhodes. I know how busy a person can get around the holidays."

"I'm sorry about your niece," said Caroline. "She seemed like a fine young person."

"You knew my Gail?"

Caroline heard the hopefulness in Elvira's voice. She needed to know more about Gail, but she couldn't outright lie to the woman.

"Not very well. But I worked with her on the day of the explosion. From what I saw of her, she'd developed quite a rapport with the patients."

"That was my Gail," Elvira boasted. "Just like her mom, caring about other people's problems before her own."

"Please give my condolences to Gail's mother. I wasn't able to attend the funeral."

Caroline assumed she'd blundered in some way when her words were met by dead silence. "Mrs. Harding? Are you still there?"

"I'm sorry. I guess there's no way you could have known about Monica. Gail's momma died when Gail was just a baby."

"Oh, forgive me!"

So that's why Gail had listed the Harding woman as next of kin. Unfortunately, it didn't explain the initials on the ring she'd seen in Gail's room.

"Don't give it another thought," Elvira said kindly. "My sister, Albina, took to her bed when she heard what happened to her granddaughter. She couldn't bring herself to call you, so I did. Can I stop by today and pick up Gail's things?"

Caroline thought fast. She hadn't yet read Gail's

diary, but she could hardly refuse the woman's request. "Of course," she agreed reluctantly. "What time would be good for you?"

"I'd like to come by now, if it's convenient."

Caroline stalled for time. "I've an appointment in ten minutes," she lied. "But I could meet you in the dormitory lobby at noon."

Mrs. Harding agreed without hesitation. Caroline hung up considering her next move. She needed to read Gail's diary before the aunt arrived, but she also wanted to talk to Carl. She dialed the professor's number.

"Damn it," she swore when the phone went unanswered. "Where are you, Carl?"

Replacing the receiver, she turned to the coffee table and found Gail's diary and letters where she'd left them the previous day. She'd just opened the slim leather volume when the phone rang again.

"Hello, Carl?" she said hopefully.

"Sorry, Mrs. Rhodes. Wrong person."

The voice didn't sound familiar. "I'm sorry. I was expecting someone else. Who's this?"

"Bill Morgan, over at Stromberg and Morgan. If it's Professor Atwater you're looking for, he left my place only a minute ago."

"I'll catch him later, I guess. So what can I do for you?"

"My son, Jim, told me you bought Martha Schoen's Jeep. I thought I'd check in and see if everything's good with the car."

"It's running beautifully, Mr. Morgan. It's nice of you to ask." Caroline wanted desperately to be rid of the man, but he appeared intent on continuing the conversation.

"That's fine. I'm glad to hear it. There's, ah, something else I need to say. It's, ah, difficult to know how to start, though."

Caroline waited, surprised by the embarrassment in the man's voice. "What's wrong, Mr. Morgan?"

"Well, like I said, Carl Atwater dropped to see me. He mentioned my mother's behavior yesterday. He said Jim acted strangely, too."

"Did he tell you that Mrs. Morgan spoke to the FBI about me?"

"Yes, ma'am, he did, and I want to apologize for that. Actually, Jim called them. Mother didn't like it, but she had to cooperate when they came to the house."

That put a new twist on things. Caroline was sure Alexsa had contacted Evans.

"I tried to explain the situation to Carl, Mrs. Rhodes. I hope you'll be as understanding as he."

"Why don't you just say what's on your mind, Mr. Morgan?" Caroline didn't even attempt to squelch the anger in her voice. Alexsa and her grandson had caused her nothing but trouble so far.

"Please call me Bill, Mrs. Rhodes. And don't judge my family too harshly. This whole mess has us tied up in knots."

Morgan certainly sounded distraught. His sincerity touched Caroline and she relented. "Go on, Bill," she said more kindly.

"You see, we thought this Jim and Monica stuff was behind us. I never realized my son would go off like a loose cannon when Gail died."

"I don't understand, Bill. Maybe you'd better start at the beginning."

The man heaved a sigh. "It all happened so long ago. Jim dated Monica Garvy before he married Liz. Monica was a little gold digger. Both Mother and I told Jim that, but he couldn't see through her. He thought the sun rose and set in that girl."

"Maybe because he loved her," Caroline suggested.

Bill snorted. "She was a hussy if I ever saw one. Dollar signs as big as saucers in her eyes. Hate to admit it, but I felt nothing but relief when she died in the fire at St. Anne's. She was finally out of Jim's life."

Caroline recalled the inferno that leveled part of the dorm in the late '70s. "Monica was a nursing student here?"

"Yeah. She roomed with Elizabeth, but only after Gail was born. You see, Monica got mixed up with some rich guy from Chicago and dropped out of school to have his kid. She went back again after her aunt offered to look after the baby. Her own mother threw her out of the house, and the baby's father turned out to be a married man. He left her left holding the bag with only her aunt to support her."

"That's sad," said Caroline. "The father refused to help?"

"Worse than that," said Bill. "The guy died in a car crash right soon after Monica became pregnant. She claimed they'd tied the knot a week before the accident, but her marriage certificate was phony. At least that's what Reverend Belding said, and he supposedly performed the service."

"Would that be Ty Belding you're talking about? A minister from this area?" Caroline felt the hairs rise on the back of her neck.

"Yeah, that's him, although I'm not sure he was a real minister. He had a farm outside of town, where he held revival meetings under a big striped tent. Lots of whooping and hollering and passing the plate."

"Did he have relatives in Rhineburg?"

"Sure he did. That fella who got killed in the explosion…"

"James Belding."

"Right. He was the preacher's nephew. I recall a niece, too, but I can't remember her name."

Caroline did. Bill should have, if he'd been reading the newspapers lately. "Why did your mother pretend not to know the Beldings?"

Bill groaned. "Monica's aunt Elvira has been my mother's housekeeper for years. Alexsa feels a loyalty to her, so she didn't want her disturbed by your questions."

That seemed a poor answer to Caroline. "What about your son? He also answered evasively when we asked him about James Belding."

"Jim hates the entire Belding family. He thinks the reverend lied about Monica's marriage. He was furious when Albina Garvy disowned her daughter. It didn't help matters that the father's family refused any financial support. They wanted proof of paternity, but Monica wouldn't allow Gail to be tested. She called it 'humiliating.' Jim figured Monica got a raw deal all the way around. He was all set to marry her when she died."

"Were Jim and Gail close?"

"No, not particularly. Monica brought the baby up to the house once in a while. Jim probably saw her then, but after Monica's death, they didn't have any real contact. The way I see it, the bombing brought back all those bad memories. Jim still thinks of Monica as some kind of martyr, and now he's placed Gail in the same category."

"So you're saying we opened a can of worms when we brought up the subject of Gail Garvy."

"Yes," Bill agreed. "Mother's caught in the middle. She feels bad for Elvira, but she wants to protect Liz and Jim's marriage."

Caroline's eyebrows rose. "It's that bad, is it?"

Bill apparently sensed he'd gone too far. He tried to cover his mistake. "Women don't like to hear about their husband's old girlfriends. Jim wants justice for Gail, but sometimes he doesn't realize how it sounds when he rants and raves about the situation. He mentions Monica a little too often, and that causes tension in the family. Oh, hell," he said heatedly, giving up any attempt at pretense. "The truth is, Liz is sick and tired of Jim's dramatics. If he doesn't cut it out, she's going to walk out on him."

Caroline recalled the haunted look on Liz's face when she'd seen her outside the Morgan house. She'd mistaken it for age, but now she knew better. Jim's wife was exhausted from contending with Monica's ghost, and Caroline doubted it was a recent phenomenon. Jim had probably carried a torch for his dead flame all his married life.

"I appreciate your explanation, Bill. It couldn't have been easy for you to tell me this."

"Well," he replied gruffly, "everybody knows some nutcase planted that bomb. I'm sorry my family caused you trouble."

"It'll all get cleared up soon." Caroline crossed her fingers. "I hope."

AT QUARTER TO TWELVE Caroline looked at her watch and frowned. Curled up on the couch with Gail Garvy's diary, she'd found herself stymied at first by the girl's unique shorthand. Eventually she'd unraveled the code, and now, fairly adept at deciphering the pages, she was hurriedly skimming the book. She had to put it back in Gail's desk before Elvira arrived, just in case the aunt knew of its existence. She'd read through half the book when the phone rang again.

Oh, damn, she thought, snapping the diary shut. She grabbed up the receiver with a curt "Hello?"

"Hello to you, too," Alan said briskly. "Have I caught you at a bad time?"

"I'm sorry, Al. I thought you were another annoying reporter. The phone's been ringing off the hook all morning."

"They've been hounding you, have they? I'm afraid I can't help you with that, but I do have the information you wanted."

"Great! I have to be somewhere at noon. Is ten minutes enough time? Or shall I call you back later?"

"Ten minutes should be fine. I'll keep it brief." Alan could be heard shuffling papers. "I'll tell you about Honeywell Industries first. An engineer named Arthur Honeywell formed the company after World War II. He parlayed a small government contract into a profitable business designing and manufacturing airplane parts. He married well, but his wife died shortly after giving birth to a son. Peter Honeywell was his father's pride and joy. Arthur brought him into the company at an early age, and the young man displayed a real knack for improving on dad's ideas. Peter doubled the company's profits before his twenty-fifth birthday."

"That's all very interesting. But where does Peter fit into the picture? I thought you were investigating Janice Honeywell."

"Patience was never your strong suit, little sister. Just stay with me and The Great Alan will reveal all."

Caroline laughed. "Of that I have no doubt. Okay, bro, I'm all ears."

"As I was saying," her brother continued, "Peter had a head for business. As his father's right-hand man, he soon became first vice president in the company. Apparently brains weren't his only assets; he also had good looks. One of our research people contacted an old friend who covered the society beat in the late '70s. According to this columnist, Peter was known as a ladies' man, a different girl on his arm every week. Then he suddenly dropped out of the social scene. Nobody could pin a name on her, but everyone figured young Honeywell had settled down with one special woman.

"Shortly afterwards, Arthur dropped dead of a heart attack. Peter was away on business, but he took the first plane back to Chicago when he heard the news. He was driving home to Lake Forest when a truck swerved into his car. He slammed into a retaining wall and died instantly."

"How tragic," Caroline exclaimed. "Father and son gone within days of each other."

"Here comes the interesting part. Arthur left everything he owned to his son, but Peter never made a will. Two days after the funeral, the Honeywell relatives met with the family lawyers. They had a knock-down, drag-out fight over the division of the estate. It looked like the courts would settle the entire mess, but then Janice Honeywell stepped forward. What happened next was enough to send shivers down the spines of conservative bankers like myself."

"Janice Honeywell, née Janice Belding, produced a marriage certificate naming Peter as her husband."

"How clever of you, Caroline," marveled Alan. "It seems you're one jump ahead of me."

"Just a good guess," Caroline admitted. She told Alan about her earlier conversation with Bill Morgan. "Bill mentioned that Monica Garvy had dated 'some rich guy from Chicago' who later died in a car crash. Monica claimed he'd married her shortly before the accident, but Reverend Ty Belding, who supposedly presided at the wedding, said the marriage certificate was phony. Reverend Belding had a niece named Janice, and she had a brother named James. Two plus two still makes four, brother dear."

"So I've heard," replied Alan dryly. "Makes you wonder if Jim Morgan isn't right when he says Monica got cheated out of her inheritance. It almost sounds like Janice Belding and her uncle engaged in a conspiracy to benefit from the will."

"How did Janice explain her marriage to the lawyers?"

"According to my sources, Janice was Peter's secretary. She claimed they'd been seeing each other for months outside of the office, and only married secretly after Arthur voiced his objection to the match. Supposedly Arthur wanted his son to marry into his own social class."

"The court must have accepted her story."

"It decided in her favor," said Alan. "The newspapers had a field day covering the legal battle. My people found loads of material on it. Apparently the marriage was duly recorded with the state of Illinois. Your Reverend Belding swore on the Bible that he himself performed the ceremony."

"If you ask me, the whole thing is very fishy. What did you find out about James Belding?"

"There's another interesting story. My people are still digging into his past, but so far they've learned that he and his best buddy joined the Army soon after graduating from high school. They served in the same unit in Vietnam, and both were declared MIA after a particularly dicey mission in the Mekong Delta. James Belding was presumed dead until this past spring when he surfaced in Thailand."

"That must have come as a surprise to his sister."

"*Surprise* isn't the word. Janice Honeywell found herself in a precarious position due to his sudden appearance. Her company had taken advantage of government trade initiatives with Vietnam. Honeywell Industries was deep in negotiations to open a factory over there."

"Her brother's appearance must have been an unwelcome reminder of the war."

"You bet. The Vietnamese were as embarrassed as hell since he apparently hid out somewhere in their country for years. They were supposed to account for as many of our missing men as possible, and here's one who slipped through their fingers. Our government was embarrassed for similar reasons. Several delegations traveled to 'Nam to look for traces of our guys. They found no evidence of survivors, but Belding's existence proved there might be some of our soldiers over there still. Honeywell Industries got caught in the middle of the whole mess. How was Janice Belding, the CEO, supposed to react when she met with the foreign officials? She could hardly forget that her brother lost decades of his life, not to mention his sanity, in the jungles of Vietnam."

"How'd you learn about this, Alan? I don't remember reading a word about Belding's rescue."

"It happened around the time Ed died," he said gently. "You weren't paying much attention to the world news back then. Of course, all the facts weren't made public right away. The government whisked him out of Thailand and into an Army hospital where they could debrief him before sending him home."

"Debrief him? The James Belding I saw was emotionally destroyed. He couldn't have told the Army anything."

"I guess they decided the same thing because they shipped him off to Janice Honeywell soon after his arrival in the States. Our people in Washington came up with this material only this morning. Folks are beginning to talk now that Belding is dead. He's no longer a threat to negotiations."

"Isn't that a pleasant thought," Caroline snapped. "A man's life doesn't hold much weight next to a business deal."

"Don't take it out on me, Caroline," Alan responded in an injured tone. "I'm only relating the facts, not what I think should have happened."

Caroline could have kicked herself. Like Belding, Alan had served in the armed forces, only his war had been Desert Storm. If anyone would be upset by the tragic story of James Belding, it would be her brother.

"I'm sorry, bro. I wasn't thinking clearly."

"It's all right," Alan answered kindly. "You've got a lot on your mind." He changed the subject. "Last but not least, we come to Mrs. Alexsa Stromberg Morgan."

"By the tone of your voice, I'd say you discovered something interesting."

"Actually, I found it more puzzling than anything else. Alexsa Morgan has holdings in several major corporations, but it appears she prefers one particular company to all others."

"Honeywell Industries?"

"Exactly," Alan exclaimed. "She holds 22 percent of the company's stock. Outside of Janice, Alexsa is Honeywell's single largest investor."

Caroline's mouth dropped open. "Then why was she so vague when I asked her about the Beldings? Surely she knows Janice is related to James."

"I put that same question to my staff, and they came up with a logical answer. Alexsa is protecting her investment."

Unschooled in the finer points of the stock market, Caroline waited for Alan to explain.

"Look at it this way. What if someone was extorting money from Janice Honeywell, using her brother as ransom against industrial terrorism, and she refused to pay? To show he means business, the killer plants a bomb at St. Anne's and *ka-pow!* There goes James Belding. The implied message is this: next time you'll be dead, or maybe I'll level a couple of your factories and simply kill your business. Honeywell Industries is denying such a possibility, but I believe the FBI is thinking along the same lines as my staff: the bomber's actual target was Honeywell Industries."

"And where does Alexsa fit in?"

"Investors are notoriously conservative. They'll pull their money out in a New York minute if they think someone's purposely sabotaging a company. The market value of Honeywell stock has depreciated since the bombing. If the slide turns into a nosedive, the company could go under. Janice is doing her best to play down any connection between her brother and the explosion at St. Anne's. Still, her people have been quietly working to reassure the stockholders, and I remind you, Alexsa is the most important of those. I'm sure she's agreed to go along with the company's version of the disaster, which is, there's a madman running loose in Rhineburg."

"That's the same explanation pushed by Charles Paine, our late administrator." Caroline recalled what Jane had told her about Janice Honeywell's contributions to the hospital. No fool himself, Paine would have cooperated completely if asked by Tony Grove, Honeywell's representative in Rhineburg.

"Here's one last bit of information. Without a doubt, Mrs. Morgan knows Peter Honeywell. As VP in charge of investor relations, he courted the more prominent stockholders, keeping them apprised of the company's success. My sources say he was constantly on the move, flying around the country to report personally to these people."

"Then he must have come to Rhineburg."

"And I'll bet he brought along his secretary, Janice Belding."

Caroline pondered the situation for several minutes after Alan hung up. If Alexsa was in cahoots with Honeywell Industries, everything she'd told them yesterday might be a lie, or at least a distortion of the truth. That meant she'd have to reconsider the importance of Thomas Adrian and May Eberle in the inquiry.

She considered the pressure being exerted on the FBI to solve this case. Janice Honeywell would move heaven and earth to influence the investigation. She's goad the police into arresting someone who presented no threat to the status quo, no menace to profits, and she'd insist he be in jail before the closing bell on the next day of trading. Not a lot to ask if you were a wealthy industrialist with friends in high places.

Caroline had no doubt the CEO of Honeywell Industries had powerful allies. Look at what happened after Alexsa talked with Evans. Caroline had gone from victim to suspect in the eyes of the police. She wouldn't be surprised if the agent wasn't out gathering proof against her right now.

It was a sobering thought, not one Caroline wished to dwell on. Determined to beat her opponents at their own game, she locked the door of the apartment and walked downstairs to await the arrival of Elvira Harding.

"MRS. HARDING? Hi, I'm Caroline Rhodes."

Caroline ushered the short, gray-haired woman into the nursing dorm lobby. Elvira was stout but not fat with a weathered face and work-worn hands. She held herself erect, adding dignity to her five-foot-three-inch frame as she nodded somberly at Caroline.

"This is my grandson Jerry," she stated matter-of-factly. "He's come along to do the liftin' and carryin'."

Caroline smiled at the boy standing behind Elvira. Barely old enough to shave, he pulled off his battered Bears cap and bobbed his head in her direction, all the while chewing on his bottom lip. She sensed his discomfort and couldn't blame him one bit. Packing up the belongings of a dead relative was no fun, as she well knew.

"Gail's room is on the second floor. We can take the elevator if you'd rather not tackle the stairs."

Mrs. Harding eyed the rickety open-cage lift with its wrought-iron doors. "I'd feel safer with the stairs," she said. "After you, Mrs. Rhodes."

Caroline led the way up to Stromberg. Elvira kept silent until they reached the room.

"I hope we're not botherin' you, showin' up like this after your trouble last night."

Caroline sighed as she unlocked the door. Word sure did spread quickly in Rhineburg! "It's all right, Mrs. Harding. It's no fun stumbling over a dead body, but since I…"

"Oh, my," Elvira exclaimed. "What a mess!"

Caroline smiled indulgently. "The students do tend to be a bit sloppy at times."

"I'd say this is a little more than sloppy," drawled Jerry. He fixed her with a cold stare. "Looks like somebody tore the place apart."

"What?" Caroline turned to look through the doorway. "Oh, no," she gasped.

The boy couldn't have been more correct in his assessment. The dorm room looked like a cyclone had hit it. Desk and dresser drawers were upended on the beds, their contents heaped around them. Posters had been ripped off the walls and books were scattered everywhere. Gail's jewelry box rested against the leg of her desk, open and empty.

Caroline felt an equal mixture of anger and bewilderment. Who had done this? How had he gained access to the room?

"We shouldn't go in," she told Elvira grimly. "I'll call for help." She walked over to the wall phone knowing she should notify hospital security first. Instead, she dialed the Archangels' number.

Michael Bruck arrived at the dormitory only minutes after her call. He took a swift look inside Gail's room before turning to Caroline. "Was it locked when you arrived?"

She nodded yes. Michael frowned, then squatted down on his heels to examine the door latch. He refrained from touching it. "Who has a key to this room besides you?" he asked as he stood up again.

"I honestly don't know," Caroline replied. "Gail Garvy and her roommate had keys, and hospital security probably has a master. They'd know if anyone else has one."

Michael looked at her thoughtfully. "Gail should have had her key with her the day she died. She wouldn't have gone off to work and left the door unlocked."

"If she did, it must have been lost in the explosion," Elvira replied bitterly. "There wasn't much of Gail left to find, much less what she had in her pockets."

Caroline glanced at a grim Michael. "The FBI must have one," she said. "Perhaps it's Gail's key."

The security man nodded and gazed once more into the room. "Most likely our intruder didn't leave any prints, but Tom Evans will want the place dusted regardless. You go home, Mrs. Harding, and I'll call you if he discovers anything."

Elvira snorted in disgust. "The FBI won't be of any help, and you know it, Michael Bruck! They haven't caught my Gail's murderer yet, have they? You think they can catch a plain old thief? Come on, Jerry!" She motioned to the boy before stalking back down the corridor.

Caroline looked helplessly at Michael, then took off after the others. Catching up with them in the lobby, she laid a hand on Elvira's arm. "Mrs. Harding, would you please answer a question for me?"

Elvira turned to face Caroline. "Seems like all I've been doing is answering questions. First the police, then the press, and today, Alexsa Morgan." She shook her head and continued toward the door.

Caroline hesitated. What was Alexsa up to now? Investigating on her own, or trying to set up more road-blocks? "Wait, Mrs. Harding!" She rushed across the lobby to where Jerry stood holding the door open for his grandmother. Pushing him gently aside, she closed it and barred the way with her body. "You have to listen to me. If you don't, Gail's killer may never be found."

Elvira tucked her arms across her chest and stared at Caroline through narrowed eyes. "What do you mean, Mrs. Rhodes?"

"Let's sit down." Caroline gestured to a couch in the lobby. "The FBI isn't getting anywhere fast because this 'mad bomber' nonsense has totally confused the issue. They're being forced to investigate physics students at Bruck and ex-employees of the hospital, all of which is a waste of time. Mrs. Harding, our murderer isn't mad in any sense of the word. He may be evil, but he's not insane."

"You seem pretty sure of yourself."

"Professor Atwater and the Bruck brothers agree with me."

That appeared to impress Elvira. Gail's aunt cocked her head to the side and studied Caroline's face. The indecision slowly faded from her eyes. "Go on," she said calmly.

"There are people in this town who would prefer that the madman theory be accepted by the police. Charles Paine was one of them." Caroline had to proceed cautiously. She still didn't have a handle on Elvira's friendship with Alexsa, so she couldn't mention the old lady's name. "Some folks have muddied the picture with innuendoes and fabrications. Others have refused to speak to the police."

"Rhineburgers don't trust them FBI types. They twist your words 'round 'til you can't remember what you said." Elvira glanced up at her grandson. "Ain't that right, Jerry?"

The boy nodded furiously. "Cops practically called me a liar when I told them about the red Jag I saw parked in the woods. They said I made it up to impress people."

"But Jerry saw that car, Mrs. Rhodes, and he saw that man walk away from it. My grandson wouldn't lie about such a thing."

"I believe you," Caroline said. She turned to the boy. "Who did you see in the woods, Jerry? Someone you know?"

The teenager shook his head. "Never met him before. I was walking down by the river, trying to figure out things in my head. Like who'd blow up a hospital, and why it had to be Gail who got killed. I mean, things were finally starting to look up for her, and then she goes and gets murdered."

"And that's when you saw this person?"

"Yeah. He came driving down the road and parked near the old logging trail past the bridge. Kids go there to neck." He glanced at his grandmother and his face reddened. "But that wasn't the reason he stopped. He got out of the car and stood looking into the woods. He didn't do anything. He just stood there."

"Then what happened, Jerry?"

"After a while he got back in the car and drove off. I wondered what he'd been looking at, so I crossed the road and walked over to where he'd parked. I couldn't see anything special about the place 'til I hiked up the trail a bit."

"Is that where you found the Jaguar?"

"Yes, ma'am," the boy said in an injured tone of voice. "I walk that trail all the time in the summer, and

I knew right away it weren't no big boulder. I brushed the snow off, and sure enough, it was a real beaut. A '93 Jag, fire-engine red."

Bells clanged in Caroline's head. Jim Morgan had sold such a car to a doctor from St. Anne's. Now, why would anyone park an expensive Jaguar in the middle of the woods? Especially in this weather.

"You said the killer was no madman, Mrs. Rhodes. Then why'd he do it?"

"Hmm? Oh, yes." Caroline pulled herself together. Elvira has lost interest in Jerry's story and now showed signs of impatience. "We think he targeted a specific person on the psychiatric ward. One of the patients, or perhaps Gail herself."

"What?" Elvira's face registered shock, then dismay. She buried her face in her hands and began to weep.

"Jerry, there should be a box of tissues on the desk." Caroline pointed across the lobby to the receptionist's area. "Why don't you get it for your grandmother?"

The boy hurried off. Caroline placed an arm around Elvira's shoulders. "Mrs. Harding, why was Gail so interested in James Belding?"

She waited while the woman composed herself. Jerry returned with the tissues, and Elvira wiped her eyes, then reached for the boy's hand.

"This is my flesh and blood, my own grandson," she whispered. "But you've got to understand. Gail was like a granddaughter to me. I raised her when her mama died in the dormitory fire. I never could understand my sister's attitude." Elvira took a deep breath. "Albina turned her back on her own daughter when that shifty minister showed up at the house with his record book. Monica tried so hard to prove she'd married Peter Honeywell. She even went to Chicago to meet with that other woman and the Honeywell lawyers. Course, she got nowhere with them."

"Did Gail think James could help her somehow?"

"I couldn't say," Elvira murmured. "I was surprised when his name showed up in the newspaper after the explosion. I didn't know he'd come back here." She raised her head and looked Caroline squarely in the eye. "But Gail must have known. She was obsessed with proving Monica had married Peter. She didn't care about the Honeywell name or the money. What mattered to her was Albina. Gail wanted to humble her grandma, make her pay for all those years of neglect." Elvira released Jerry's hand and took a deep breath. "I don't know why I'm telling you this, Mrs. Rhodes. You're a stranger here in town, unfamiliar with our history."

"That's true. I didn't know about Gail's mom until this morning. No one told me someone died in the fire."

Elvira twisted a tissue in her gnarled hands. "My niece worked part-time at St. Anne's to pay her tuition. Everyone else went home for the holidays, but Monica stayed 'cause of her job. She was alone here when the fire broke out. The police said she must have lost her footing on the fire escape. They found her on the ground beneath the ladder."

And the daughter followed in her mother's footsteps, thought Caroline. Both in nursing and in death.

"Was Gail searching for evidence of her mother's marriage here at St. Anne's?" she asked Elvira. "Is that why she enrolled in nursing school?"

The old woman nodded wearily. "I begged her to let it go, but Gail figured Monica hid the marriage certificate where nobody else could find it. It never turned up after Monica's death. I searched high and low at the house. Peter's letters were gone, too. They must have been in her dorm room."

"Gail refused to believe they'd burned in the fire?"

"Like I said before, Gail was on some kind of holy mission to clear her mama's name. Mind you, I believed what Monica told me, but I couldn't see how Gail would ever convince Albina. She'd only get hurt worse."

Jerry shifted from foot to foot and gazed longingly at the door. Caroline sympathized with the boy, but she needed more answers. "Were you good friends with your cousin?" she asked him.

Jerry shrugged his shoulders in a noncommittal way. "Sometimes she got on my nerves with all her talk about Aunt Albina. Gail could be pretty weird when it came to her grandma, but I liked her well enough."

"Did she ever confide in you?"

"I guess you could say so," the boy replied hesitantly. "She told me about the Belding fella and the funny things he said."

"What things?"

Caroline tried to restrain her excitement, but the boy sensed it in her voice. He glanced at his grandmother, suddenly wary of sharing a confidence with a stranger. She nodded encouragement to him.

"If you know something that'll help this lady, you speak up," Elvira told the boy. "Maybe she's right about Gail being the killer's target. Maybe them Honeywells were behind it."

Caroline held her breath. The boy's eyes darted back and forth between her and his grandmother.

"If you say so, Gram. But remember, Mrs. Rhodes might've been the one who ransacked Gail's room."

"I promise I had nothing to do with it, Jerry." Caroline spoke firmly. She had to assure the boy that she presented no threat to his family. "Michael Bruck wouldn't have let me come downstairs with you if he thought I was a dangerous person."

She'd pushed the right button. Evidently even Jerry trusted the three Archangels.

"Okay," he said with a nod. "I don't see how it will help, but here goes. Gail and I had lunch together a few days before the explosion. She talked about Aunt Albina like usual, but she seemed happy. She said she planned on givin' her a real Christmas present this year. I told her to quit being stupid. Aunt Albina would throw any present of hers right out the door. Gail must have thought that was funny 'cause she laughed real hard and said, 'Not this one!'" Jerry frowned at the memory. "I couldn't figure out what she was up to, so I just listened. She told me about James Belding and how he did this." He made a fist, then uncurled the fingers of his right hand one by one until only his thumb remained tucked in his palm. "It didn't make any sense to me, especially when Gail whispered 'Four to go' and then started laughing again."

Elvira grunted. "It doesn't make sense to me either. Sounds like Gail was joshin' you, Jerry."

"Maybe, Gram," the boy grumbled. "But you said I should tell Mrs. Rhodes about it, and I did."

"And I thank you, Jerry." Caroline rose to her feet. She wanted nothing more than to race upstairs and read Gail's diary, but she first had to get rid of these two. "I appreciate your candor, Mrs. Harding. You've been very open about Gail and Monica."

Elvira pulled herself up from the couch. "No reason to keep it a secret. With both of 'em dead, none of it matters anymore." She turned to her grandson. "Take me home, boy. There's too many bad memories here."

Jerry took his grandmother by the elbow and led her to the door. A black sedan turned into the driveway as he helped her into the truck.

"Oh, no! He's here already."

Caroline turned and fled upstairs, anxious to be gone before FBI agent Tom Evans entered the lobby. If he'd doubted her innocence before, he'd be doubly suspicious once he heard she had a master key for the dorm. And Gail's diary, lying on the couch in her apartment, proved she'd been inside the girl's room.

The noose grows tighter around my neck, she thought grimly as she took the steps two at a time.

CAROLINE OPENED HER DOOR a crack and peeked down the hallway. The third floor was quiet as a tomb. Evans must still be busy downstairs.

"Let it stay that way," she said quietly before slipping into the corridor, a briefcase dangling from her hand. She crossed to the laundry room, scraped frost off the window above the dryer, and peered out at the driveway below. A state police car stood parked next to Evan's sedan. One officer lounged against its door while a second one approached the dormitory.

"Damn! I'm trapped!"

Her plan to escape through the tunnel linking the dorm to the hospital seemed doomed now due to presence of police in the lobby. She had to find another way out of the building. Refusing to panic, she forced herself to concentrate on the problem. There had to be… Caroline snapped her fingers.

"Why not try it? It'll look like I never even returned to my rooms."

Caroline hurried down the corridor to the student lounge. Inside, she closed and locked the door, then tugged open the window facing the hospital. A fire-escape ladder led from the window to the ground below. It took less than a minute for her to scramble down the rusty iron steps. Someone had shoveled the sidewalk encircling the dormitory, and Caroline left no traces as she made her way to a side door and entered St. Anne's. Five minutes later she exited through the emergency department and headed for the hospital's parking garage.

The guard was nowhere in sight. Caroline pulled away from St. Anne's unobserved and circled the Green at a leisurely pace. She picked up speed after turning onto the highway leading to Rhineburg. Inside the town limits she slowed down again, reluctant to attract the attention of a radar ranger with a quota to fill. Best she keep well away from the police until she'd talked with Carl and, perhaps, a lawyer.

With that thought in mind, she pulled into the parking lot next to the German restaurant where she'd lunched with the professor. She was probably indulging in wishful thinking, imagining Carl inside wolfing down a huge meal, but Caroline decided to look for him there anyway. As it turned out, she'd only just missed him.

"He left about five minutes ago," the waitress told her. "But I don't know where he went."

Caroline crossed to the telephone booth and called Carl's office. The machine took her message and she hung up, dialed again, and waited while the phone rang at his home. Once again she reached only an answering machine. Frustrated, she gave up and walked over to a booth.

She signaled to a waitress, ordered a Coke, then put her briefcase on the seat next to her and unlocked it. She withdrew the letters she'd found in Gail's room and unfolded the first one. The paper looked old, its edges crinkled and tinged brown. She lifted it to her nose and sniffed. The musty odor of smoke still clung to the letter.

"Here's your drink, Mrs. Rhodes."

Caroline looked up expecting to see the waitress. Instead, a thin woman in a fur parka stood over her, an icy glass in one hand, a cigarette dangling from the other. The newcomer placed the glass on the table and slid into the seat opposite Caroline.

"I'm Elizabeth Morgan," she said as she shrugged off the coat. She extended a bony hand to Caroline. "I saw you the other day up at the house. You were grilling Alexsa about the bombing."

Caroline laughed. "I wouldn't call it grilling, Mrs. Morgan. We were seeking advice."

"Call me Liz. Or Elizabeth if you prefer. There's only one 'Mrs. Morgan' in this town, and that's Jim's grandmother."

Caroline ignored the sarcasm in Liz's voice. "Then you can call me Caroline. We'll cast formality to the wind and pretend we've known each other for years."

Liz blew a ring of smoke into the air and watched it disappear before shifting her gaze back to Caroline. Her eyes glittered mischievously.

"But we haven't, have we? We're nothing more than strangers in a very strange town." She held up a hand. "Now don't start prattling on about the rustic charm of Rhineburg. It's little more than a rural hellhole, and you know it."

"It's certainly not Chicago. I wouldn't call it 'strange,' though. I suppose it's typical of small towns everywhere."

Liz threw back her head and laughed scornfully.

"Obviously you haven't been around long enough to appreciate the truly unique character of our village." She leaned across the table, and the odor of whiskey floated to Caroline's nose. "Stick around, my friend, and you'll soon come to hate this place as much as I do. The only people who truly belong here are the wealthy and the old. The rest of us are looked down on as peons."

"You're wealthy," Caroline reminded her.

Liz shook her head. "Jim is wealthy. I'm a hanger-on, a poor girl from the wrong side of town who married well. Doesn't count, you know." She took another drag on her cigarette. "What did Alexsa tell you? Did the old girl provide you with a few clues?"

"She told some fascinating stories," Caroline replied carefully. "But nothing she said actually helped us."

Liz raised her eyebrows. "Really? You mean you're no closer to a solution than before?"

"I wouldn't say that. Alexsa tried her best to lead us astray—her comments about Thomas Adrian and May Eberle were truly inspired—but the professor and I aren't stupid. We know how to separate truth from fiction."

"So tell me, who did it?" Liz asked casually. She ground out her cigarette in the ashtray, her eyes downcast.

"Come on. You don't expect me to answer that, do you? Suffice it to say, you won't be surprised by the name."

Caroline waited for a reaction to the ruse, but Liz didn't rise to the bait. Instead, she continued to gaze downward. Suddenly her face went pale.

"Where'd you get that?" she whispered, pointing to Gail's letter. She reached for it, but Caroline reacted quickly.

"It's a note from an old friend," she said, folding the paper and thrusting it back into the briefcase.

"Liar," Liz screamed. She slid out of the booth and nearly fell as she grabbed for the briefcase. A waitress hurried over.

"Let me help you, Mrs. Morgan."

"Let go of me!" Liz tore her arm free from the girl's grasp and whirled to face Caroline. "Liar," she hissed. "I know what you're up to, but it won't work. You can't frighten me, or Alexsa!" She straightened up with effort and lifted her chin. "We're Morgans. Our kind don't frighten easily."

"Please, Mrs. Morgan. Let me drive you home."

A broad-shouldered fellow in a greasy apron approached the booth. He reached for Elizabeth's coat and placed it gently around her shoulders. Her fury spent, she didn't resist him. Caroline watched him guide her toward the door. Elizabeth's shoulders sagged as she stepped outside.

"I'm so sorry," the waitress said. "Sometimes she doesn't know when to quit."

"It's all right," Caroline replied with a smile. She slid out of the booth and handed the girl a five-dollar bill. "Keep the change. It's the least I can do to make amends for the ruckus."

The waitress protested, but Caroline gathered her things and left the restaurant. She needed to be alone to think things over. Liz Morgan had abruptly emerged as another piece of the complicated puzzle. Where she fit in, Caroline didn't know. Liz had certainly recognized Gail's letter, and that must mean something.

Caroline climbed into the Jeep and sat there considering her options. She couldn't drive back to the dorm; the police would surely be waiting for her. Martin's apartment was off-limits also. No fool, Evans would guess she'd head in that direction. She had no idea where Carl lived, and he worked too near the hospital to risk a visit. The only other place she could think of was certainly secluded, but would she get lost trying to find it?

"God only knows," she muttered, throwing the Jeep into Drive. "It's the last choice left to me."

With that cheery thought in mind, Caroline pulled into traffic and headed out of Rhineburg.

THE AFTERNOON SUNLIGHT did nothing to improve the appearance of the Blue Cat Lounge. If anything, the exterior looked more decrepit than ever with its peeling paint and warped windows. The roof was an eyesore of multicolored shingles layered haphazardly bottom to top, and the wooden gutters were pockmarked by rot. Caroline viewed the building with a critical eye. *Dilapidated* might be too kind a description.

Carl should consider some repairs, she thought as she passed beneath the sign of the cat. Inside, the smell of beer and peanuts permeated the empty lounge. The overhead lights were off, but a glow emanated from the diamond-shaped window in the door leading to the kitchen. Caroline walked toward it hesitantly.

"Hello? Is anybody here?"

"Not for another half hour," came a voice from behind her.

Caroline spun around. "Who's there?" she cried out.

"My goodness. Aren't you the jumpy one."

A young man strode out of the shadows behind the stage, a mop in one hand and a bucket in the other. He set them down next to a table and grinned at her. "Did I spook you?"

"I'm afraid so." Caroline blushed as she backed away from the bar. "I thought someone was in the kitchen. I didn't expect to find you behind me."

The youth glanced over his shoulder. "I guess it's a bit dark in the corner. Sorry if I surprised you."

"Forget it. I'm just a little on edge."

"Life can be that way sometimes." He glanced at his watch, then smiled at Caroline. "Like I said, we're not open yet. But since it's the holidays, I'll make an exception. You look like you could use a drink."

Caroline thought of Elizabeth Morgan and quickly shook her head. "Nothing alcoholic. I'd love a Coke, though."

"How about one of our world-famous roast beef sandwiches to go along with it?"

"Well…"

"Don't say no, or I'll take it as an insult." The young man walked toward the bar. "By the way, my name is Shiloh."

"I'm Caroline Rhodes." She slipped into a chair and watched the boy build her sandwich. Medium tall with chestnut hair pulled back in a ponytail, Shiloh moved about behind the bar with an efficiency of motion that indicated his familiarity with the place.

"Would you mind if I sat here awhile? I have some paperwork to do."

"No problem." Shiloh walked over and placed a tray on the table. "Stay as long as you like. I've got some work to do in the kitchen. If you need anything, holler." He flashed another smile and turned away.

Caroline hadn't realized how hungry she was. Or how tired. Leaning back in the chair, she closed her eyes and let the fatigue drain from her muscles before tackling the two-inch-tall sandwich. The beef tasted delicious. After two bites she decided it deserved the designation "world famous." Or at least, "best in Rhineburg."

Finished with the meal, she opened her briefcase and withdrew Gail's letters. She unfolded the first one and spread it on the table. It appeared to be a typical love letter.

"Dearest," it began. "I don't think I can stand another minute of separation from you." The body of the note contained a rather emotional protestation of devotion concluding with the words "All my love, Peter."

Caroline folded the paper and put it aside. The second and third letters were similar in content and mood, but the wording in the fourth reflected a somber intensity.

"Father refuses to approve of our marriage. I'm tired of arguing with him, dearest. Perhaps we should give up and make a new life for ourselves somewhere else."

Peter sounded even less hopeful in the fifth letter. The sixth one, though, indicated a plan had evolved between the two lovers. "You're right when you say I simply can't break with Dad. It would kill him and hurt me deeply. Better to do it your way. I'll meet you next weekend in Rhineburg. The reverend can marry us then. Father may come around in time."

Caroline remembered her brother's words. Arthur Honeywell wanted his son to marry into society. Unfortunately, Monica stood low on the social ladder, making her an unsuitable match for Peter. The same could be said for Janice Belding, but then, the letters weren't written to her.

Elizabeth Morgan's pale face invaded Caroline's thoughts. Why had the woman gone berserk in the restaurant? She'd been cocky at first, but her confidence quickly degenerated into belligerence when she saw Peter's letter.

The episode disturbed Caroline. Had Liz recognized Peter's handwriting? If so, she'd seen the letter before— or others like it—when she'd roomed with Monica at St. Anne's. And that meant Liz could have supported her roommate's claim. But Bill Morgan had never even hinted at such a possibility. Neither had Elvira Harding. Surely one of them would have mentioned it if Liz had spoken up on Monica's behalf.

Then again, the letters didn't prove Peter had married Monica Garvy. They indicated the young man's intentions, but fell short when it came to confirming the deed. As long as Reverend Belding disputed the authenticity of Monica's marriage certificate, Janice had the upper hand in the battle for the Honeywell name.

Of course, records could be falsified. The minister might have substituted his niece's name in the ledger, then registered the supposed marriage with the state. If so, Janice probably instigated the move. Ty Belding had nothing to gain by working the scam alone. If the switch was accomplished before Peter's death, it indicated an even greater crime in the works. Janice and Rev. Belding must have plotted Peter's demise. The plan wouldn't have worked if Peter lived to refute his secretary's claims.

It made no sense to say the change occurred after Honeywell's death. Reverend Belding couldn't tamper with records already held by the state. Unless, that is, he'd never registered the marriage in the first place. But why not? Once again, one could only believe that Janice planned to kill Peter, then pass herself off as his wife.

Either way one looked at it, Janice Belding and her uncle were after Honeywell Industries. They'd gotten it, too, despite the collective wisdom of the firm's lawyers and a circuit judge.

Caroline fumed with frustration by the time she opened Gail's diary. She still didn't see where James Belding fit into the plot. If he didn't fit, neither did the bombing. Maybe she was probing a crime other than the one she'd intended to investigate. Or maybe the puzzle was simply too complicated for an amateur like herself.

With her confidence ebbing by the minute, Caroline scanned the diary. She saw nothing of note until an entry dated late in September.

"I managed to change the student schedule. Halsey left it in her desk—she doesn't lock her office!—and I penciled in my name for the first psych rotation. What luck that she picked St. Anne's for her brother."

Caroline frowned. Gail had broken into the nursing director's office and tampered with school records. The girl's action spoke volumes about her integrity.

"This is impossible!" the next entry stated. "I finally get near to Belding, and he's totally out of it! He doesn't speak at all. I can't believe I went through all this trouble just to be disappointed again."

Caroline flipped through the diary, skimming page after page of vitriolic comments aimed at James Belding, Janice Honeywell, and Albina Garvy. Gail's impatience grew more evident with each passing day as she made no headway with her chosen patient. Then, in an entry dated mid-November, the girl wrote something curious.

"That watchdog Grove is here again. He seems to be coming more often and staying longer. I have to be careful when he's around. I don't want to give myself away."

Farther on Caroline noted a change in Gail's attitude. "I'm getting through now to Belding. He looks me in the eye when I talk to him. But is there anything of value going on in his head? Of value to me, that is."

Gail mentioned Tony Grove on the next page.

"He's back again—Honeywell's little spy. I know he's watching me. I have to avoid Belding when he's around. The good news is, I got the nurses' aide job. Now I have an excuse for coming in late at night. I can snoop around the dorm while everyone's sleeping."

A few days later Gail wrote: "Another night of adventure. One would think the maintenance men would occasionally check the lock on the sealed-off wing. Their stupidity is my good fortune. As long as they don't know it's broken, they won't install a new one. And our housemother is so dense! She never checks rooms after midnight."

Caroline grimaced. Apparently both she and the maintenance department had fallen down on the job.

"I think I've found the right room. The window overlooks the spot where the sidewalks meet, like Mom described in her diary. The place is a mess, but I'll find where she hid it."

"Hid what?" Caroline murmured. She turned the page, engrossed in the diary.

"Belding did something strange today. I repeated the names—Mom's, Peter's, and Janice Belding's—the same as I do every day. This time he reacted to them. He raised four fingers and whispered, 'Four to go.' I don't know what it means, but I aim to find out. Fortunately, no one saw him talk to me. Garner would tell the doctors if she knew, and then they'd be all over Belding. I'd never get near him again."

"Poor James," murmured Caroline. Perhaps he'd be alive today if Gail hadn't been so self-centered. She read on.

"Success at last! I found the letters tucked away behind the baseboard beneath the window. Mom must have been terrified of that bitch if she went to such great lengths to conceal them. If I could only find the marriage certificate! Tomorrow, Albina. Maybe tomorrow."

At least Caroline knew why the letters reeked of smoke. They'd been in hidden in Monica's burned-out dorm room.

"Belding continues to behave strangely," a later entry noted. "I no longer have to mention the names to get a reaction from him. He only has to see me and he starts with the 'four to go' business. I have to be very careful the other nurses don't notice. I'm afraid Grove may have seen him do it today. Old Tony was hanging around the rec room. He looked at me so oddly, it frightened me. But I think I know the meaning of Belding's message. I'm so close to the truth that I refuse to give up. And after all, what can Grove do to stop me?"

The last entry was dated five days before the explosion.

"This is driving me crazy! I want to blow Albina out of the water, but I've hit a dead end. I can't find the marriage certificate anywhere. I know that minister killed my mother. He must have stolen it from her before he set the fire."

Caroline sat back and stared at the ceiling. Could Gail's theory be correct? Was Rev. Belding not only a con man but also an arsonist? Well, why not? If he'd conspired with Janice to defraud the Honeywell family, he'd already lent his hand to Peter's murder. What difference would another death make to a man like that? Especially if it could be hidden under the guise of a fire?

Caroline read Gail's last words.

"Grove's been here constantly this week. He's watching me like a hawk. I'm staying far away from Belding now that I know his words are a warning. Is Grove dangerous? I don't think so, but I'm sure he reports directly to Janice Honeywell. She wouldn't hesitate to come after me like she came after Mom. I wish I could tell her I don't care about the money or the Honeywell name. It's Albina that matters. Only Albina."

"Did you enjoy the sandwich?"

"Hmm? Oh, Shiloh. I didn't see you standing there." Caroline closed Gail's diary and smiled up at the boy. "You have a habit of catching me unawares."

"That's twice today, isn't it? Would you like a refill?" Shiloh pointed to her empty glass. Caroline nodded, grateful that the boy seemed in no hurry to be rid of her. She needed more time to unravel the secret of Belding's message to Gail. Four to go. Was it really a warning?

"You've been to the Blue Cat before, haven't you?"

Caroline nodded. "Professor Atwater brought me here the night Andy Parker's band played. They were very good."

"Yeah, they always pack the house."

"I'm surprised the fire department allows such a crowd in here. This building looks like it's ready to collapse."

Shiloh grinned broadly. "It's supposed to look that way. At least on the outside. But Professor Atwater sank a lot of money into the place when he became a partner in the business. Behind the ramshackle exterior we have solid brick walls and a reinforced roof."

"Why in the world…"

"I know what you're going to say." Shiloh held up one hand, interrupting her. "Why would we rehab the inside and leave the outside looking like hell? Well, it

goes like this. The Blue Cat is a refuge of sorts. Folks
come here to relax, converse with their friends, maybe
hear some good music on the weekends. Pretty up the
façade and we'll attract all those yuppie types who sail
through Rhineburg on their way to someplace else.
They'd start pulling off the highway thinking, 'Now,
isn't this a quaint little place.' Pretty soon they'd be taking pictures of the locals and congratulating themselves
on finding 'rustic America.'"

Caroline laughed despite herself. Ed and she had
done the same thing themselves while on vacations. The
temptation to experience rural living as one imagined it
to be was strong among urban dwellers. City folks had
been romanticizing the countryside every since Tho-
reau popularized Walden Pond.

"I get your point. A little deception prevents a lot
of trouble."

Shiloh ambled off after pouring another Coke for
Caroline. She leaned back in her chair, watching the
young man as he wiped down the bar preparatory to the
start of business. The afternoon shadows were lengthen-
ing outside, and patrons began to drift in for predinner
drinks. Caroline glanced at her watch. Four o'clock.
Almost quitting time for Agent Evans.

Gathering up Gail's letters and diary, Caroline de-
posited them in the briefcase, then extracted a notepad
and began to write. A half an hour later she completed
her task. Aside from a few missing details, she had the
whole story of the bombing down on paper. Now all she
needed to do was make several quick phone calls. She
dialed the university security building from the privacy
of the lounge's telephone booth.

"Hello, Michael? I'm glad I caught you in."

"Is that you, Mrs. Rhodes? I got to tell you, Tom Evans is one angry man! He's on the warpath, searching all over for you."

"I figured he would be, but I had to clear up some unfinished business first. Michael, will you do me a favor?"

"Depends on what it is. You shouldn't have left the dorm, Mrs. Rhodes. It makes it look like you're hiding something."

"In a way I am. Or was." Caroline explained about the diary and letters. She gave Michael a concise summary of her deductions. "If we can clear up the loose ends, we can take the whole story to Evans and let him make the arrest. Will you help me now?"

"What do you want me to do?" Michael was all business now. Caroline sighed with relief. She could finally see a light at the end of the tunnel.

"I need a name." She told him what she knew about the person. "Perhaps someone at the high school remembers him."

"Don't worry," Michael assured her. "One of the counselors there is an old friend. He'll help me."

"My next request may prove more difficult to accomplish. Can you locate the records of a marriage? It may have taken place in Illinois, but it's more likely they were underage at the time. They probably crossed state lines."

"Tom Evans has better resources for ferreting out that kind of information. Once you tell him your theory, he'll nail down any records that exist."

"All right, we'll leave it to him. The last thing I need to know is the circumstances surrounding Rev. Belding's death. How'd it happen? Who found his body?"

"I'll talk to my dad. He was hunting that day and arrived on the scene right after Belding went down. My brothers and I were in school, but I remember him discussing it at home."

"How soon can you get back to me?" Caroline asked.

"Not before tomorrow. Are you going back to your apartment?"

"Not if I can help it. I'd prefer to steer clear of the FBI until I have the answers to those questions. I'll call you again in the morning. Say around ten o'clock."

Michael sighed. "I could be in big trouble for doing this, but all right. I won't tell Evans that I've heard from you."

"Thanks, Michael. You're a real friend."

"Don't mention it. We Rhineburgers have to stick together."

Caroline smiled as she hung up the phone. She'd never been called a Rhineburger before. Oddly enough, the designation bolstered her spirits. With renewed confidence in the ultimate success of her mission, she placed her second call.

"Mrs. Harding? This is Caroline Rhodes."

"What can I do for you, Mrs. Rhodes?"

Caroline noted the exhaustion in Elvira's voice. She hated having to add to the poor woman's misery.

"Earlier today you mentioned speaking with Alexsa Morgan. You said she asked you a lot of questions."

"What of it?" Elvira responded sharply. "Alexsa and I are old friends."

"Please, Mrs. Harding. Would you tell me what she wanted?"

"I'm not sure it's any of your business."

"It might help the investigation," Caroline pleaded. "You do want Gail's murderer caught, don't you?"

"Of course I do! But Alexsa..." Elvira hesitated, then suddenly gave in. "It's not like either one of us has something to hide. We were only discussing that awful minister."

"Rev. Ty Belding?"

"Yes, that's him. He caused so much trouble for poor Monica with his lies. I told Alexsa, he got his just desserts being killed that way."

"He died in a hunting accident."

"Sure did. They never found who done it either. I always said that was a blessing. Whoever shot him deserved a medal, not a jail cell."

"Did Alexsa agree with you?"

"She said she was real glad I felt that way. Alexsa knows how my husband and I loved Monica. Charlie wanted a little girl of his own, but the Lord gave us three sons instead. Monica was the closest thing we had to a daughter."

"Your husband must have been pretty upset when she died."

"*Upset* ain't the word. Charlie went half out of his mind with grief. He blamed the fire on that preacher. He was angrier than a 'coon when the cops couldn't pin it on him. Charlie said Belding set the fire to stop Monica from claiming her rightful inheritance. He figured the reverend was in cahoots with his niece."

"Jim Morgan shares that belief."

"Of course. That's why he stood up for Charlie after the accident. It didn't look real good, my husband being the one who found the preacher's body."

Caroline hadn't known that.

"Your husband was out hunting that day?"

"First day of deer season, Mrs. Rhodes. Practically every man in town toted a gun into the woods that morning. Thank God, Charlie never got off a shot. The police checked his rifle. It was clean as a whistle."

"It must have come as a shock when he discovered the corpse. Did your husband happen to hear or see anyone else in the forest?"

"Now you sound like Alexsa. She asked me about that, too."

"Why?"

"She figured Gail's death would stir up unpleasant memories for some folks. It sure did for Charlie and me. Doesn't seem a day passes without one of us mentioning Monica. But Charlie won't discuss Rev. Belding, or the accident. He said all along he knew nothing about it, and he ain't gonna change his statement now."

"He's sure he didn't see another man that day? Maybe a stranger to these parts."

"Charlie saw nobody. He was alone when he heard the shot and alone when he found the body. He always hunted on private property, so he didn't expect to see anyone else."

Caroline had hoped for more information, but she'd have to be satisfied knowing Alexsa had also been stymied. The old woman had learned nothing new from Elvira. Thanking Gail's aunt, she hung up the phone and dialed Carl's number. The answering machine clicked on and she hung up in disgust. Shiloh hurried over when she returned to her table.

"You don't look too happy. Is there anything I can do to help?" he asked.

"Not unless you know someone who attended Rhineburg High twenty years ago." Caroline replied flippantly.

"My grandfather was the school's principal back then."

Caroline stared openmouthed at the boy. "I can't believe this!" She gathered him up in a bear hug. "You're the answer to my prayers."

"I don't know about that," Shiloh replied in embarrassment when she released him. "But I appreciate the thought. Now tell me who you're looking for."

Caroline described the person she sought, giving Shiloh the approximate date of his graduation.

"Granddad will probably remember him. He's been following the progress of the investigation in the newspapers. He still can't believe someone would bomb St. Anne's."

Caroline waited patiently while Shiloh poured drinks for several customers. She watched him walk to the telephone booth where he carried on an animated conversation with someone for several minutes. He was smiling when he returned.

"My grandfather has a good memory. He gave me three names, any one of which could be your man."

He handed Caroline a list. She drew a blank on the first two names, but the third one practically leaped off the page at her.

"You tell your grandfather I owe him big-time," she exclaimed before leaping to her feet. "I've got to get hold of Professor Atwater. Could you tell me how to get to his house?"

"Sure, but he won't be there." Shiloh lifted Caroline's jacket off the back of her chair and held it while she closed and locked the briefcase. "Tonight's the Winter Festival."

"Winter Festival? Oh, right. Rhineburg's annual holiday bash. My daughter-in-law mentioned it this morning." Caroline pushed her arms into the parka. "You think the professor will be there?"

"Of course," the boy replied with a grin. "They couldn't hold a Christmas parade without Santa Claus."

It took a minute for the words to sink in before it dawned on Caroline what the young man meant. She began to chuckle as she pictured Carl perched atop a sleigh pulled by eight prancing reindeer.

"So that's what Jim Morgan meant when he said his father was buying Carl a new suit."

"It's about time," Shiloh laughed. "Professor Atwater is the best darned Santa in the county, but his old suit fit mighty tight in the waist."

Caroline zippered the parka, hugged Shiloh again, and left the Blue Cat Lounge. Preoccupied with finding Carl, she never noticed the red Jaguar when she pulled out of the parking lot. It followed a safe distance behind her, its lights dim, its driver hidden by the darkness of the winter night.

WILHELM ROAD SPARKLED with hundreds of Christmas lights. Strung tree to tree, they formed a manmade Milky Way above Rhineburg's main thoroughfare. Normally, Caroline would have reveled in the holiday decorations. Tonight she focused her attention on navigating the Jeep safely though a crush of pedestrian traffic. It looked like half the county had come out to celebrate the Winter Festival. Parking was at such a premium that by the time Caroline found a spot, the festivities were already under way in the town square.

Hoping to find Carl before the start of the parade, she skirted the crowds on the sidewalk and jogged west down Wilhelm to City Hall. The sights and sounds of Christmas surrounded her. Stores south of the square teemed with last-minute shoppers searching for the perfect gift. Some of the more clever merchants had set up tables outside their shops and were offering hot chocolate and cookies to passers-by. At the end of the block the local theater advertised Santa's arrival in foot-high neon letters while green-suited elves hawked fliers listing coming attractions.

Caroline glanced over to where children were gathering around a large wooden gazebo in the square. The gazebo served as a bandstand in the summer, but tonight it would be home to Santa. An enormous gilt chair cushioned in red velvet rested on a raised platform inside latticework walls. Garlands of balsam and holly encircled the gazebo's railings, and two life-sized toy soldiers guarded the steps leading up to the entrance. The laminated figures saluted smartly in the glow of several floodlights suspended from the roof.

She reached City Hall simultaneously with Mayor Schoen. Terrible Teddy, as she'd come to think of him, pushed through the mass of humanity gathered on the walk and climbed the half-dozen stairs to the Hall's entrance. There in the shadows of the town seal, he waved his arms for quiet.

"It's my great pleasure," he solemnly intoned, "to announce the official opening of Rhineburg's annual Winter Festival. The City Council and I, your elected servant…"

A mighty drumroll drowned out the mayor's last words. All heads turned, and the crowd let out a roar as from behind the building the high school marching band emerged. Trumpets blaring, they swung into a lively rendition of "O Tannenbaum."

Caroline dismissed any hopes she'd had of reaching Carl before his grand entrance in the parade. Instead, she squeezed into a space near the curb and joined the locals in cheering on the Rhineburg Marching Maniacs. Splendid in bright red uniforms with gold capes and gleaming black shakos, the band members dipped and swayed in exaggerated movements, performing a series of choreographed dance steps down the center of the street. The spectators urged the band on with shouts and whistling before they circled the square and disappeared once more behind City Hall.

Puzzled by the brevity of the performance, Caroline was about to turn away when she glimpsed two familiar faces across the street.

"Martin! Nikki!" She waved frantically in an effort to attract their attention. Nikki saw her first, grabbed Marty's arm, and pointed. The two of them dashed across the street.

"Hi there. Where've you been hiding?" Martin gave Caroline a peck on the cheek. "Professor Atwater's been trying to reach you."

"I'm sorry. It's been a rather busy day."

Nikki smiled. "Christmas shopping, I bet. How'd you like the band? Aren't they fantastic?"

"They sure are, but the program was too short," Caroline complained. "Don't they know any other Christmas songs?"

"Just wait," Marty laughed. "The best is yet to come."

The words were hardly out of his mouth when the brassy wail of a trumpet split the night. Caroline craned her neck to see over the heads of the people in front of her. The music seemed to be coming from behind City Hall. It intensified to a fever pitch as the unseen performer raced up and down the scale, concluding on a piercingly high C. The note died on the wind, and for an instant, all was still. Then a dozen snare drums shattered the silence. Their staccato tattoo rose to a crescendo of sound before three columns of majorettes high-stepped onto Wilhelm Road, flags and batons held at the ready. Behind them appeared the Marching Maniacs.

A collective roar went up from all sides. Each band member sported a snowy-white beard and fur-trimmed hat. They tore into "Santa Claus is Coming to Town" with a passion befitting their image.

"Look, Mom," Nikki cried. She pointed down the road. "Here comes Professor Atwater."

Caroline drew in her breath. Decked out in a red harness dotted with fist-sized silver bells and led by the most unlikely trio of elves imaginable, eight genuine reindeer pranced down the middle of Wilhelm. They pulled an emerald-green sleigh emblazoned with the letters *SC* in gold on both sides. The sleigh was decorated fore and aft with snow-frosted garlands tied in place by scarlet ribbons. A dusting of silver in the paint caused the sleigh to sparkle in the glow of the streetlamps. Piled high on the backseat were brightly wrapped boxes of every shape and size, while perched up front, handling the reins as if he was born to it, rode Professor Carl Atwater, a.k.a. Santa Claus.

Dress in crimson fur from head to toe, a black satin sash encircling his massive girth, Carl waved and "ho, ho, ho'd" his way down Wilhelm Road. The crowd cheered wildly when the elves cleared a path into the square. They led the reindeer straight to the illuminated gazebo where Santa climbed down from the sleigh carrying a large canvas sack. He nodded his thanks to the elves and the reindeer and carried the sack into the gazebo. A horde of children immediately surrounded him.

"That old ham," Caroline chuckled.

"You bet," said Martin. "My boss lives for this Christmas parade. Those 'ho, ho, hos' come naturally to him."

Nikki laughed. "I like the new Santa suit. The professor barely squeezed into last year's outfit."

"He does look better," Martin agreed. "But those elves are something else. I never thought I'd live to see the Archangels in tights! Kind of ruins their image, don't you think?"

The three of them watched Carl hand out gifts to a long line of Rhineburg children. After a while they drifted over to the steps of City Hall where the choir of St. Mark's Lutheran Church competed with their Catholic rivals from St. Mary's in a program of Christmas carols.

"Dueling choirs," joked Martin.

Caroline enjoyed the singing, but her toes were almost frozen. She suggested they abandon the outdoors for a bit. Martin and Nikki readily agreed. A north wind had sprung up, bringing with it the first flakes of yet another winter storm. The three revelers beat a hasty retreat to the Sugar Bowl Café where they ordered hot cider and watched the snow begin in earnest.

"There's a streak of practicality in these Rhineburgers," Caroline observed. Wilhelm had opened to traffic again, and she noted how easily the pickup trucks and popular four-wheel drives handled the snow-encrusted road. "Look at the sturdy vehicles they own."

"That one looks out of place," said Nikki. She pointed to a red Jaguar slipping into a parking spot across the street. "What's a little sports car doing out in this weather?"

Caroline checked out the auto. Ed had been an auto aficionado, a passion he shared with her brother, Alan. Although she'd showed minimal interest in the subject, they'd insisted on teaching her how to recognize a gem when she saw one.

This particular vehicle fit the description. It was a late-model Jag, dirtied by the weather but classy nonetheless. Ed would have given his eyeteeth to own it. Caroline only wanted it to go away.

"Are you okay?" Nikki had seen her mother-in-law shiver.

"I'm fine, dear." Caroline couldn't tear her eyes from the car. Without a doubt, here was the Jaguar Jim Morgan had sold and Jerry had found hidden in the woods. There could be only one reason for its presence in Rhineburg: the hunter was on the prowl.

"He's looking for someone," said Martin. "With the streets this crowded, it's like searching for a needle in a haystack."

A man had climbed from the car and stood with his back to the restaurant. He surveyed the crowd in the square, then turned and stared directly at the Sugar Bowl. Caroline's heart skipped a beat. Chances were slim he could pick her out in the café through the falling snow. Still, the very thought of it frightened her. This man was an accomplished killer, adept at disposing of threats. Unfortunately, Caroline presented the most immediate threat to him. She'd seen him on the psych ward on the day of the bombing, and as of tonight, she could put a name to his face. She was a liability he couldn't afford to ignore.

"He's lost," said Nikki. "Can't decide which way to go."

The man had stepped away from the Jaguar. Like a snake searching out its prey, his head swiveled left and right as he inspected the knots of people on the sidewalk. He began to cross the street, then switched directions, turning instead toward the town square.

A prickle of fear ran through Caroline. She wasn't the only one who posed a problem for the owner of the Jag. Carl had made himself anathema by prying into the bomber's identity. The killer wouldn't neglect an opportunity to silence his second adversary.

She watched the man fade into the crowd and thought of Carl playing Santa in the gazebo. The man would approach him, and Carl, unaware he was facing a murderer, would look up and smile, his fate sealed by his own ignorance. Caroline refused to let it go down that easily. She slid out of the booth, grabbed her coat, and dashed to the door.

"What's wrong, Mom?"

"I forgot something in the Jeep. I'll be back in a minute."

Now wasn't the time to confide in Martin. He'd try to stop her, or at least insist on coming along. Whichever way it went, they'd spend precious minutes arguing over a course of action. Much as she regretted lying to her son, Caroline had no choice. She had to reach Carl before he left the safety of the gazebo.

The deteriorating weather complicated things mightily. The snow fell heavier now with wind gusts causing blizzardlike conditions up and down Wilhelm Road. Despite visibility being practically nil, Caroline threw caution aside as she stepped from the curb. She scurried across the street, dodging cars full of families abandoning the party. Her search suddenly took on a new urgency. A deserted square meant greater danger for Carl. Dressed in his bright red Santa Claus suit, he'd be a sitting duck for a man with a gun.

Her heart beat faster now as she pushed her way

through the departing crowds. The lights from the gazebo glowed like a beacon pointing the way to the professor. She shielded her eyes with a gloved hand and squinted at the wooden structure, hoping to catch a glimpse of Carl. As if in answer to her prayer, the snow suddenly lightened in intensity. In that brief moment Caroline saw him standing alone beside a laminated toy soldier at the entrance to the gazebo. His solitude cheered her. Either the killer had been swept up by the crowd, or he was as blinded by the snow as she. Determined to reach Carl first, she hurried on.

In her haste, Caroline forgot the ice lurking beneath the surface of the new snow. Her foot hit a slick spot on the path and she slid forward, crashing in a heap against a tree. She scrambled up, brushed the snow from her shoulders, and turned again toward her goal. One glance at the gazebo and her heart sank. True to the tradition of Santa Claus, Carl had vanished into the winter night.

SNOWFLAKES TUMBLED against Caroline's cheeks, melted on her eyelashes, and blurred her vision as she desperately searched the nearly deserted square. Carl should have stood out clearly in his red fur, but the blizzard had changed everything. Colors vanished beneath a blanket of white. Wet flakes clung to everyone, and Caroline could barely distinguish men from women as the last of the festivalgoers trudged by in their snow shrouds.

Think, she told herself angrily. *Where did he go?*

Forcing herself to concentrate, she turned in a tight circle and examined the routes leading out of the square. Her eyes came to rest on City Hall. For the first time she noticed that the first-floor lights were on in the building.

"Of course," she cried out in relief. Carl wouldn't have driven into town in the Santa suit. He would have changed clothes somewhere in Rhineburg, City Hall being the logical place. That's where the band had assembled, where they must have stored their instruments after the parade. The mayor had stood on the City Hall steps to issue his proclamation, and the sleigh had emerged from behind the building. Having served his stint in the gazebo, Carl would surely return to what served as headquarters for the Winter Festival.

Caroline began to run. She abandoned the sidewalk and cut across the square, plowing through the ever-growing drifts of snow. Her left ankle ached. She'd twisted it when she fell against the tree, but the cold and her own anxiety had numbed the original pain. The pressure on the stretched ligaments increased now as she tramped over the uneven ground. Each step became more difficult. Only fear drove her on.

Halfway across the square Caroline stepped on a discarded mitten embedded in the snow. Crusted with ice, the glove slid along the snow taking her left foot with it. She flailed at the air uselessly before pitching sideways into a mound of snow. She landed heavily on the injured foot.

"Ahhh!" Pain lanced through her left leg. Gritting her teeth, she brought her knee to her chest, unlaced her boot, and slid her hand inside. Warm blood greeted her fingers where a fracture had sliced through the skin leaving a bone protruding against the leather.

"Damnation!" she murmured grimly.

Caroline recognized the desperateness of her situation. Somewhere nearby walked a killer. She'd have no chance of escape if he suddenly appeared at her side. She couldn't run, much less walk, with her ankle twisted and broken. Even worse, she was sinking deeper into the snow with every move she made. She'd been a fool to cut across the square. The snow on the path had been manageable, but out here in the open the drifts were waist high. The one she'd fallen into threatened to suffocate her. She had to get back on her feet. But how?

She rested until the pain in her ankle became more manageable. Then she wiped the wetness from her eyes and inspected her surroundings. She sat in a sea of whiteness. Like waves, the snow rose and fell in uneven drifts around and beyond her. Even the sky appeared white with snowflakes swirling aimlessly in an unrelenting wind. She thought of calling for help, but what if the killer heard her? No, she decided. Silence would serve her best, silence and her own inner strength.

An idea came to her and she stretched out on her back, extending both arms. With slow, deliberate movements, she brushed angel wings in the snow. Each sweep flattened the drift a little more until it was packed down solidly on either side of her. She rolled to the right; the angel wing held.

Pulling her good leg beneath her, Caroline raised herself on one elbow and pushed down with her hands until she could kneel. She brought her right foot forward and planted it firmly on the ground. No way could she crawl out of the drift; she had to somehow stand up and walk.

"Okay, here we go," she whispered. Willing her right leg to hold her, she lurched upright. Pain shot from her ankle to her hip when she put weight on the injured left foot. She grimaced in agony.

"I have to do this," she gasped. Balancing precariously on one good foot, she clenched her teeth and hauled the injured leg forward. Cold sweat ran down her face. She managed another two steps, alternately hopping on one foot and dragging the other, before she tumbled back into the snow. Tears of pain and frustra-

tion stained her face as she rolled back into a sitting
position.

I haven't a chance, she thought with sudden clarity.
I'll never got out of this alive.

The notion so panicked her that Caroline never heard
the man approach. It wasn't until he squatted down a
foot away that she even realized he was there.

Looking into his cold eyes, she felt her heart sink.
Death no longer waited on the sidelines. It stared
straight at her.

"WELL, WELL. WHAT do we have here?"

The man stood up and walked a slow circle around
Caroline. She could almost feel his breath on her neck
when he passed behind her.

"Another accident, Mrs. Rhodes? How unfortunate."
He halted in front of her. "But then accidents do happen, especially in weather like this. Snow can be so
deadly. An injured person, someone like yourself perhaps, could fall facedown in a drift and smother." He
hunched down in the snow. Rocking back on his heels,
he smiled at her. "A terrible way to die, wouldn't you
say?"

Caroline shuddered. Trapped by her own pain and
fear, she struggled to remain calm.

"You won't get away with it. An autopsy would show
I didn't die naturally."

The man straightened up and slowly shook his head.
"I doubt it." He gazed around the empty square. "How
convenient. We seem to be all alone."

Caroline drew her legs in and leaned back straight
armed, supporting her weight on her hands. *I refuse to
die this way,* she thought to herself. How incredible to

have survived the ordeal of Ed's death only to end up a corpse in the snow.

"Why'd you do it?"

The killer tipped back his head and laughed.

"You've been watching too many movies, Mrs. Rhodes. You can't buy time that easily." He moved forward, his gloved hands reaching for her throat. "After all, time is a luxury I no longer have, thanks to… Ahhh!"

Stimulated by a rush of adrenaline, Caroline had pushed down on her bad foot and lashed out and up with the good one. The toe of her boot caught the man squarely between the legs. He doubled up in agony and she kicked again, this time hitting him in the chest. He grunted as the air shot out of his lungs and he tumbled backward into the snow.

Caroline scrambled to her knees, her ankle on fire with pain. She managed to crawl a few feet toward the gazebo before her good leg jerked out from under her and she went sprawling to the ground. The man had both hands wrapped around her right boot and was pulling her toward him.

She shook the cobwebs from her brain and struggled to twist away. Rolling onto her back, she caught a glimpse of her attacker before a gust of wind whipped ice crystals into her face. She instinctively raised a hand to shield her eyes.

As she did so, something sharp slashed at her wrist. She cried out in pain and flung herself sideways on the ground. Looking up, she saw the man crouched over her. Sweat and melting snow ran down his face. His eyes glittered with hatred.

"Bitch," he screamed. His hand flew up and she saw the knife poised above her head. For a split second something else came into view, something she vaguely remembered seeing earlier that evening. Long and thin, it swirled through the air, dancing in the wind as it rushed toward them. Then the knife came slicing down.

Caroline heard a loud crack and saw the knife waver only inches from her face. She reached up and shoved the man's hand away as he came tumbling forward, his skull crashing into her ribs and knocking the wind out of her lungs. Gasping for breath, she dragged herself from under his now still body. Waves of nausea swept over her. She pushed back the urge to vomit and crawled crablike across the snow, clawing at the drifts until several feet separated her from the killer. Then she collapsed in exhaustion.

Minutes passed. Caroline's heart slowed its frantic beating and she eased herself up on one elbow. She looked over at the "mad bomber" of Rhineburg.

Tony Grove lay sprawled in the snow, dead. His head twisted upward at an impossible angle and an expression of surprise transfixed his face. His open eyes stared blindly at the starless sky.

Off to the right, Caroline's pint-sized savior leaned against the drooping branch of a pine tree. He sported a lopsided smile and his right arm was cocked in a jaunty salute. Giddy with relief, she waggled her fingers at the silent figure.

A sudden gust of wind seemed to whisper her name. Intent on the vision of her rescuer, Caroline paid no attention. The sound came again, this time louder and more insistent. It tugged at her brain and she sat up, looked around, strained to hear above the sound of the storm. *It's not the wind,* she thought. *Or is it?* No. A human voice called to her. She opened her mouth, tried to call out, but could only manage a strangled sob.

Then strong arms encircled her and she looked up into a face as ashen as the trampled snow.

"Mother! Are you okay?"

She heard the emotion in Martin's voice as he hugged her to his chest. She nodded, looked past his shoulder, and saw Carl striding toward them. The professor knelt down next to Martin, murmured something, then took her hands and warmed them in his own huge paws. She saw his eyes go wide with fear when he noticed blood on the snow.

"She's hurt, Marty. We have to get her to the hospital."

"Let me help."

Michael Bruck had arrived. He pushed Carl aside and locked wrists with Martin. Together they lifted Caroline from the ground. She glanced over her shoulder as they carried her to a waiting police car.

"Nice going," she whispered softly.

The toy soldier who'd guarded the gazebo could say nothing in return. He simply stood at attention, his back against the tree, his duty clearly done.

SIX

December 31

"HAPPY NEW YEAR!" Caroline waved a fried chicken leg at Professor Atwater as he hung his coat in the closet. "Sorry we didn't wait for you, but the men were starving. The aroma from Nikki's kitchen simply overwhelmed them. As you can see, we ladies weren't much better at controlling our appetites."

The three freckle-faced redheads seated on the couch giggled in unison. Carl bowed to them before turning to Caroline.

"So you've met the Archangels' wives. A trio of beauties, aren't they?"

The triplets shared a blush.

"Oh, Professor!" exclaimed Faith. "You're embarrassing us."

"Yes," agreed Hope. "You and your blarney!"

"There must be some Irish in you," insisted Charity.

"Only on my mother's side," quipped Atwater.

The three women giggled again.

"His mind is affected by hunger," Faith told her sisters. "Let's get him something to eat." She motioned the others to their feet. With broad grins aimed at Carl and Caroline, they giggled their way into the dining room.

"What a group," Caroline said with a wry smile. "Those three pairs of green eyes never stop twinkling."

"They're a jolly lot all right. And just what the Bruck

boys need. A little Irish humor may temper their German sobriety." Carl collapsed on the couch. "How was your Christmas?"

"Absolutely wonderful. Kerry and Krista drove in from Chicago on Christmas Eve. We had dinner here with Martin and Nikki. We sat up all night talking about Ed and the fun times we had in Chicago. By the time we left for church in the morning, we were talked out."

"You must have been bushed."

"I was," conceded Caroline. "But it was a pleasurable tiredness. You see, it turns out I wasn't the only one feeling guilty after Ed's death. The kids were carrying their own individual burdens, blaming themselves for what happened to me. 'If I hadn't gone back to school so soon!' 'If we hadn't gone back to Rhineburg!' 'If I hadn't left you alone!'" Caroline shook her head. "It took a while to persuade them that my depression had nothing to do with them. In the end, I think they believed me. We turned a corner sometime between Christmas Eve and Christmas morning. We're talking freely now, without bitterness or remorse. And all of us are truly ready to get on with our lives."

"That conversation might have been the best Christmas present you ever gave each other," said Carl. "I'm happy for you, Cari. So tell me, when did your daughters leave?"

"Yesterday. They had to get back to work and their boyfriends. And how about you? I wanted to call you on Christmas morning, but Martin said you'd gone out of town."

"I spent Christmas with old friends. I had a nice time, but it's good to be home again. I certainly didn't want to miss Martin and Nikki's New Year's Eve party."

"I'm glad you're back, and even more glad you arrived

when you did. The Bruck women were bubbling over with absurd compliments. Talk about being snowed."

"Have they sufficiently bolstered your ego?"

"Inflated is more like it. Those three are suffering from an extreme case of hero worship."

Carl chuckled. "Your prowess as a detective is a matter of record, Cari."

"Sheer luck, Professor. Sheer luck."

"I disagree, although Elizabeth Morgan seems to share your viewpoint."

"Oh?" Caroline shifted the pillow under her broken ankle. The cast was cumbersome and her foot kept slipping to the side of the footstool. "When did you talk to her?"

"Here, let me help you with that." Carl plumped up the pillow on both sides of the cast. "I stopped by Alexsa's before coming here. She called this afternoon, all apologetic about her conversation with Agent Evans. She thought she was helping him, Cari."

"Right," said Caroline sarcastically. "She may be an old friend of yours, Carl, but Alexsa sure made a mess of things for me. But let's forget her for the time being. I'm more interested in what the junior Mrs. Morgan had to say."

"Liz and Jim were at the house when I arrived. Jim asked a thousand questions about the night of the Winter Festival. Liz seemed totally annoyed with him. She made several disparaging remarks."

"Like what?"

"For one thing, she called Jim a busybody. Said he sounded like an old woman gossiping over the backyard fence."

"The comparison must have riled Alexsa."

"Strangely enough, it didn't seem to bother her. In

fact, she told her grandson to drop the subject. They'd been playing bridge when I arrived. She seemed anxious to resume the game."

"She's probably embarrassed," said Caroline. "Doesn't want to admit her theory bombed."

"Did I hear the word *bomb?*" Jane Gardner appeared in the living room carrying two plates of food. She handed one to Carl. "Faith told me to give you this. Michael waylaid her under the mistletoe." She settled down in a chair across from Caroline. "So, my friend, when do we get to hear all the gory details?"

"Not you, too!"

"But of course. Do you expect me to believe everything I've heard at the hospital? According to the grapevine, you're a combination of Miss Marple and Bruce Lee."

Caroline laughed. "Don't I wish. I'm just fortunate to be alive. If it hadn't been for the wooden soldier..."

"I heard about that. Tell me, Caroline. Did it really come flying out of nowhere right when Grove was..." Jane paused and rolled her eyes.

"About to kill me? Yes, it happened exactly that way. The plywood soldier broke loose from its moorings by the gazebo and the wind caught hold of it. I spotted it spinning toward us right before it smashed into Grove's neck."

"And I can testify that the toy soldier caused Grove's death." Dr. Paul Wakely entered the living room along with Martin, Nikki, and the entire Bruck contingent. He elaborated while the others dug into their food. "It must have careened into him at a good speed and the right angle because it severed his spinal cord. Mr. Grove was dead before he hit the ground."

"According to the weather service, that storm packed

gusts of fifty miles an hour," said Michael. "Those laminated decorations are pretty sturdy. Given the force of the wind, it's not surprising our toy soldier killed the man."

"What I'd like to know is how you figured it out, Caroline. I would have never suspected Tony Grove."

"You would have, Jane, if you'd known all the facts. Once I read Gail's diary and the letters Peter Honeywell wrote to her mother..."

"Wait a minute," exclaimed Paul. "How'd you get hold of them?"

Caroline explained about her search of the dead student's dorm room. She was describing the ring in Gail's jewelry box when the doorbell rang. Martin went to answer it.

"The letters *MGH* puzzled me at first, but after..." Her voice trailed off as Martin reentered the room with Jim Morgan.

"Look who's joined the party!" Martin motioned Jim to a chair.

"We were at my grandmother's house tonight playing cards when Liz developed a migraine," Jim explained. "I drove her home, but it seemed too early to call it a night. Professor Atwater mentioned you were holding a party, Martin. I figured you wouldn't mind if I dropped by." He flashed a nervous smile at the others. "You're taking about the bombing, aren't you?"

Caroline and Carl exchanged glances. Jim's presence complicated matters concerning his and Alexsa's role in the case.

"Mrs. Rhodes is a genius," gushed Hope. "They way she figured it out when the FBI were totally confused!"

"That's not quite true," Caroline said gently. "They'd have broken the case soon enough. Tony Grove got careless. He made a huge mistake when he ransacked Gail's room."

"He drew attention to the girl's part in the mystery," said Michael.

Caroline nodded. "After my accident, Carl and I came to the conclusion that the killer was after someone on the psych ward. I worked there that day. I must have seen or heard something that would have revealed the killer's identity. We began inquiring into the victims' pasts."

"That's why you went to see my grandmother."

"Yes, Jim. But Alexsa wasn't much help. She distracted us with stories about May Eberle and Thomas Adrian. She denied even knowing the Belding family."

"You make it sound like she purposely lied."

Caroline ignored the Morgan heir. "At first, May and Thomas Adrian headed our list of possible targets. After Grove broke into the dorm, it dawned on me that Gail's diary and the letters must hold incriminating evidence. Why else would someone search the girl's room? The only other thing missing was the ring, and that by itself meant nothing."

"You mentioned the ring earlier," said Paul. "What's its significance?"

"The letters *MGH* were engraved on the inside of the band," replied Caroline. "I assumed it to be a family heirloom. Nevertheless, the condition of the ring bothered me. It didn't look worn like an old ring should. Nor did it look especially valuable. The only thing setting it apart was the engraving. Those initials had to be important to someone."

"I still don't get it," muttered Jane.

"Neither did I until I read the letters. You see, Gail's mother, Monica, fell in love with Peter Honeywell of

Honeywell Industries. Peter's father opposed their
union, so they married secretly here in Rhineburg. I'm
not positive, but I think the missing ring was Monica's
wedding band."

"MGH. Monica Garvy Honeywell."

"That's right, Jane. Gail had her mother's ring. She
also found Peter's love letters in Monica's burned-out
dorm room. The only thing she didn't have was the
marriage certificate."

"Back up a bit," said Paul. "I've been reading the
newspapers every day since Grove's death. They've
never mentioned Monica Garvy. Where does she fit
into all this?"

"Honeywell Industries probably threatened to sue the
papers if they printed what, at this point, is still speculation. The FBI should be coming out with a statement
soon, though. They still have to tie up a few loose ends."

"One of them being Monica," said Carl.

Caroline nodded. "We believe Grove planted the
bomb to keep Gail from proving that Janice Honeywell is the illegitimate heir to the Honeywell fortune."

"You're kidding," exclaimed Jane. "All that money
doesn't belong to her?"

"Not a cent of it," said Carl. "Gail was about to blow
her out of the water. Janice conspired with Grove in the
bombing of the psych ward."

"That's a drastic solution to her problems," said Paul.

"Yes," said Caroline. "But Gail had made contact
with James Belding. He also was a threat to Janice."
She could tell by the looks on her friends' faces that
they needed a detailed explanation. "The story starts
over twenty years ago when Peter came to Rhineburg
to meet with Alexsa Stromberg Morgan. Alexsa is a
major investor in Honeywell Industries. Peter's job was

to court the stockholders and keep them happy. Monica Garvy often visited the Morgan house because her aunt worked there as Alexsa's housekeeper. Monica was attracted to Jim, but she fell for Peter after they met. Alexsa never approved of Gail, so she probably introduced the girl to Honeywell.

"The two started seeing each other and, according to his letters, Peter eventually proposed. Peter's father didn't approve of the match. He wanted his son to wed someone within his own social circle. They argued about it continuously. In the end, the couple opted to marry in secret. Peter asked Reverend Ty Belding to perform the ceremony here in Rhineburg."

"Did they actually go through with it?" asked Jane.

"Of course they did," exclaimed Jim angrily. "Monica wouldn't lie about a thing like that, no matter what that damned preacher said!"

Caroline's sympathy for Elizabeth grew by leaps and bounds. She continued to ignore their uninvited guest.

"Arthur Honeywell died suddenly of a heart attack. Peter flew back to Chicago from a business meeting after hearing the news. While driving home from the airport, he was killed in an auto accident. Father and son were buried the same day."

"How tragic," Hope said softly.

"Peter's mother died young," said Caroline. "And he had no siblings. Relatives came crawling out of the woodwork after the funeral, all of them claiming a piece of Honeywell Industries. The company might have gone under except that Janice Belding came forward with proof of inheritance."

"Was she related to the minister?" asked Paul. "The one who married Peter and Monica?"

"She was his niece," said Carl. "She and her older

brother, James, lived with Ty Belding on a tiny farm outside of Rhineburg. James entered the Army after high school. Janice moved to Chicago after graduation."

"She got a job at Honeywell Industries," continued Caroline. "She proved herself there and soon assumed the role of Peter's private secretary. She accompanied him on trips, including the ones to Rhineburg. After Peter's death, she produced a marriage certificate signed by her uncle. She insisted she was young Honeywell's wife."

"But I thought Peter married Monica!"

Jane's eyes were wide with astonishment. Caroline couldn't help but laugh.

"Confusing, isn't it? Imagine how the lawyers reacted when Monica showed up with another marriage certificate signed by the same minister. Ty Belding denied having performed a ceremony for Monica and Peter, insisting Janice had married him instead. He had records to back his assertion which he later showed to Monica's mother, Albina Garvy."

"That old bitch," Jim swore. "She disowned her own daughter on the word of that shyster preacher!"

"Be that as it may, a court of law named Janice the legal heir and awarded her full control of Honeywell Industries. Monica later made a futile attempt to solicit financial support for Gail, claiming Peter had fathered the girl."

"He did," growled Jim. "Monica told me that herself."

"She wouldn't submit the baby to genetic testing, Jim," Caroline replied testily. "Do you really think the Honeywell lawyers wouldn't demand proof of paternity?"

Morgan muttered something under his breath that

Caroline didn't catch. Unwilling to be drawn into an argument, she ignored him.

"Monica dropped out of nursing school for a while. She returned to St. Anne's as a live-in student after Elvira Harding offered to care for Gail. Then came the fire that destroyed part of the dormitory. Monica was the sole casualty. She fell running down the fire escape ladder and died of a head injury. Carl and I believe Ty Belding set the fire."

"We think Ty was working for his niece," said Carl. "Monica had already made two attempts to get money from the Honeywell estate without the help of a lawyer. If she sued Janice, Ty Belding's records would have been examined more thoroughly, exposing any alterations he made. Both he and Janice could have landed in jail."

"The FBI subpoenaed old records from the Rhineburg Bank," said Caroline. "They found that shortly after the fire, Ty Belding began making payments into his account that exceeded his usual deposits. We think Janice paid him to commit arson."

"So Belding killed Monica." Jim jumped up from the sofa and began pacing the room. "Her name was mud in this town for years. People bad-mouthed her because they believed that son of a bitch preacher!" He pulled up and turned to face Carl. "Rhineburg owes Monica a public apology. I'll be damned if I don't see she gets it!"

Caroline recalled Bill Morgan's phone call and what he'd said about his son's infatuation with Monica. *"Jim thinks of her as some kind of martyr. If he doesn't cut it out, Liz is going to walk out on him."* Watching the younger Morgan parade about the room like a madman, she began to understand what Bill had been saying. No wonder Liz drank to excess. Her husband was obsessed with the ghost of his former lover. How could any woman compete with the saint he'd created in his mind?

Alexsa's motivations became clear to her now. The matriarch of the Morgan clan had thrown out red herrings hoping that Caroline would concentrate on May Eberle and Thomas Adrian instead of Monica's daughter. Alexsa had sensed the terrible destructiveness of Jim's emotions. She knew how fragile her grandson's marriage truly was. Better that Caroline stumble around in the dark than expose the truth and leave Liz to reap the consequences.

Caroline couldn't blame Alexsa for what she'd done. The old lioness was only protecting her cubs.

Michael broke the uncomfortable silence that followed Jim's outburst. "The FBI is building a case against Mrs. Honeywell. It won't be easy because Ty Belding died in a hunting accident years ago."

"Are you sure it was an accident?" asked Jane

"You're beginning to sound like Mrs. Rhodes," said Michael with a smile. "Much too suspicious for your own good. But you ask a good question, one the FBI are asking, too."

"Ty might have been Tony Grove's first victim," said Caroline. "The police investigated his death, but they couldn't prove anything one way or the other."

"My dad headed the security department at Bruck back then. He also hunted. He was the first person with any police experience to arrive on the scene after the shooting."

"Did he suspect murder, Mike?" asked Paul.

"Belding had dressed in an orange jumpsuit. Hard to believe anyone could have mistaken him for a deer. He'd been shot in the back and the bullet passed straight through his heart. My father didn't think it was accidental. He believed someone took deliberate aim at the minister."

"The police questioned Elvira Harding's husband," said Caroline. "He blamed Belding for Monica's death."

"Harding found Belding's body. My father checked Charlie's gun. It hadn't been fired that day."

"Of course it hadn't," snorted Jim. "Charlie couldn't hit the broadside of a barn. He was as poor a shot as my wife. He only went hunting to get away with the boys."

"You're probably right," Michael conceded. "Still, he had a pretty good motive. Everyone knew he hated Belding." He shook his head in frustration. "It took a real marksman to nail Belding that way. Hunting season is a popular time around here, but not every Rhineburger who handles a gun is an expert. Jim here could have done it. Alexsa was a sharpshooter in her day and taught her grandson a thing or two about rifles."

"I'd gone to work, and you know it," said Morgan angrily. "Both my father and I had alibis. Anyway, Mrs. Rhodes thinks Tony Grove did it."

"That's what I suspect, Jim, but I have no proof," said Caroline. "It's possible Belding got greedy and demanded too much money from his niece. He might have become a liability to Janice, so she had Grove kill him."

"When did Grove enter the picture?" asked Jane.

"At the very start of things," said Carl.

"Tony Grove grew up in Rhineburg," Caroline explained. "Only then he was known as John Anthony Grovelli. Tony was a high school buddy of James Belding. They joined the Army together and served in the same unit in Vietnam. The two of them went missing during a mission in enemy territory. It's believed James was captured and held somewhere in Vietnam. He only recently surfaced in Thailand. My brother mentioned

Grove while passing on some information to me, but he didn't call him by name. Shiloh, a waiter at the Blue Cat Lounge, discovered Grove's true identity. Shiloh's grandfather used to be the principal at Rhineburg High. He remembered both Belding and Grovelli."

Gabriel Bruck jumped in with a piece of the story. "The Army listed Grovelli as MIA along with James Belding. We know now that he was alive and running drugs out of Southeast Asia. The authorities were aware of him only as 'Dr. G.' They assumed a rival had eliminated him when he suddenly dropped out of the trade. The truth is, he saw a magazine article about Honeywell Industries with a picture of its CEO, Janice Belding. That article sent him packing straight back to Chicago."

"How'd you find out about the Asian connection?" asked Paul

Rafael Bruck answered for his brother. "Tom Evans filled us in. The FBI contacted both the Army and other government agencies when they learned of Grove's dual identity. As for the magazine, Grove kept it when he returned to Chicago. The FBI found it while searching his apartment."

"But why did Grove come back? What was so important about the article?" asked a mystified Jane.

"Tony returned because he knew Janice when she had yet another name," exclaimed Nikki. She clapped her had over her mouth. "Sorry, Mom. I didn't mean to steal your thunder."

"That's all right," said Caroline with a smile. "Martin and Nikki already know the full story," she told the others. "I'm surprised they're not bored with it by now."

Paul waved off the interruption. "Go on, Caroline. You've got me on the edge of my seat."

"Me, too," said Jane. "Explain what Nikki said."

"Between Belding and Honeywell, Janice bore the title of Mrs. John Anthony Grovelli, a.k.a. Mrs. Tony Grove."

Caroline saw she'd shocked her friends from St. Anne's. Paul and Jane wore twin looks of surprise.

"Janice wed Grovelli when they were teenagers. She knew about his MIA status, and may have thought he'd died in Vietnam. Nevertheless, she was still his wife when she inherited Peter's company. Tony's sudden appearance jeopardized her position as the Honeywell heir. She wasn't about to lose her fortune, so she used it to buy Tony's silence. She's admitted to the FBI that she supplied him with a cushy job in the company. Tony did nothing in the way of real work, but his title covered the enormous salary Janice paid him."

"He blackmailed her."

"In a way, Paul. Remember, though: Janice is no innocent victim. She manipulated the truth to get where she is today. And we believe she conspired with Grove to bomb the psych ward."

"Tell us how you uncovered the plot," demanded an eager Faith.

"I'm dying of curiosity," said Hope.

"Me, too," exclaimed Charity.

Caroline smiled at the three women. "Gail mentioned Grove several times in her diary. I wondered what his ties were to Janice since he seemed to be her right-hand man. I also wondered about James's Army buddy. Was it possible he also made it out of Vietnam? It all began to fall into place when Shiloh gave me Grovelli's name. I asked Michel to check the neighboring states for records of a marriage between Janice Belding and John Anthony Grovelli, and bingo! There it was, in black-and-white. The two of them tied the knot in Hazard County, Kentucky, before Janice reached legal age in Illinois."

"Unfortunately," added Michael, "I didn't learn this until after Grove attacked Mrs. Rhodes."

Jane asked, "Getting back to the bombing, what's your theory on that?"

"I think Grove meant to kill Gail Garvy and James Belding," said Caroline. "It's possible James recognized Tony. If so, Janice needed to tuck him away where he could do her no harm."

"She figured a hick town like Rhineburg was the perfect place to hide him," Jane said bitterly. "She paid off Charles Paine with donations to St. Anne's, then moved her brother onto the ward. No wonder Grove knew about the tree. He visited the unit a lot those last few weeks."

Caroline nodded. "Gail popped up as an unexpected complication. She enrolled in nursing to gain access to the dormitory. Elvira said the girl was obsessed with revenge. She wanted to shame Albina into admitting she'd wronged Monica. To do that, Gail needed to find Monica's marriage certificate. Elvira assumed it had burned in the fire, but Gail thought her mother hid it somewhere in the dorm."

Caroline told them about Gail's midnight journeys to the third floor. "She found Peter's letters, but the certificate eluded her to the end. When she heard James Belding had been admitted to the psych ward, she contrived to get herself assigned there. She hounded the poor man, convinced he knew about Janice's scam."

"Do you blame her?" demanded Jim. "Gail got a raw deal from her grandmother."

"Pipe down," Michael said softly. "We all feel bad about Gail."

Jim glowered at Bruck, then walked over to the window and stared out at the snow. Caroline nodded her thanks to Michael and continued her story.

"Gail constantly repeated the names Monica, Peter, Janice, and Ty Belding to James. She got no reaction from him until a few days before the bombing. He raised four fingers, one by one, and whispered 'four to go.'"

"I'm still angry that Gail didn't report this to me," said Jane.

"James seemed only to confide in Gail," said Caroline. "I think he was trying to warn her off."

"How?" Faith frowned in puzzlement.

"'Four to go' are the last words of a nursery rhyme. If you think about the rhyme, each line could refer to someone involved in the case. 'One for the money' would be Janice Honeywell. She feathered her nest by pretending to be Peter's wife. 'Two for the show' may allude to Janice and Ty Belding. They worked together to fool the Honeywell lawyers. 'Three to get ready' might indicate Tony Grove had joined Janice and her uncle in the deception. I think 'four to go' pertains to those who had to be eliminated for the plan to work. Monica and Peter were already dead. The only threats left were James and Gail Garvy."

"Too bad Gail didn't heed the warning," said Jane. "She must have realized Grove was dangerous. She always backed off when he arrived on the ward."

"He made her nervous," Caroline replied. "But she was unrelenting in her quest to clear her mother's name. It was the only thing that mattered to her. In a way, Gail needed psychiatric help as much as James Belding."

"It must have worried Grove to see Gail hanging around James."

"The explosion conveniently disposed of both of them. I became a problem when I saw Grove leave the rec room only seconds before the bomb went off." Caroline described bumping into him near the doorway. "I thought he was a patient attempting to leave the ward. I followed him down the hallway before he turned into another room."

"But you didn't recognize him.'

"No, Paul, I didn't. But I'd never heard of the man until Jane pointed him out to me in the cafeteria. He seemed familiar to me then, but I couldn't place where I'd seen him."

"Tony handled explosives in the Army," said Carl. "The damaged Christmas tree provided him with the inspiration for his plan. He couldn't rig the bomb here, so he drove to Chicago in the red Jaguar he'd bought from Jim."

"Grove was the rich doctor!"

"Yes, Jim. Tony didn't dare take his rental car because the mileage would have shown on the odometer. And he couldn't take the company plane because the authorities could track it. Buying the Jag was brilliant. Sure, the car stood out in a crowd, but if you saw something like that tooling down the highway, would you stare at it or the driver?"

"Forget the driver. I'd be too busy admiring the car!"

"Exactly, Paul," said Caroline. "Tony counted on that kind of reaction. While he drove the Jag, his own car sat in the hospital's garage. Everyone assumed that because the car was in town, so was Grove."

"And once he made it to Chicago," said Carl, "Tony knew precisely where to go to buy the ingredients for the bomb."

"Are explosives that easy to get in Chicago?" Faith asked in astonishment.

Michael slipped an arm around his wife's shoulders

and hugged her. "Maybe not for you, honey. But you've got to remember, Grove wasn't exactly what you'd call an upstanding citizen. With his past experience as a drug dealer, making contact with the right people would be no problem for him."

"The FBI is working on the Chicago connection even as we speak," said Caroline. "Getting back to Tony, he rigged the tree and shipped it from Chicago, then hurried back to Rhineburg and hid the Jag on the old logging trail near the bridge. A couple of days after the bombing, he made his first real mistake. He was worried someone might find the car, so he drove back to the woods to check on it. That's when Jerry, Elvira's grandson, saw him. Grove's behavior seemed peculiar to Jerry. He waited until Grove left, then hiked up the trail and found the Jag buried under a snowdrift.

"I didn't connect Jerry's story to the bombing until the afternoon of the Winter Festival. That's when I mentioned to Shiloh that the Blue Cat Lounge looked awfully dilapidated on the outside. He said they'd purposely made the exterior of the building look bad as a ruse to discourage tourists from dropping in. The structure itself is sturdy, but the locals prefer not to share their favorite watering hole with outsiders. The conversation got me to thinking about the red Jaguar. Maybe its purpose similar, to deceive the FBI."

"Grove was a master of deception," said Michael. "Look at the deadly weapon he created from a Christmas tree. Those steel branches shot out like arrows when the bomb detonated. No one near it stood a chance of surviving."

A hush fell over the group as each person considered the havoc wrought by Tony Grove. Finally Jane broke the silence.

"Why did Grove kill Charles Paine?"

"Paine relied heavily on Janice Honeywell for financial support for St. Anne's," said Caroline. "He was probably worried she'd back off because of her brother's death. I think he tried to enlist Grove's aid in persuading Janice to continue funding the hospital. Maybe he tried to bribe Tony. Or maybe he mentioned James Belding's name in a way that seemed suspicious to Grove. Whatever the reason, I think Grove panicked and killed Paine while he had the opportunity."

"It makes sense," said Jane. "Our late administrator liked getting his own way. I could see him pressuring Grove and not knowing when to back off."

"So many people dead, and all because of greed." Nikki shook her head sadly. "Not a nice way to start out the New Year, is it?"

"You forget, Mr. Grove is safely six feet under," Martin reminded her. "I'd say the world is better off without him."

"And your mother is alive and well," added Carl. "That's something to be thankful for!"

Caroline smiled at the professor. She might need a little repair work physically, but mentally, she was in tip-top shape. She felt whole and alive again, and much of that was due to Carl's friendship. She was the one who ought to give thanks.

"The past should be left in the past," she said. "Why don't we all make that our New Year's resolution?"

"Sounds good to me!" Martin sprang to his feet and headed for the kitchen. "How about champagne, everyone? It's almost midnight. Gotta start the countdown."

Jim looked glassy-eyed with fatigue. He excused himself, and when no one objected to his leaving, he slouched out head-down like a beaten man. The others were content to put aside all thoughts of murder and celebrate instead the beginning of happier times. Carl led them in a toast.

"To life! May we all live it well."

"Amen," agreed Caroline with a smile.

SEVEN

January 1

CAROLINE PICKED UP the remote control and switched channels on the television. The Rose Bowl parade had ended and it would be several hours before the game itself started. Fortunately for football fans, of which she was one, there were other bowl games on TV today. She found the team selection particularly good for the one coming up. Prepared to enjoy herself, she settled back on the sofa to await the kickoff.

Caroline knew she was considered an oddity among her sex. Football was considered a man's sport. Nevertheless, she regarded New Year's Day as the ultimate pigskin holiday when she could revel in the game from noon until late at night. No one in her family shared her fanaticism, which meant she'd be alone this holiday. But she didn't mind. Her ankle was still mending after a surgical repair the night of the Winter Festival. And although the sutures were gone from her head, the ones in her wrist itched while the bone itself still ached from the thrust of Tony Grove's knife. Alone, she could lounge to her heart's content, whereas if Martin and Nikki had joined her, she'd feel obligated to play hostess.

The phone rang as a Colorado special teams player caught the football. Caroline ignored it. The runner was surging up the field, following his blockers through a swarming defensive line. He slipped tackles like a snake shedding its skin while curling in and out of openings.

The clamor continued, and Caroline covered the phone with a pillow. The runner crossed the thirty, the thirty-five, the forty-yard line. The opposition crumbled before him.

Her caller would not be denied. Caroline snatched up the receiver on the seventh ring. The Colorado player was at midfield with only the kicker left blocking the end zone.

"Hello," she muttered distractedly, her eyes glued to the TV.

"Cari? Is that you?"

The runner curved toward the side of the field. He evaded the kicker's flying tackle and scampered across the goal line.

"Touchdown," Caroline hollered, throwing both arms up over her head. The time-honored gesture of victory sent the receiver clattering to the floor. It skittered across the rug and crashed against the leg of the coffee table.

"Oh, my goodness." Caroline hobbled off the sofa and grabbed the phone. "Carl, I'm so sorry. I'm watching a bowl game and I got carried away."

"I apologize for bothering you," the professor replied tersely.

"It's no bother," Caroline lied. "I've been relaxing on the couch, babying my ankle." Her eyes strayed back to the screen. The point-after attempt was up—and good! The score blinked on the screen, then the picture switched to a beer advertisement. She pushed the mute button on the remote control. "What are you up to today?"

"Bill Morgan called, Cari. Something's happened."

The hairs rose on the back of Caroline's neck. She braced herself for the worst.

"What is it, Carl?"

"Elizabeth Morgan drove her car into the river early this morning. The bridge iced over and apparently she was speeding when she approached it."

"She's dead, isn't she?" It was more a statement than a question; Caroline already knew the answer.

"The river's running high with all the snow we've had. The water's terribly cold."

Caroline grabbed a crutch and carried the phone over to the window. Below her, Bruck Green lay blanketed in white. The morning sun tickled the frozen landscape and a million icy diamonds reflected upward. Too beautiful a day to die.

"Accidents can happen to anyone," she said. "Sometimes they're…unavoidable."

"That's true." A hint of formality cast a hollow ring to Carl's words. "It's a tragedy for the entire Morgan family. Liz was a lovely young woman."

And a troubled one, thought Caroline. But then, considering her life with Jim, who could blame her?

EIGHT

January 3

"HOW'D YOU SPEND your morning?"

Carl placed his empty glass on the table and smiled at Caroline. At loose ends after Liz's funeral, he'd wandered back to her apartment and invited himself to lunch. They discussed the service over salami sandwiches and beer, Carl telling her how Jim had snubbed him at the cemetery and how greatly Alexsa had aged since the accident. He appeared depressed when he first showed up on her doorstep, but his mood improved with every sandwich he consumed. Now, having polished off his fourth, he was almost his old self again. Caroline regretted spoiling his meal. He had a right, though, to know about the letter.

"Did a little of this, a little of that. Went downstairs to pick up my mail. Among other things, I received a note from Liz Morgan."

Carl appeared dumbfounded. "When did she write it?"

"New Year's Eve. Or early New Year's morning. Jim went home and told her everything we'd discussed at the party. Liz wasn't thrilled with his reaction to the news about Monica. Apparently his feelings for his old flame were pretty evident."

"Damned fool," Carl grumbled. "I suppose Liz blamed you for telling him the truth."

"Not really. It seems, though, that some of my conclusions were a little off base."

"What do you mean?"

Caroline pushed away from the table. Using her crutches, she walked to the living room and opened the top drawer of the desk. She withdrew an ivory envelope and carried it back to the kitchen.

"You'd better read this."

Carl frowned, but he took the envelope and withdrew from it three sheets of paper covered in spidery handwriting.

"This is too much," he growled after perusing the first paragraphs. He tossed the letter on the table. "You're not responsible for Liz's suicide, regardless of what's in this…this…piece of garbage! And let's stop beating around the bush. We both know her death was no accident."

"Yes, we do, even if we've been reluctant to admit it. But don't tell me you haven't felt the slightest bit guilty since hearing of Liz's death. I know I have. At least," she added, "I did until today."

Carl stroked his beard, something he did habitually when pondering a problem. "I've wondered if things wouldn't have turned out differently had we only left it in the hands of the police. If Liz wanted to blame anyone, it should have been me."

"Forget the first part of the letter," Caroline said with a wave of her hand. "That's nothing more than the ranting of an angry woman. Read the rest of it." She pushed the pages toward him. "We were wrong about a lot of things, Carl. Liz led a secret life. She couldn't reveal what she knew without destroying herself."

Curiosity got the best of Carl. He flipped the first

page aside and concentrated on the second one. He suddenly went deadly pale.

"This can't be true!"

Caroline was saddened by the horror she saw in her friend's eyes. "Liz wasn't lying. That's the confession of a woman who could no longer live with herself." She took the pages from Carl's hand and began to read aloud.

"'Let me set you straight on a few details. Number one, Monica never married Peter Honeywell. I know because I made the biggest mistake of my life when I helped her steal a blank marriage certificate from Reverend Belding's office. I saw her forge Peter's signature on it.'"

"It's sheer vindictiveness, Cari. Jim hurt Liz. She wrote those words for revenge."

"Come on, Carl! You don't believe that. Listen to what Liz says. 'Money was all Monica wanted. When Peter died so suddenly, she saw a chance to get rich quick. In exchange for my help, she promised to leave Jim alone. He was crazy about Monica, but I loved Jim and thought he'd eventually love me, too. All these years I've put up with that woman's ghost. I can't fight her any longer. She's finally won.'"

Carl wasn't convinced. "If the whole thing was a hoax, how come Peter wrote those letters to her? How do you explain that?"

In answer, Caroline began to read again.

"'That little bitch refused to let Janice Belding stand in her way. She broke into Janice's Chicago apartment, hoping to find and destroy her marriage certificate. It wasn't there, but Monica did find letters from Peter. She used them to back up her claim.'"

She looked up at Carl. "Those are the letters I found

in Gail's desk. Because Gail had them, I assumed they were written to Monica. I now realize they could have been sent to anyone. They all started with the words *dearest* or *darling,* never with a name."

"That doesn't prove anything," argued Carl. "Monica could have told Liz about the letters. Then Liz saw them when she accosted you in the restaurant. She could have made up all this nonsense."

"You're a stubborn man, Carl, but you're wrong. Remember how Monica died in the fire?"

"Ty Belding set it."

Caroline shook her head. "Another mistake on our part. Liz set it after she murdered Monica."

Carl's mouth sagged. He couldn't have looked more surprised, or distressed. Caroline explained.

"The Honeywell lawyers demanded proof of Gail's paternity, but Monica refused to have her daughter tested. She knew Peter wasn't the father and she told Liz that the night she died. Monica had been seeing Jim again. Liz went to the dorm to persuade her to leave Jim alone."

"Bill Morgan told me Monica brought Gail to the house once or twice. But Jim was dating Liz then." Carl frowned. He might be stubborn, but he wasn't a fool. "Tell me what happened."

"According to the letter, Monica and Liz quarreled, then Monica dropped her bombshell. She claimed Jim was Gail's father. She said if she couldn't have the Honeywell fortune, she'd settle for the Morgan money. Liz became so enraged that she attacked Monica. The girl fell and hit her head on an iron radiator. Then Liz panicked. She pushed Monica's body off the fire escape and set the fire to cover her tracks."

Carl traced a circle on the table with his knife.

"Did Liz show any remorse for what she did?"

"No. The letter ended abruptly with Liz's signature."

"That's odd," said Carl. "Liz must have been distraught when she wrote this letter. You'd think you'd get an inkling of what came next. Her suicide, I mean."

"I had the same thought. She never mentioned ending her life. But she wouldn't have mailed the letter to me if she weren't contemplating suicide. You can't make this kind of confession and then expect nothing to happen. Still, the letter seems incomplete. It's as if she lost interest in the story and just stopped writing."

"Maybe that's exactly what happened," said Carl.

Neither one of them believed it, but the alternative was too grisly to even imagine. Caroline scooted her chair to the refrigerator and took out two bottles of beer. She opened them and offered one to Carl.

"You realize we have a problem here."

"Definitely," said Carl. "We assumed Janice was in cahoots with Grove because Gail could prove she'd never married Peter. Now we know Gail wasn't a threat at all. Unless, of course, she knew about Janice's earlier marriage to Grove."

"No, she didn't have the means to check the records the way Michael did. And according to her diary, James Belding didn't tell her. Which brings us to the meaning of his warning. Why did Belding repeat those words to Gail?" Caroline racked her brains for an answer. She couldn't believe she was too far off from the truth.

"Maybe he tried to communicate fear for his own life," said Carl. "He knew about the marriage. That made him a walking time bomb."

Caroline didn't buy it. "James was totally out of it. Do you think anyone would have believed him if he said Tony and Janice were married?" She leaned her elbows on the table and massaged her forehead with the fingertips of both hands. "I'm afraid I had it all wrong. Janice would never have brought him to Rhineburg if she feared he'd reveal her past. Better to lock him up at home where nobody could get to him."

"We should have thought of this before we talked to Agent Evans. He's ready to arrest Janice."

"There's so much we didn't know." Caroline slumped down in her chair. "And there's another thing. Why did Alexsa lead us down the garden path with her innuen-does about Thomas Adrian and May Eberle? Was she protecting Liz when she refused to discuss Gail Garvy? And why did she lie about the Beldings? She's hiding something, Carl. I feel it in my bones."

"Then why don't you ask her about it? She's bound to be home. Let's go there."

Caroline hesitated. "It's not the right time to question Alexsa. She's worn out. You said so yourself."

"Maybe she's worn out because she's burdened with secrets." Carl gazed intently at his friend. "I've known Alexsa for years. There's little in this town that gets past her. I wonder if she didn't know all along that Gail was Jim's daughter."

"It would explain her evasiveness. I think Alexsa would do anything to protect her family."

Caroline wasn't easily persuaded, but in the end, she accompanied Carl to the Morgan home. Bill Morgan answered the door and ushered them in. He appeared glad to see them.

"I hoped you'd stop by," he said as he led them into the living room. "My son's behavior this morning was unforgivable. I want to apologize for him."

The professor waved it off. "Jim's been under a lot of strain. Is he here now?"

"Naw! He's driving around trying to sort things out. Unfortunately, he had a terrible argument with Liz only hours before the accident." He pointed to a bottle of Scotch on the table next to his chair. "Would you like a drink?"

When they declined, he poured one for himself. Caroline guessed it wasn't his first of the day.

"He came home from your party and insisted on telling us all about the bombing. Talk about wound up! He kept mentioning Monica's name, over and over again, like a man possessed." He took a pull on his drink. "I'm not the most romantic guy in the world, but even I know you don't rave about another woman in front of your wife. I didn't blame Liz for being upset."

"Is that when they argued?" asked Carl.

"No. Liz was one classy lady. She'd never fight with Jim in front of my mother or me. She went to her room and Jim stayed here drinking. It must have been a good hour later when I woke up to the shouting. Frankly," he confided, "I don't believe in interfering in other people's lives. I pulled the covers over my head and shut it out."

Caroline grimaced. What a night it must have been.

"I didn't see Liz the next morning and Jim looked like he hadn't slept a wink. I figured it wasn't my business, so I let it alone. I was watching football when the police called." Bill frowned and swirled the whiskey in his glass.

"Jim left the cemetery before I could extend my condolences," said Carl.

"He didn't leave," Bill retorted. "He took flowers over to Gail's and Monica's graves. I told you, he's obsessed!"

Carl nodded sympathetically. "Alexsa appeared very upset. Do you think she's up to visitors?"

"You're not a visitor, Carl. You're the closest thing to family we've got." Bill led them upstairs to a small library at the end of the corridor. "Mother's in her bedroom. Wait here and I'll get her."

Carl sank down on a flowered sofa while Caroline examined the room. Potted plants lined the two windowsills and sat atop a glass curio case displaying delicate figurines. In the far corner stood an antique writing desk bearing a box of lavender stationery. A scent of gardenias hung in the air reminding Caroline of the perfume Alexsa had worn the last time she'd visited. The library had been decorated with a woman in mind and was obviously Mrs. Morgan's private haunt.

"Good afternoon."

Caroline spun around. Alexsa stood inside the doorway, leaning heavily on her cane. Her face looked drawn and her voice quavered. Carl rose to greet her, but she motioned him back into his seat.

"Do you like my little hideaway?" she asked. She smiled tightly when Caroline nodded. "I thought so. You're a woman of good taste."

Caroline sensed a challenge in the words. She reminded herself that regardless of her present condition, Alexsa was still a force to be reckoned with.

"We came to extend our sympathy."

"How interesting." Alexsa sank down on a straight-backed chair behind the desk. "And why else have you come?"

She knows, thought Caroline. *Somehow she knows about the letter. Well, why beat around the bush?*

"I received a letter from Elizabeth today. She wrote about her role in the Honeywell fiasco, how she helped Monica fake her marriage certificate. She also explained how Monica died."

Alexsa pursed her lips as if she'd tasted something sour. "I must say, it surprised me when Jim didn't find a note. Liz wasn't the sort to leave loose ends."

"You mean a suicide note," Carl murmured.

"They're calling it an accident, but we know better, don't we." Alexsa flicked a piece of lint from the breast of her silk suit, then ran a hand over her skirt, slowly smoothing away imaginary wrinkles. She appeared totally bored with the conversation.

She's playing with us, thought Caroline. *It's a game of chess to her. Check and checkmate.*

"What we told the FBI was incorrect. We can't change their minds without showing them the letter."

"Why would you do that, Mrs. Rhodes?" Alexsa looked puzzled. "What good will it do to harm this family further?"

"It might save Janice Honeywell's life," Carl retorted. "The police think she's a murderer!"

Alexsa shrugged. "She has many fine lawyers at her disposal. They won't allow her to be prosecuted."

You old lioness, thought Caroline. *You'll sacrifice anyone to shield the Morgans.*

"She'll be ruined nonetheless," she snapped. "You of all people should realize how easily reputations can be destroyed."

"Oh, I do. That's precisely why I'm not going to risk ours."

"You'll have no choice if I give that letter to the FBI," said Caroline. "I could also send a copy to Janice. Her 'fine lawyers' will have a field day with it!"

Alexsa's eyes narrowed. She glanced at Carl and he nodded in agreement with Caroline. She hesitated less than a minute before saying, "What is it you want of me?"

"The truth."

Alexsa's hands fluttered in annoyance. "How simple you make it sound. And what do I get in exchange for 'the truth'?"

"Partners in damage control." Caroline saw she'd taken Alexsa by surprise. She pushed on. "I admire you for protecting Liz, but I won't stand by and watch an innocent woman prosecuted. The police shouldn't hound Janice if she was ignorant of Grove's plans. Let's look at the facts, toss out what's irrelevant, and find some answers."

Alexsa appeared to be weighing her options. Caroline figured none of them looked attractive.

"Where shall I start?" she said in a resigned tone of voice.

"When did you first learn of Monica's murder?" asked Carl.

"The day Liz shot Ty Belding."

"What?" Carl jerked upright on the sofa. "Are you saying Liz killed him, too?"

"I thought you knew," Alexsa whispered. Her face twisted in agony. "I thought she told you everything!"

Caroline pushed the letter into the old woman's hands. "You'd better read this. Evidently, Liz left out some things."

She glanced at Carl as Alexsa skimmed the letter. She could tell they were thinking the same thing: the letter was incomplete. Liz had ended it abruptly. But why?

A subdued Alexsa handed the pages back to Caroline. The fight had gone out of her.

"Everything Liz wrote happened as she said. What you don't know is that Ty Belding saw her leave the dormitory that night. He guessed she'd set the fire. He began blackmailing her after she married Jim.

"Liz paid, but it was difficult hiding the truth from Jim. She became desperate. The last time Belding demanded money, he suggested they meet in the woods. Liz went, but she took Jim's rifle with her. She shot the preacher in the back."

Alexsa sighed and shook her head. "I remember it clearly. I looked out my bedroom window and saw her coming up the path from the woods, carrying the rifle. When I went downstairs, I found her cleaning the gun in the mudroom. She was crying. I questioned her, and she broke down and told me the whole story." The matriarch of the Morgan family raised her eyes and glared at them. "Monica was an evil person. She'd have ruined Jim's life. Liz saved him from that and earned my eternal gratefulness. I couldn't let her suffer for what she'd done."

Carl huffed into his beard in what sounded to Caroline like outraged empathy. He obviously felt Alexsa had been faced with a difficult choice: expose Liz, or become an accessory to murder. Caroline wasn't buying any of it.

"That's quite a story," she murmured, aware that Alexsa had now lured Carl to her side. She was on her own, but she wasn't beaten. "Let's go over what we know," she said crisply. "We'll separate the facts from, shall we say, the fantasy."

She summarized the events of the past two weeks. Alexsa roused herself and appeared to listen intently. Carl also perked up, adding information until the picture seemed complete.

"What we don't know is why Grove killed Belding and the others."

"Honeywell's marriage to Janice was invalid," said Alexsa. "Tony Grove never died in Vietnam."

"Yes," Caroline admitted. "But Tony had nothing to gain by exposing his wife as a bigamist. That would be like killing the fatted calf and then missing the feast."

Alexsa chuckled at the comparison. She was acting more like her old self now. Caroline mentally applauded her nerve.

"It's absurd to think Janice felt threatened by her brother. As I told Carl, no one would have believed James if he suddenly claimed Tony as his brother-in-law. His experience in 'Nam traumatized him to the point where he hardly even spoke. He was a very troubled man."

An idea flashed through her mind, but it vanished before she could grasp it.

"I agree," said Carl. "He was lost in another world. I doubt he even recognized Grove."

"But would Grove have realized that?" Alexsa said quietly. "You made the mistake of thinking James remembered him. Considering all they'd been through together, wouldn't it have been natural for Grove to assume the same thing?"

Stunned by the simplicity of Alexsa's argument, Caroline sank back on her chair and stared at the woman. They'd been dodging around the truth, concentrating on the marriage angle rather than Belding's personal history. They'd needed Mrs. Morgan's input to trigger an epiphany.

"But for a very different reason," she exclaimed. "We've been looking at this all wrong, Carl. Tony wasn't worried about being recognized as Janice Honeywell's husband. He was afraid James would remember him as his old pal from the Army!"

Carl looked puzzled, but Alexsa nodded her head. She understood what Caroline meant.

"Desertion is a treasonable offense, Carl. Somehow Grove escaped when the Vietcong captured James. Rather than go back to his unit, he deserted and started trafficking in drugs. If James came to his senses and fingered him, Tony could have spent the rest of his natural life in prison."

The light began dawning for Carl. "He never would've revealed his past to Janice. He couldn't trust she'd keep such a dangerous secret."

"A secret worth killing for." Caroline was on a roll with everything suddenly clicking into place. "Now I'm convinced Janice wasn't involved in the bombing. Tony planned it to get rid of James. Gail's attention to James may have worried him, but Belding was the primary target."

"Grove muddied the waters by including so many victims," said Alexsa.

Caroline agreed with her. "The police had to broaden their investigation. That took time, and time was Grove's biggest ally. It allowed people, myself included, to forget he'd been in the recreation room that day. He was the one who called out for Belding to light the tree. As soon as he saw James pick up the cord, he scooted out of there. And because there were multiple victims, no one knew who the real target was," Caroline added. "Janice might have feared for her company, but she had no reason to suspect Tony."

"If we can convince the FBI of this, they may drop their investigation of Janice," said Carl. "That would let you off the hook, Alexsa. There'd be no need to pry into the past."

"I still have a few friends in high places. A word in

the right ear may change the direction of the investigation." Alexsa rose from her chair. "And now, if you'll forgive me, it's been a long day."

Caroline and Carl accompanied her to the door. At the last moment, Caroline asked for a word alone with Alexsa and she agreed. Carl went downstairs to wait.

CAROLINE FLIPPED ON the lights in her apartment.

"I need to find James Belding's obituary," she told Carl. She hobbled over to the desk and rummaged through the newspapers piled there. "Alexsa said something strange when we were alone upstairs. I was about to leave when she suddenly began talking about James Belding and how his capture in 'Nam occurred only days before he was scheduled to ship home. It got me to thinking... Ah, here it is!"

She pointed to a boxed column in the death notices and read aloud.

"'James Belding, a former sergeant in the U.S. Army and brother of Janice Honeywell of Honeywell Industries, was laid to rest yesterday at Roseland Cemetery after a private service. Sgt. Belding was presumed captured in Vietnam four days before his scheduled return to the States.'"

She turned to Carl and said excitedly, "Don't you see? Belding's words had nothing to do with Grove or Janice or anyone else in Rhineburg. He was simply talking to himself!"

Carl threw himself down on the sofa. "You've lost me, Cari. This old brain of mine has absorbed way too much information today."

"Four to go, Carl! Four to go!" Caroline closed the paper and sat down across from the professor. "Gail thought the words were a cryptic message about her mother. Tony thought James was whispering about him. We assumed both were correct, but we should have been listening to Jane. She said James was too ill to be rational. Emotionally, he remained a prisoner of the jungle."

She willed Carl to understand. "Think of the years he spent in captivity. He must have gone over it in his mind a hundred thousand times. 'Four days and I would have been out of here. Four days to go. Four to go.'"

Carl sat up straight, a grin splitting his face. "You're right, Cari. With nothing else to hang on to, those four words became a personal mantra to him."

"And his only way to communicate. How stupid of me to think a man that ill could take a nursery rhyme and twist it into a complex omen."

"Don't be so hard on yourself. It was only logical to build on Gail's theory."

"I guess so," Caroline said grudgingly. She changed the subject. "We should call Tom Evans."

"Can't it wait 'til later? All this talk has made me hungry."

Caroline grinned when Carl rubbed his stomach. "You don't look particularly starved to me."

"I have to stay in training, Cari. What would the children say if a skinny Santa showed up at the Winter Festival next Christmas?"

"That's true," said Caroline, giving in to the professor's wishes. Leaving him to make dinner reservations, she went off to change her clothes. She was bone tired, more exhausted than she'd let on, and once in her room, she slumped wearily on the bed. Her one-on-one face-off with Alexsa had exacted a heavy and unexpected toll.

Unbeknown to Carl, she'd gone into league with the

Morgan matriarch, an accomplice to yet another cover-up that must be kept secret even from the professor. The curious partnership had formed after he'd gone downstairs, when Caroline had confronted the old woman with her lies.

"You convinced Carl that Liz shot Ty Belding. But I'm not so gullible, Alexsa. The letter ended too abruptly. I know she wrote another page."

Alexsa stood still as a rock. She appeared unmoved by Caroline's words.

"Bill told us Jim argued with Liz the night of her death. I think he found her writing the letter and saw the part about the dorm fire. He must have gone crazy knowing she'd killed Monica. He hit Liz, didn't he? It became another 'accident,' like the one so many years ago."

Alexsa turned away. "You have no proof," she said coldly.

"An autopsy would show Liz died long before she hit the water."

"There was no autopsy. The county coroner is a friend of the family. He knows how dangerous that bridge is in winter. Others have gone off at the same spot."

"How convenient. You can shield your grandson like you shielded Liz."

Alexsa refused to answer. She walked to the window and stared out at the fields in the distance. Caroline stood rooted in the center of the room, determined not to loose this battle of wills.

"You knew about Monica and the blackmail long before Ty Belding's death. It must have been humiliating watching Liz pay him off each month."

"No need to be dramatic," Alexsa said with a wave of her hand. "Make your point, then get out of my house."

"My point is, you're the one who shot Reverend Belding."

Alexsa arched an eyebrow but said nothing.

"Liz didn't know how to shoot. Your grandson told me that on New Year's Eve. But Michael Bruck spoke favorably of your marksmanship. Seems you were quite good in your day."

"That was a long time ago. I haven't touched a gun in years."

"You knew Belding would bleed Liz dry. You're a strong woman who makes difficult decisions. You made a very difficult one the day you killed that blackmailer." Caroline paused, waiting for some reaction from Alexsa. One never came. "You ran into Charlie Harding in the woods that day. He saw your rifle and suspected you'd shot Belding. But Charlie covered for you because he hated the preacher with a passion."

Alexsa smiled and shook her head. "Charlie will never support your theory."

"If you're so sure of that, why did you call Elvira and question her about Charlie? You were afraid he'd spill the beans after Gail died."

"I'm not afraid," said Alexsa. "I know who my friends are."

"You're a stubborn old woman, Mrs. Morgan. Liz understood what you did for her. But in her desire to make a clean breast of it, she included details of Belding's death in the letter. Jim mailed the confession after engineering Liz's plunge into the river. If the police didn't accept his wife's death as an accident, he expected me to come forward with proof of suicide.

"But he couldn't allow you to be arrested for Belding's murder. He could forgive you where he couldn't forgive Liz. Ty Belding meant nothing to Jim. Monica did. To save you, he kept the last page and forged Liz's name to what remained."

"A very clever story, Mrs. Rhodes. And what do you intend to do about it?"

"Nothing, for now."

Alexsa appeared visibly startled. Caroline pressed on.

"I don't think Jim meant to kill Liz, but he made a stupid mistake trying to hide what happened. He compounded it by sending me that letter."

Caroline said it would be senseless to punish Jim's daughters for what he'd done.

"They've already lost their mother. They'll only suffer more if their father is arrested. They'll always be known as 'the girls whose dad murdered their mom.' I see no justice in that. Neither do I think Jim will ever harm anyone again. Living with what he did will be punishment enough."

Then Caroline listed her demands.

"Convince your Washington friends to squelch the investigation of Janice Honeywell. Tell them what we know and back us with all the power you wield in this state. Do that and I'll keep quiet. Not even Carl will hear what I've told you."

Alexsa bowed her head.

"And one other thing," Caroline added. "I have a feeling Jim kept the last page of that letter. If I were you, I'd destroy it." Alexsa nodded. She didn't bother to thank Caroline, but in exchange for her silence, she offered her a clue to James Belding's last words. It was a unique but acceptable way of sealing the bargain.

Now, alone with her thoughts, Caroline took a long

hard look at herself in the mirror. She'd changed since arriving in Rhineburg. She'd put the painful part of her past behind her and was stronger for having done so. Her immediate plans included proving Janice Honeywell's innocence. After that, who could tell? Perhaps she'd stay in Rhineburg, or maybe she'd move on. Whatever she did, it would be her own choice, a decision made not because she had to but because she wanted to. That was the beauty of life; one always had second chances.

"And I'm going to take mine!"

Caroline winked at her reflection, then turned from the mirror and began dressing for dinner.

* * * * *

REQUEST YOUR FREE BOOKS!

2 FREE NOVELS
PLUS 2 FREE GIFTS!

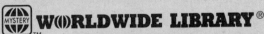

WORLDWIDE LIBRARY®
MYSTERY ™

Your Partner in Crime

YES! Please send me 2 FREE novels from the Worldwide Library® series and my 2 FREE gifts (gifts are worth about $10). After receiving them, if I don't wish to receive any more books, I can return the shipping statement marked "cancel." If I don't cancel, I will receive 4 brand-new novels every month and be billed just $5.24 per book in the U.S. or $6.24 per book in Canada. That's a saving of at least 34% off the cover price. It's quite a bargain! Shipping and handling is just 50¢ per book in the U.S. and 75¢ per book in Canada.* I understand that accepting the 2 free books and gifts places me under no obligation to buy anything. I can always return a shipment and cancel at any time. Even if I never buy another book, the two free books and gifts are mine to keep forever.

414/424 WDN FEJ3

Name _____ (PLEASE PRINT)

Address _____ Apt. #

City _____ State/Prov. _____ Zip/Postal Code

Signature (if under 18, a parent or guardian must sign)

Mail to the **Reader Service:**
IN U.S.A.: P.O. Box 1867, Buffalo, NY 14240-1867
IN CANADA: P.O. Box 609, Fort Erie, Ontario L2A 5X3

Not valid for current subscribers to the Worldwide Library series.

Want to try two free books from another line?
Call 1-800-873-8635 or visit www.ReaderService.com.

* Terms and prices subject to change without notice. Prices do not include applicable taxes. Sales tax applicable in N.Y. Canadian residents will be charged applicable taxes. Offer not valid in Quebec. This offer is limited to one order per household. All orders subject to credit approval. Credit or debit balances in a customer's account(s) may be offset by any other outstanding balance owed by or to the customer. Please allow 4 to 6 weeks for delivery. Offer available while quantities last.

Your Privacy—The Reader Service is committed to protecting your privacy. Our Privacy Policy is available online at www.ReaderService.com or upon request from the Reader Service.

We make a portion of our mailing list available to reputable third parties that offer products we believe may interest you. If you prefer that we not exchange your name with third parties, or if you wish to clarify or modify your communication preferences, please visit us at www.ReaderService.com/consumerschoice or write to us at Reader Service Preference Service, P.O. Box 9062, Buffalo, NY 14269. Include your complete name and address.

WWLI1B

FAMOUS FAMILIES

YES! Please send me the *Famous Families* collection featuring the Fortunes, the Bravos, the McCabes and the Cavanaughs. This collection will begin with 3 FREE BOOKS and 2 FREE GIFTS in my very first shipment—and more valuable free gifts will follow! My books will arrive in 8 monthly shipments until I have the entire 51-book *Famous Families* collection. I will receive 2-3 free books in each shipment and I will pay just $4.49 U.S./$5.39 CDN for each of the other 4 books in each shipment, plus $2.99 for shipping and handling.* If I decide to keep the entire collection, I'll only have paid for 32 books because 19 books are free. I understand that accepting the 3 free books and gifts places me under no obligation to buy anything. I can always return a shipment and cancel at any time. My free books and gifts are mine to keep no matter what I decide.

268 HCN 0387   468 HCN 0387

Name _____ (PLEASE PRINT)

Address _____ Apt. #

City _____ State/Prov. _____ Zip/Postal Code

Signature (if under 18, a parent or guardian must sign)

Mail to the **Reader Service**:

IN U.S.A.: P.O. Box 1867, Buffalo, NY 14240-1867
IN CANADA: P.O. Box 609, Fort Erie, Ontario L2A 5X3

* Terms and prices subject to change without notice. Prices do not include applicable taxes. Sales tax applicable in N.Y. Canadian residents will be charged applicable taxes. This offer is limited to one order per household. All orders subject to approval. Credit or debit balances in a customer's account(s) may be offset by any other outstanding balance owed by or to the customer. Please allow 4 to 6 weeks for delivery. Offer available while quantities last. Offer not available to Quebec residents.

Your Privacy— The Reader Service is committed to protecting your privacy. Our Privacy Policy is available online at www.ReaderService.com or upon request from the Reader Service.

We make a portion of our mailing list available to reputable third parties that offer products we believe may interest you. If you prefer that we not exchange your name with third parties, or if you wish to clarify or modify your communication preferences, please visit us at www.ReaderService.com/consumerschoice or write to us at Reader Service Preference Service, P.O. Box 9062, Buffalo, NY 14269. Include your complete name and address.

FFBPA12

REQUEST YOUR FREE BOOKS!

2 FREE NOVELS
FROM THE SUSPENSE COLLECTION
PLUS 2 FREE GIFTS!

YES! Please send me 2 FREE novels from the Suspense Collection and my 2 FREE gifts (gifts are worth about $10). After receiving them, if I don't wish to receive any more books, I can return the shipping statement marked "cancel." If I don't cancel, I will receive 4 brand-new novels every month and be billed just $5.99 per book in the U.S. or $6.49 per book in Canada. That's a saving of at least 25% off the cover price. It's quite a bargain! Shipping and handling is just 50¢ per book in the U.S. and 75¢ per book in Canada.* I understand that accepting the 2 free books and gifts places me under no obligation to buy anything. I can always return a shipment and cancel at any time. Even if I never buy another book, the two free books and gifts are mine to keep forever.

191/391 MDN FEME

Name _____ (PLEASE PRINT) _____

Address _____ Apt. # _____

City _____ State/Prov. _____ Zip/Postal Code _____

Signature (if under 18, a parent or guardian must sign)

Mail to the **Reader Service**:
IN U.S.A.: P.O. Box 1867, Buffalo, NY 14240-1867
IN CANADA: P.O. Box 609, Fort Erie, Ontario L2A 5X3

Not valid for current subscribers to the Suspense Collection
or the Romance/Suspense Collection.

Want to try two free books from another line?
Call 1-800-873-8635 or visit www.ReaderService.com.

* Terms and prices subject to change without notice. Prices do not include applicable taxes. Sales tax applicable in N.Y. Canadian residents will be charged applicable taxes. Offer not valid in Quebec. This offer is limited to one order per household. All orders subject to credit approval. Credit or debit balances in a customer's account(s) may be offset by any other outstanding balance owed by or to the customer. Please allow 4 to 6 weeks for delivery. Offer available while quantities last.

Your Privacy—The Reader Service is committed to protecting your privacy. Our Privacy Policy is available online at www.ReaderService.com or upon request from the Reader Service.

We make a portion of our mailing list available to reputable third parties that offer products we believe may interest you. If you prefer that we not exchange your name with third parties, or if you wish to clarify or modify your communication preferences, please visit us at www.ReaderService.com/consumerchoice or write to us at Reader Service Preference Service, P.O. Box 9062, Buffalo, NY 14269. Include your complete name and address.

SUS11

REQUEST YOUR FREE BOOKS!
2 FREE NOVELS PLUS 2 FREE GIFTS!

H HARLEQUIN®

INTRIGUE®

BREATHTAKING ROMANTIC SUSPENSE

YES! Please send me 2 FREE Harlequin Intrigue® novels and my 2 FREE gifts (gifts are worth about $10). After receiving them, if I don't wish to receive any more books, I can return the shipping statement marked "cancel." If I don't cancel, I will receive 6 brand-new novels every month and be billed just $4.49 per book in the U.S. or $5.24 per book in Canada. That's a savings of at least 14% off the cover price! It's quite a bargain! Shipping and handling is just 50¢ per book in the U.S. and 75¢ per book in Canada.* I understand that accepting the 2 free books and gifts places me under no obligation to buy anything. I can always return a shipment and cancel at any time. Even if I never buy another book, the two free books and gifts are mine to keep forever.

182/382 HDN FV54

Name	
	(PLEASE PRINT)

Address	Apt. #

City	State/Prov.	Zip/Postal Code

Signature (if under 18, a parent or guardian must sign)

Mail to the **Reader Service:**
IN U.S.A.: P.O. Box 1867, Buffalo, NY 14240-1867
IN CANADA: P.O. Box 609, Fort Erie, Ontario L2A 5X3

**Are you a subscriber to Harlequin Intrigue books
and want to receive the larger-print edition?
Call 1-800-873-8635 or visit www.ReaderService.com.**

* Terms and prices subject to change without notice. Prices do not include applicable taxes. Sales tax applicable in N.Y. Canadian residents will be charged applicable taxes. Offer not valid in Quebec. This offer is limited to one order per household. Not valid for current subscribers to Harlequin Intrigue books. All orders subject to credit approval. Credit or debit balances in a customer's account(s) may be offset by any other outstanding balance owed by or to the customer. Please allow 4 to 6 weeks for delivery. Offer available while quantities last.

Your Privacy—The Reader Service is committed to protecting your privacy. Our Privacy Policy is available online at www.ReaderService.com or upon request from the Reader Service.

We make a portion of our mailing list available to reputable third parties that offer products we believe may interest you. If you prefer that we not exchange your name with third parties, or if you wish to clarify or modify your communication preferences, please visit us at www.ReaderService.com/consumerschoice or write to us at Reader Service Preference Service, P.O. Box 9062, Buffalo, NY 14269. Include your complete name and address.

HIDIR12